LETHAL QUESTS
Sinister Fantasy Becomes Deadly Reality

BERNIE FAZAKERLEY MYSTERY 15

by
Judy Ford

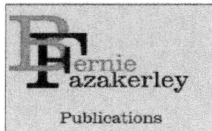

Bernie Fazakerley Publications

COPYRIGHT

Lethal Quests

Published by Bernie Fazakerley Publications

Copyright © 2024 Judy Ford.

ISBN: 978-1-911083-94-8

DEDICATION

Dedicated to all those people who live in fear or anxiety because they are perceived by those around them as different, and to all those of every faith and none who are trying to make the world a fairer, more inclusive place.

وَلَمَن صَبَرَ وَغَفَرَ إِنَّ ذَٰلِكَ لَمِنْ عَزْمِ ٱلْأُمُورِ

Though if a person is patient and forgives, this is one of the greatest things.

(Qur'an 42:43)

WHO'S WHO?

Although this book can be read as a standalone novel, it features many people from my earlier books. In particular, it could be viewed as a sequel to "Lethal Mix", in which a group of Muslim students are sprayed with acid by an unknown attacker. For readers who are new to my cast of characters, here's a handy list of the main players in this story.

Bernie Fazakerley – "Our Bernie", Liverpudlian now living in Oxford.

Lucy Paige – Bernie's daughter by her first husband, studying Medicine at Liverpool University.

Peter Johns – Bernie's second husband, a retired police officer

Jonah Porter – Retired police officer, friend of Bernie and Peter, disabled in the course of duty by a bullet in the neck.

Joey Fazakerley – Bernie's cousin.

Ruth Fazakerley – Joey's wife.

Dominic Fazakerley – Joey's and Ruth's son, works as a Religious Studies teacher.

Ibrahim Ali – Lucy's fiancé, works as an engineer.

Mariam Ali – Dominic's fiancée, studying Medicine at Liverpool University. She was injured in the acid attack which left her with scars on her head and neck.

Tahira Siddiqui – founding member of the Feminist Sisterhood of Islam, Liverpool university graduate and scholar of Shariah, assistant imam at Stanley Mosque and Islamic Centre.

CONTENTS

1. PRELUDE

July 2022

The stupid bitch! Who did she think she was – calling him a racist! All he said was if people want to come over and live here, they shouldn't expect to change everything to be like the places they came from. And she had to come out with all that woke nonsense about respecting other people's cultures. What about British culture? When does anyone ever show that any respect?

Guy strode down the road, head down, shoulders hunched. An empty beer can lay on the pavement in front of him. He gave it a violent kick, sending it skittering downhill ahead of him.

She was so young, so naïve! But she thought she knew it all. She wouldn't listen when he tried to tell her about his nan in Bolton, who always said she felt like a foreigner in her own country, now that she was the only white face on her street. What did she know about actually living in this "multicultural society" that she was always banging on about? How many immigrants were there down there in Hemel Hempstead?

He stopped at the traffic lights, waiting to cross Lime Street, unsure where he was going except that he wanted to get away from Nicole and her university friends. He looked across at Wellington's column and then, turning his head to the left, at the classical frontage of St George's Hall. A bus moved off allowing him to see the mounted statue of Queen Victoria surrounded by parked cars.

That's what she didn't understand! Liverpool used to be a great city at the heart of a great empire. Now, according to her, we were supposed to apologise for it all. What about all the lives that have been saved because people in Africa have access to western medicine instead of relying on witch doctors? What about democracy and justice systems and technology? All those places would be a lot worse off if they were still ruled by tribal chiefs who might kill you or cut off your hand at a whim! And if everything about Britain is so bad, why do so many people want to come here?

The lights changed and he crossed the street. As he walked slowly down William Brown Street, between the magnificence of St George's Hall on his left and the pillared splendour of the Walker Art Gallery and the Museum on the right, he thrust his hands deep into the pockets of his jeans in an attempt to hide his despondency with a devil-may-care swagger.

She had no right to dump him like that – after all the things he'd done for her! He'd even bought tickets for that concert she'd been banging on about – "Celebration of Musical Diversity"! A load of overseas students showing off in front of people like Nicole who wanted to show how "multi-cultural" they were. He'd have gone along to it with her too – even though it was bound to be a load of …!

Still wandering purposelessly, he turned into the gardens at the back of St George's Hall. The grass was neatly cut and the beds were bright with summer flowers. There were plenty of people there enjoying the sunshine. Some were sauntering alone or in groups admiring the flowers and trees or staring up at the statues representing the great and the good of Liverpool's past glories. *How long before someone dredged up a link to slavery or some other misdemeanour and there were calls for them to be torn down, like that statue in Bristol?*[1] Others were walking briskly, probably using the gardens merely as a short cut. Most of the benches were occupied – tourists eating ice creams and contemplating which landmark to visit next, shoppers with bulging carrier bags taking a breather before heading back to find their next bargain, young people walking with heads bowed over their phones.

Guy walked up the broad path towards the memorial in the centre of the gardens: a stone pedestal with a statue of Britannia on top, surrounded by bronze figures of soldiers. There were more benches standing against the circular stone wall surrounding the monument, and sitting alone on one of them was a young woman. Her brown face, framed by a hijab in black fabric edged with something shiny, told him that she was a Muslim and what his grandfather would have described as a "dirty Paki".

Of course, Guy would never use such derogatory language. That was what Nicole didn't understand! Real racists treated people differently depending on the colour of their skin. He wasn't like that. He didn't care what someone looked like, so long as they recognised that they were living in this country, not the one they'd chosen to leave, and they had to fit in – learn the language so they could chat to their neighbours, keep the smells of their spicy cooking to themselves, not have ten kids in a two-up-two-down next door to his nan.

The young woman was reading a book and jotting down notes on an A5 pad. Guy watched as she put the book down on her lap and reached inside a small backpack, which lay on the bench beside her. She took out a bottle of water and drank deeply before returning it to the bag. Her fingers were slender with neatly-

---

[1] In June 2020, the bronze statue of city benefactor Edward Colston, was taken from its plinth and pushed into Bristol harbour as a protest against his involvement in the trans-Atlantic slave trade.

trimmed nails. Her skin was smooth and unblemished. Guy took a step towards her. She returned to her book without looking up.

This was his chance! He would show Nicole that he wasn't a racist. He would ask this girl to go to the concert with him. She looked well fit, and, the chances were, she'd jump at the idea of going out with a white guy. With any luck, Nicole would be at the concert too – she'd made enough fuss about how she absolutely had to be there – and she'd see them together and then she'd know what a mistake she'd made.

He sauntered over to the bench.

'Anyone sitting here?'

'No.' She looked up and smiled. 'Feel free.' Then her head went down again and she turned a page in her book.

'I'm Guy,' he ventured. 'And you are …?'

'Mariam.'

He sat down, leaving just a few inches of the bench between them. 'Mariam?' he repeated. 'That's an interesting name – different.'

This observation elicited no reply, so he tried again. 'Hot again today, isn't it?'

'Yes,' Mariam agreed, without looking up. Then she shuffled a little way along the bench to expand the space between them.

'But I don't suppose you feel it, being from …?'

'Blackburn.' She lifted her head at last and looked straight at him, an expression of amusement on her face. 'Yes. The heat is terrible there. Sometimes we have to put away our winter woollies as early as … June – or even May!'

'No, but I mean. Where you *really* come from – India or Pakistan or …'

She took a deep breath and let it out in a long sigh. 'I was born in Blackburn. That *is* where I'm really from.'

'But your family – your Mum and Dad?'

'Are both from Manchester.'

PRELUDE

Guy fell silent, conscious that he had not made a good start with this conversation. Mariam crossed her legs, turning her body away from him slightly and putting down the pad of paper between them on the bench.

'Are – are you doing anything tonight?' Guy asked in desperation. 'I mean – I've got tickets for this concert. Would you like to go with me? It's music from around the world. I expect you'd know some of it. Maybe you'd be able to help me appreciate it better.'

She lowered her book into her lap again and turned towards him just enough to look him in the eye.

'You're asking me out?' she said in tones of deep scepticism, one eyebrow raised. *Was she laughing at him?*

'Yes. I saw you sitting here on your own, and I thought how – how – nice you looked.' Guy hesitated over the adjective, unsure which words he could safely use to describe her. Nicole was always telling him off for "objectifying women" when he was intending to compliment her on her appearance. 'And I've got two tickets, so I thought ...'

Mariam stared at him with an amused expression. 'Well, that's very ... flattering, but I think my fiancé would take a dim view of me going out with a stranger that I met on a park bench.'

She was definitely laughing at him now. She thought it was funny that he was showing an interest in her. She was as bad as Nicole! What was the matter with girls these days? Or maybe ... Maybe she was frightened of what her family would do if they found out she'd been speaking to a man in public. They had all sorts of rules about that, didn't they?

'Your fiancé? I suppose your parents found someone for you. That's how your people do it, isn't it? But you don't have to go along with it. You're in Britain now. We have laws about forced marriage.' *That was another of Nicole's hobby-horses: saving ethnic minority women from out-dated societal norms.*

The woman laughed outright now. 'Forced marriage! You have no idea, do you? I'm not some sixteenth century princess who has to marry into the correct royal family in order to seal some international alliance and preserve peace in Europe! When it comes to who I get hitched to, *I* make the decisions.'

'But you let them tell you what to wear, don't you?' Guy countered, nettled by her derision. He reached out and took hold of the loose end of her hijab. 'You go along with this thing!' He gave it a shake, leaning towards her so that his face was close to hers. She shrank back, taking hold of the hijab and trying to pull it out of his grasp. 'It's a sign of male oppression,' he continued. 'Let me take it off for you and let's see what's underneath!' He grabbed at the length of fabric with both hands now, rising to his feet to get better purchase.

'No, you don't!' A loud shout from behind him coincided with an excruciating pain in his right arm as something hard and heavy hit it. The next thing he knew, his other arm had been twisted round and pulled up painfully behind his back. He struggled to get free, but his assailant was strong and had him at a disadvantage. Without knowing quite how, he found himself pinned up against the wall behind the bench, his face only millimetres from the stonework.

'Right! I've got him.' It was a female voice, but strong, confident, in control. 'OK, Mariam, call the police.'

2. OPENING GAMBIT

April 2023

'When it comes to the *Mahr*, or marriage gift, there are lots of misconceptions. Many people think that it is a "bride price", which the groom pays to the bride's father in order to essentially buy her, as if she were a piece of his property. But nothing could be further from the truth. The Mahr is, in fact, a way in which Islamic marriage provides security and financial independence for the wife, who traditionally would have been prevented by her domestic duties from working outside the home.'

Tahira Siddiqui, the young assistant imam at the Stanley Mosque and Islamic Centre, looked round to check that her audience was paying attention. She had never prepared a couple for matrimony before and now she had two mixed marriages to oversee – or rather a double marriage. Mariam Ali, a close friend from Tahira's university days, was to marry Dominic Fazakerley, a Roman Catholic; and her brother Ibrahim was marrying

Dominic's cousin Lucy. This was an opportunity to dispel some myths about the nature of Islamic marriage and the status of women within her faith community.

'So, we can't expect Ibrahim to give us a nice little nest egg to keep us in our old age?' a voice commented brightly. It was Bernie Fazakerley, born and raised in Liverpool, but now living in exile in Oxford. She was the mother of the bride and very interested in the proceedings, which were entirely novel to her.

'Mam!' her daughter Lucy growled, giving her mother a dig in the ribs. 'Be quiet! I can't take you anywhere, can I?'

Tahira acknowledged the interruption by grinning in Bernie's direction before resuming her prepared speech.

'The misconceptions are often based on the fact that the Mahr is traditionally negotiated by the bride's father, or another male relative, on her behalf. Her *Wali*, which means "protector" or "helper", is entrusted to make sure that she is appropriately provided for in the marriage contract. In the past, women often married at a young age and lacked the experience to make the detailed negotiations that could be required and the legal knowledge to ensure that she was given her rights under Islamic law.'

'So, who's Lucy's Wali,' asked Peter, Bernie's husband. 'She won't let me give her away when it comes to the church ceremony, but I'd be happy to step into the breach and negotiate for Ibrahim to hand over all his worldly wealth.'

'Of course, these days,' Tahira resumed, flashing another grin in the direction of Lucy's family, 'many women come into a marriage with their own income and capital, so the Mahr may be more symbolic than substantive; and part of the marriage contract – the Nika Nama – may be concerned with ensuring that both parties are able to retain control over an appropriate portion of their own wealth and income.'

'So, how much will Dom be expected to give to Mariam?' asked Dominic's mother Ruth, a touch of anxiety in her voice.

'It doesn't have to be a monetary gift,' Tahira explained, 'and it doesn't have to be given all at once. All or part may be deferred to a later date, perhaps only payable in the event of divorce.'

'A bit like a pre-nuptial agreement,' commented Lucy.

'Yes,' agreed Tahira. 'The rest of the world seems to be beginning to catch up with Islamic law in that respect. But, as I was saying, the Mahr need not include any cash. Jewellery is a popular choice, for example.'

'Like a ring?' Lucy suggested, mischievously.

'But you won't … I mean, Ibrahim's going to give you that in the wedding service, isn't he?' Ruth queried anxiously. 'After the ceremony in the mosque is over.'

'That's right,' Lucy agreed. 'I was just pointing out that *our* traditions include the bridegroom giving the bride some jewellery too. We've already agreed what my Mahr is going to be,' she went on. 'Ibrahim's got this beautiful Qur'an: in Arabic, with an English translation on the opposite page; and a fantastic prayer mat, with my name on it in English and Arabic.'

'And, following their example, Dom's giving me a Bible and a rosary,' Mariam added. 'And a ring, of course.'

'Will that be OK?' Ruth asked anxiously, looking towards Mariam's parents. 'I mean … isn't that sort of thing forbidden?'

'Well,' Tahira intervened firmly, 'since there's a body of opinion that says that Muslim women aren't allowed to marry non-Muslim men at all – even though Muslim *men* are explicitly permitted to marry Christians and Jews – I don't think that this will raise any additional hackles!'

She looked towards Mariam and Dominic, sitting side-by-side between the two sets of parents. 'It is going to be difficult for you both sometimes,' she warned, 'and for you too,' she added turning to Lucy and Ibrahim.

'And I'm sure it won't all be coming from one side,' Bernie added. 'But we're backing you all the way, and I'm sure you're all strong enough to ride out the storms when they come. Just be sure and tell us if you're having a tough time.'

'That's right,' agreed Tahmina Ali, stretching out her arms to place a hand on the shoulder of each of her children. 'We'll deal with any trouble from your aunties and uncles. I'm proud of you both, and I'm very pleased that you've found partners who will make you happy.'

'OK then,' Tahira looked down at her notes again, 'let's look at the other elements of the Nika Nama. We always recommend using this standard template, which includes giving both partners equal rights to divorce the other and a space for adding any special conditions that either party may want: a ban on polygamy, for example. Of course, you're also going to have the additional safeguard of a legal marriage, which provides access to the courts in the case of–'

She broke off as the door opened and a woman came in. She was dressed in a black hijab with an apron tied round her waist over trousers and a long-sleeved blouse. 'Tahira? I'm sorry to interrupt, but it's the police. They say they need to speak to you urgently.'

'Excuse me.' Tahira got up and went out of the room into the welcome area at the front of the centre. Fragments of her conversation with the police officers could be heard through the part-open door.

'... bad news, I'm afraid ...'

'Yasmeen? Dead?'

'... found this morning ... suspect foul play ...'

'Strangled? Like Rania? Is it the same killer?'

'We don't know ... all speculation at the moment ... formal identification.'

'Yes. I'll come right away. Just excuse me a minute.'

The door swung back and Tahira came back in.

'I'm sorry,' she said in a shaky voice very different from her usual confident tones. 'I'm afraid we're going to have to postpone this. Something rather awful has happened.'

By this time Ruth was on her feet. Taking Tahira by one arm, she guided her to a chair. The younger woman sat down gratefully, wiping a hand across her face as she struggled to take in what the police had just told her.

'I'll get you some water,' Tahmina said, heading out of the door, past the two uniformed officers who were waiting discretely just outside.

'It's Yasmeen,' Tahira told them. 'She's dead – strangled, just like Rania.'

'Rania?' echoed Bernie. 'What–?'

'Someone else who goes to this mosque,' Lucy explained. She was killed a couple of weeks ago. Someone strangled her with her own hijab and left her by the bins outside one of the JMU[2] buildings.'

'Why didn't you tell us about it?' demanded Peter. 'If there's a serial killer picking off students, you ought to have let us know. I hope you've all been being extra careful since it happened.'

'We didn't know it was a serial killer,' Lucy pointed out with exaggerated patience. 'How could we, when it was the first one? I didn't want to worry you. And I didn't want Jonah dragging you both up here so he could investigate personally. You know what he's like. You won't tell him about this, will you?'

---

[2] Liverpool John Moores University is one of the "post-1992" universities, created when former polytechnics were granted royal charters with the ability to award their own degrees.

'Well, thankfully Jonah is safely up in Durham for another ten days and Reuben will keep him there, whatever fancy ideas he gets about coming here to help,' Peter observed.

Their great friend, retired DCI Jonah Porter, was spending two weeks with his son Reuben and his family, giving Bernie and Peter a well-earned rest from their responsibilities as his full-time carers, which they had fulfilled since his disabling injury some fourteen years before. Lucy, who had only been nine when he moved into their home, had embraced her role in attending to his needs, and they had developed a close and lasting bond. It had been her association with him and his many murder investigations that had prompted her to choose forensic pathology as her career ambition.

'Here you are.' Tahmina was back, accompanied by the woman in the black hijab, who handed Tahira a glass of water. 'Just sip it slowly and take a few deep breaths. There's no rush. Just take your time.'

'Thanks, Khadija – and Tahmina.' Tahira took the glass, but did not drink. She held it on her lap as she looked round the room.

'They want me to go and give formal identification of the body. I was wondering if you would come with me, Lucy? I've never seen … someone dead before.'

'Or perhaps one of the older ladies might come?' one of the police officers suggested, stepping into the room.

'Lucy's a final year medical student,' Bernie clarified. 'And she's aiming to become a forensic pathologist. She's quite familiar with this sort of thing.'

'Oh, I see.' PC Janet Morecambe looked taken aback, but soon recovered her poise. 'In that case. Yes, by all means she can come too. When you're ready,' she added turning to Tahira.

'I think I'd like to get it over with.' Tahira handed the glass back to Tahmina as she got to her feet. 'Then I'll be sure ….'

PC Morecambe looked round the room. 'This community support officer will stay here,' she said, 'If you have any questions, you can ask her. And she'll be checking out security measures with the people in charge. There's no reason to believe that this place will be a target, but we recognise that some people may need reassurance.'

'Oh, Natasha's always welcome here!' Khadija said warmly, smiling towards PCSO Natasha Lyons. 'She often drops in for a coffee and a natter.'

'The best coffee on my beat,' Natasha declared with a grin, 'and cakes you could die for!'

Tahira and Lucy followed the police officers out of the room, leaving the others staring round at one another, not knowing what to say.

'There's coffee and cakes in the welcome area,' Khadija said at last. 'I suggest you all come out there where it's more comfortable – or I can bring some in here for you if you'd rather?'

'That's OK, Khadija, we'll come through,' Mariam answered. 'If you're sure you wouldn't rather we left.'

'No, of course not. This sort of thing is what we're here for. Stay as long as you like. And when you're settled, I'll give Imran a ring. He'll want to speak with you all, I'm sure.'

They came out of the side room where they had been meeting with Tahira and into a large open area furnished with a dozen or so tables. Groups of people were sitting around them, chatting and eating cake. Natasha was standing at one side, a large slice of cake in her hand, talking to two women in matching blue-and-white hijabs who were supervising a group of toddlers playing on a mat on the floor. Conversations stopped abruptly and Bernie felt everyone's eyes on them as the little party made its way across the room.

Khadija led them to a large table in the far corner. It was deserted, although the chairs here were upholstered and looked more comfortable than the plastic stacking chairs elsewhere in the room. Bernie deduced that she had probably asked whoever had been sitting there to move to make room for her guests.

'Imran?' Ruth asked, once they were all seated and Khadija and Tahmina had gone off to prepare drinks and fetch cake.

'He's Khadija's husband,' Mariam explained, glad of something to say unconnected with the tragic news that had just hit them. 'He's the principal imam here. Tahira's his assistant, and strictly-speaking, she's an *imaama,* which is the female equivalent of an imam. This mosque is very unusual in allowing a woman to lead prayers where there are men present. We're very lucky to ….' She tailed off as she realised that this was not the time to expound on the role of women in Islam.

They sat in silence for several minutes, too shocked to know how to begin a conversation. Dominic put his arm protectively around Mariam's shoulders and hugged her tight to him. Tahmina and Abdul Ali looked anxiously across the table at their daughter.

Ruth turned to her son. 'Why didn't you tell us you knew that girl who was killed outside John Moores?'

'We didn't want to worry you,' Dominic answered sheepishly. 'We thought, if we told you that she came here, to this mosque, you might think that Mariam could be a target too.'

'And it looks very much as if your mother would have been right if she did think that,' retorted his father.

'I did, actually,' Ruth added. 'I did think that. And I said as much, didn't I Joey? But you said not to say anything to them in case thinking about it triggered flashbacks to … you know.'

Four years earlier, Mariam and some of her fellow students had been the subjects of an Islamophobic attack, in which one of her friends had died and she herself had suffered serious injury.

'Tell us about this other girl who was killed.' Peter directed his request towards Dominic. 'We didn't know about it at all. It can't have made the national news. What happened?'

'Her name was Rania – Rania Ansari,' Mariam told him. 'She was studying Computer Forensics at JMU, which gave her lots in common with Lucy. They were always talking about court cases and evidence and that sort of thing. She always came here for Salah al-Jummah on Fridays and she belonged to our women's group.'

'The Feminist Sisterhood, you mean?' asked Bernie.

'That's right.'

Tahira was the leader and founding member of a group of Muslim students who styled themselves "The Feminist Sisterhood of Islam". Most of the original members had now graduated and some had moved away, but several were still living in the Liverpool area and, together with new recruits from among the current student population, continued their quiet – and occasionally not so quiet – campaign for gender equality.

'The day she was killed, she went to a sort of careers evening thing at the Henry Cotton building,' Mariam continued. 'They had some JMU computer science graduates speaking about what they'd done with their degrees since they left. One of the other students found her body the next morning, pushed into a corner behind the rubbish bins. She'd been strangled with her own hijab. It must've happened as soon as she left the building, because her room was only in the building next door. It's almost as if someone was lying in wait for her.'

'Or as if she'd arranged to meet someone,' Bernie suggested. 'Couldn't it have happened later on – after she'd been back to her room. If the killer is someone she knew, they could have called on her later and then the two of them gone out together.'

'What have the police said about it?' asked Peter.

'Nothing much,' Dominic told him. 'Just that she was strangled sometime that evening and for women, particularly students, to be extra vigilant when they're out at night.'

'Someone from Radio Merseyside asked if it was an Islamophobic attack,' Ruth added. 'But they just said they were keeping an open mind.'

'I should think they'll be revising that opinion now,' Bernie observed. 'Or public opinion will be revising it for them!'

'The weird thing is the way it happened so close to where she lived,' Mariam mused. 'I mean, the two buildings are next door to one another. She only had a few yards to walk. And there'd have been other people around – other students coming out from the talks. They surely couldn't have attacked her until after everyone had dispersed.'

'Which does suggest that there could be something in Bernie's idea that she came back out again later,' Peter agreed, becoming interested in spite of his inner determination not to interfere in an investigation that ought rightly to be left to the local police.

'Did she have a boyfriend?' Bernie asked.

'Not the sort who would kill her and dump her body behind the bins!' Mariam retorted quickly. 'She wasn't stupid – or a masochist.'

'I was thinking it could have been an accident.' Bernie tried to be conciliatory.

'How do you accidentally strangle someone?' Dominic demanded scornfully. 'It's not like she fell and hit her head. It *must* have been deliberate!'

'And now it's happened again,' his mother added. 'And Mariam could be next – or Lucy,' she added, looking pointedly at Bernie.

'Do you think whoever it is is targeting people from this mosque?' Joey asked, 'rather than just Muslims in general?'

'You mean, it could be sectarian?' asked Bernie. 'Someone who doesn't approve of their Western, liberal approach? A Muslim fundamentalist, perhaps, who sees them as betraying Islam?'

'I wasn't really thinking of that. I was thinking more: someone who lives round here and doesn't like the idea of having a mosque on their street,' Joey replied. 'But, thinking about it, they'd be more likely to attack people on their way to and from the mosque, wouldn't they?'

'I think there could be something in the radical Muslim idea,' Dominic said. 'There do seem to be a lot of people out there promoting a very traditional form of Islam. Mariam's had to close down her Twitter account; she was getting so much trolling from people who think it's haram for her to marry a non-Muslim.'

'You never told us about that,' Tahmina reproached her daughter.

'I didn't want to worry you,' Mariam shrugged. 'It's not a big deal. I never used Twitter that much anyway. I was only really on it because I liked to see what the university and the hospital trust were putting out there.'

'Could the attacks be directed more at the Sisterhood, rather than the mosque?' Bernie suggested, and then immediately cursed herself inwardly when she saw the look of alarm that appeared on Ruth's face.

'Or it could just be a coincidence,' Joey said firmly, fixing his cousin with a stare that told Bernie very clearly not to pursue this line of reasoning.

'Yes,' Peter agreed quickly, picking up on Joey's desire to quieten Ruth's anxiety. 'The two deaths may not even be connected. This sort of thing does sometimes happen at random – and when it does, it makes the investigating officers' job harder, because you make all sorts of assumptions based on them both having the same perpetrator and the same motivation.'

Abdul drained his mug of tea and set it down on the table in front of him. 'I think we've trespassed on your hospitality for long enough,' he said to Khadija. 'Thank you for the tea and that cake was absolutely delicious, but it's time we went.' He turned to his daughter, 'Come on Mariam, we still haven't seen this house you've found for you and Dom to move into.'

'Your dad's right,' Tahmina agreed, getting to her feet. 'Obviously Tahira won't be wanting to discuss the wedding any more today. 'I suggest we all go for lunch somewhere and then you and Dom must show us the house. We're going to have to go back home this evening because we're both working tomorrow.'

'I'll text Lucy to see how they're getting on,' Bernie said, reaching for her phone. 'We'd better wait for her, seeing as she and Tahira will presumably come back here when they're done at the mortuary.'

'And I'll wait too,' Ibrahim nodded. 'Lucy and I have got a lunch for everyone at *our* new house. We were expecting everyone would go back there.'

'Well, *we* certainly will,' Bernie assured him. 'That's what we're up here for: to help you get it decorated ready to move in. We were expecting to get stuck in right away – once we'd got the marriage plans sorted here.'

Bernie's phone buzzed. It was a message from Lucy saying that they were on their way back to the mosque. That settled things: everyone sat down again and Khadija went off in search of fresh drinks and more cake, ignoring Ruth's protestations that it was nearly lunch time. She was a great believer in comfort eating in times of stress and in the importance of hospitality.

3. NEXT MOVE

'Come this way.'

Lucy and Tahira followed the mortuary assistant along a corridor and into a rather bare room, very clinical with spotless surfaces and harsh overhead lighting. In the centre, a mound roughly the shape of a human form lay on a trolley covered by a very clean white sheet.

Lucy and PC Morecambe stood back against one wall, watching sombrely as Tahira and the assistant took up their places on either side of the trolley. Tahira gave an involuntary gasp as the assistant drew back the sheet to reveal the face of a young woman.

'Yes,' she nodded, 'That's her. That's Yasmeen.'

Lucy, unable to contain her curiosity, came up alongside her friend and peered down at the dead woman, noting marks of bruising on her neck and a slightly bluish tinge to her skin. She bent lower, hoping to see the tell-tale petechial haemorrhages that typify death by strangulation, wishing that she could lift the lids to inspect the eyes, where they might be more evident.

The assistant replaced the sheet and stepped back, looking towards PC Morecambe who nodded briefly in his direction and then put out her hand to touch Tahira on the shoulder.

'I'll take you home now,' she said gently.

They turned to go, but then Tahira turned back. 'How soon …?' she asked the mortuary assistant. 'I mean, when will we be able to take her away?'

'It's the tradition for Muslims to be buried as soon after death as possible,' Lucy added helpfully.

'I'm afraid that's above my pay grade,' the assistant answered apologetically. 'I'm afraid there will have to be a post-mortem, and then it's up to the coroner to decide when the body can be released. I can ask for the PM to be done as soon as possible, but that's about all, I'm afraid.'

'OK. I see.' Tahira and Lucy started for the door again, but they were stopped in their tracks as it flew open and a tall man in a white coat came striding in.

'Is that the–?' he began. Then, 'I'm sorry, I didn't realise … And Lucy! What are *you* doing here?'

'I came with Tahira,' Lucy answered. 'She's been identifying her cousin. Tahira, this is Professor Charles Mortimer. He teaches forensic pathology at the university. I'm hoping to train with him after I qualify. Professor, Tahira Siddiqui, assistant imam at Stanley Mosque and Islamic Centre.'

'My condolences on your loss.' The professor held out his hand towards Tahira. 'And I'm so sorry to have intruded.'

'That's OK, we were just leaving.' Tahira shook his hand, looking up briefly and then lowering her eyes again.

'The family are anxious to have the body released for burial,' the mortuary assistant told the pathologist. 'When were you planning to do the PM?'

'I was thinking of first thing this afternoon. That's why I'm here, checking everything's ready for me.'

'Can I watch?' Lucy asked eagerly. 'I mean, the more experience I can get the better,' she added, looking round at the array of surprised faces that were suddenly all gazing at her.

'No, Lucy, you can't,' Professor Mortimer said firmly. 'I have an unbreakable rule that nobody who knows the deceased is ever present at the post-mortem examination.'

'OK.' Lucy thought for a moment. 'Can I read the PM report afterwards? I'm going to need to know how to write them and interpret them, aren't I – if I'm going to be a forensic pathologist?'

'My report is for the police and the coroner.'

'You've shown us extracts from some of your old cases in your lectures,' Lucy pointed out.

'Anonymously,' the professor countered. 'Alright, Lucy, if you're really keen to see what a whole PM report looks like, I'll sort out a few for you to look at. Come to my office at nine-thirty on Monday morning. Now I must–'

There was a knock at the half-open door and a tall woman with short brown hair looked in. 'Professor?'

'DCI Latham!' Professor Mortimer turned his attention to the newcomer. 'Come to see our latest arrival, I assume? I'll be starting the PM at one thirty this afternoon. Can I expect you to be there?'

'Either me or DS Simpson, but I was really here because I was told that the vict– I'm sorry!' Sandra Latham broke off as she spotted Tahira standing unobtrusively in a corner of the room. 'You must be Tahira Siddiqui. Yasmeen Osmani was your cousin – is that right?'

'Yes. Our mothers are sisters.'

'I'm DCI Latham. I'm with Merseyside Police CID. I was wondering if I could ask you a few questions?' She paused, a puzzled look on her face. 'But haven't we met before? And …,' she turned to look at Lucy. 'it's Lucy Paige, isn't it? You're one of DCI Jonah Porter's friends.'

'That's right,' Lucy smiled back. 'I'm Lucy and you know Tahira because she was a witness to the acid attack four years ago when Salma Rahman was killed.'

'Yes, of course! I'm sorry, Miss Siddiqui, I should have remembered you. And I'm very sorry for your loss. I can't imagine how you're feeling after another violent death so soon.'

The usually self-assured Tahira nodded her acknowledgement of the condolences but did not trust herself to speak. Lucy noted silently that the police officer had not mentioned the obvious fact that both deaths appeared to have been motivated by hatred towards young Muslim women.

'Would it be alright for us to speak now?' Sandra asked gently. 'Or …?'

'Now will be fine,' Tahira said quickly. 'Anything that will help to find whoever did this.'

'I'll show you to a better room,' the mortuary assistant suggested. 'And would you like some tea?'

Soon Lucy and Tahira were sitting together in a small room facing PC Morecambe and DCI Latham across a low table on which stood four mugs of tea and a plate of digestive biscuits.

'I won't keep you long,' Sandra assured them. 'I just need you to fill in a bit of background for me. Your cousin was in her first year at the university. Is that right?'

'Yes. She was studying Dentistry.'

'And had she settled into university life OK? I know how hard it can be for teenagers being away from home for the first time.'

'Oh yes! She'd made some friends at the place where she was living – in Greenbank Student Village – and she also had friends at the mosque.'

'Where you are an imam, I hear,' Sandra nodded. 'That's unusual for a woman, isn't it?'

'Yes,' Tahira agreed, becoming more animated as the conversation moved on to her favourite subject, 'but we're challenging those patriarchal stereotypes. Islam is really a very feminist religion, but it's been corrupted for centuries by the male hierarchy. Khadijah, the wife of the Prophet, peace be upon him, was something of a leader in her own right. Another of his wives, Aisha, is the source of over two thousand hadiths and was crucial in spreading Islam after the death of Muhammad, peace be upon him. There have been many female scholars of the Qur'an and the Hadith. The Qur'an gave married women the right to own and manage their own property hundreds of years before the British government did. But, just as in the West, men have been reluctant to give up their privilege and allow women equal rights.'

She paused to draw breath, and then looked round rather sheepishly.

'Tahira is a very passionate feminist,' Lucy explained with a smile.

'Well, you're with friends here,' Sandra assured her, smiling back. 'Janet and I are very familiar with the patriarchy and male privilege. But, to get back to your cousin: when was the last time you spoke to her?'

'Yesterday afternoon, after Friday prayers.'

'How did she seem?'

'Just like normal,' Tahira shrugged. 'She didn't stay for long. She was in a rush because she was going out with friends in the evening, and she had some work she needed to get done first.'

'Did she say where she was going?'

'I think they were having a meal somewhere in town. It was someone's birthday – one of the girls at her hall.'

'OK. We'll be able to check with them.' Sandra paused, unsure how her next question would be received. 'Did she have a boyfriend at all?'

'Not that I know of.' Tahira shook her head. 'But I suppose if she had, she might not have told me. She knows that her parents expect weekly updates from me, letting them know she's alright.

And they would definitely not have been pleased. Her father is rather ... traditional, in outlook. He wasn't at all keen on allowing her to go away from home to study, but Aunty Marina persuaded him to let her come because I was here to keep an eye on her. They were trusting me to ... They – they ...'

All of a sudden Tahira's natural poise and confidence seemed to evaporate. Her voice choked to a halt and her face crumpled into tears.

DCI Latham moved a box of tissues, which the mortuary assistant had thoughtfully left on the table, towards her. 'Take your time. There's no rush.'

Tahira wiped her eyes and blew her nose. 'I'm sorry. I don't usually ... It's just ... I feel so guilty that I didn't do anything after Rania was killed. I mean, I just told everyone to be careful, but I tried to make out that was just a one-off. I should've made sure she never went out alone – especially at night.'

'So, you knew Rania Ansari?' Sandra asked.

'Yes. She came to Friday Prayers at the mosque most weeks.'

'And to meetings of the Feminist Sisterhood,' Lucy added.

Sandra looked puzzled for a moment and then smiled. 'Oh yes! I remember that now. So that's still going strong, is it?' She looked towards Lucy, appearing to take in for the first time the lime green hijab covering her luxuriant blond curls. 'And are you a member now?'

'A sort of honorary one,' Lucy smiled back. 'I'm marrying Mariam Ali's brother in July – and she's marrying my second cousin Dominic – so they let me come to meetings even though I haven't converted to Islam.'

'You haven't?' Janet Morecambe sounded surprised. 'So why the ...?' She too stared at Lucy's striking head covering.

'Solidarity,' Lucy answered. 'After Mariam started wearing one to hide the way that half her hair's gone. It deflects attention. By the time people have finished asking what a nice white girl like me

– only usually they don't actually quite *say* that in so many words – is doing dressed up in something they associate with Asian women, they've lost all interest in wondering why there's a brown woman with a stethoscope round her neck studying their medical notes.'

'Mariam? Oh yes! She was injured in the acid attack, wasn't she?' Sandra cut in. 'She had some quite nasty burns. I hope she's fully recovered now.'

'Pretty much,' Lucy nodded. 'There'll always be scars, but … well so far it hasn't prevented her doing anything she wanted to. Do you think the killer could be targeting people who attend the Stanley Mosque?'

'It's too early to draw any conclusions about that,' Sandra said firmly. 'But that will be something to consider. On the other hand, the two deaths may not be related at all or, if they are, the link could simply be to do with them both being young women or young women in Muslim dress or just female students. But I will make sure there's a greater police presence around the mosque and I'd advise you to be extra vigilant and not to let in anyone you don't know.'

'But we're a Community Centre,' Tahira protested. 'We host all sorts of activities for local people. We can't start turning people away from our debt counselling service or our foodbank and community café! People are relying on us.'

'I know PCSO Lyons will be making a point of calling in every day,' Janet told them. 'And I'll pop in as often as I can too – any excuse for a coffee! You community café sounds like a great idea.'

'It is!' Lucy declared enthusiastically. 'It's staffed mainly by volunteers, and it gives them a chance to learn new skills. Some of them are asylum seekers, who aren't allowed to work, but they can volunteer. And it's a lifeline for people on low incomes. You can get a hot meal at lunchtime, and coffee and cake from nine in the morning until four. And you just pay whatever you can afford. Last winter, with the energy crisis, lots of older people came in and sat there all day just to save putting the heating on at home.'

'OK.' Sandra looked down at her notes. 'Was there anything else to connect Rania and Yasmeen – apart from attending the mosque and belonging to the Sisterhood? Were they particular friends, for example?'

'No, I don't think so,' Tahira shook her head. 'Rania was in her third year at JMU and Yasmeen was a first year at the dental school. Their paths hardly crossed, except at the mosque. And Yasmeen didn't even get to many meetings of the Sisterhood. She was dreadfully conscientious about her studies. They always came first.'

'What do the more … er … traditional members of the Muslim community think of the Sisterhood?' Sandra asked cautiously.

'You mean, could they have been killed by some fundamentalist firebrand who doesn't approve of women thinking for themselves?' Tahira asked sharply. 'No. I don't think that's at all likely. For a start, why pick on Rania and Yasmeen? Why not go for one of the real rebels, like me? They never did anything to draw attention to themselves. They didn't go out in public with their heads uncovered or post a blog about giving women back the status they used to have in the time of the Prophet, peace be upon him, or dare to lead men in prayer!'

Sandra studied the young women opposite: blue-eyed, fair-skinned Lucy in her lime green hijab with just a few strands of blond hair visible across her forehead; and Tahira, brown-skinned, her dark brown eyes flashing beneath a fringe of shiny black hair, cut in a pageboy bob. Which of them would be a more likely target for an attack from either pro- or anti-Islam extremists?

'And do you ever receive criticism from fundamentalists?' she asked at last.

'Oh yes! All the time. Especially on Twitter, because they can hide behind a cloak of anonymity. But it's all just talk. It doesn't frighten me. Usually, it's silly young men repeating things their fathers and grandfathers have told them and showing off that they know a few verses from the Qur'an. None of them have actually studied it properly.'

'All the same. I'd like one of my officers to check out the profiles of anyone who has said anything abusive about the Sisterhood or about the mosque having a female imam. And you should be extra vigilant over your own personal safety. As you've pointed out, as one of the leaders of local Muslims, you could be a particular target.' Sandra slid a business card across the table towards Tahira. 'Now I won't keep you any longer. If you think of anything else that could help us, there's a number on this where you can ring me.'

She got to her feet. 'We can arrange for the local police to notify Yasmeen's parents ...'

'No. No, I'll ring them. It ought to be me.'

$$***$$

'It looks like lunch time. I'll come in with you and give your community café a try,' Janet said, as she pulled up outside the Islamic centre. She got out and went round to help her passengers out. Lucy, however, was too quick and by the time Janet reached the door she already had it open. She climbed out followed by Tahira and together they walked to the front of the centre and pushed open the glass doors.

Lunch was in full swing. A diverse range of people were sitting around the tables, some chatting in groups, others apparently alone, eating in silence. Perhaps half were of South Asian appearance, a few in traditional baggy trousers and loose-fitting tunics, but most wearing clothing indistinguishable from that of their white neighbours. A good number of the women had their heads covered, but that was by no means universal.

Looking round, Janet spotted Natasha sitting with a group of young women at a table near the centre of the room. She went over to join them.

Lucy meanwhile was making a bee-line for the big table at the side of the room where the others were still sitting, apparently deep in conversation with Imran.

'Guess who the SIO is! It's Sandra Latham,' she announced. 'She was at the mortuary. That's why we were so long. She wanted to ask Tahira some questions about Yasmeen. She agrees that the two murders may be linked. They wouldn't say how Yasmeen was killed, but it looked like strangling to me. I'm sure ...' she stumbled to a halt as she realised that nobody was listening to her. All eyes were on her companion.

'Are you OK?' Ruth was on her feet looking anxiously towards Tahira and gesturing towards the seat that she had just vacated. 'You sit down here. Dom: get her a glass of water, and Joey: another couple of chairs.'

Dominic and Joey sprang obediently into action. The others shuffled their chairs backwards to make more room round the table. Imran got to his feet and waved across the room to attract his wife's attention. Khadija looked up from the table where she had just delivered three bowls of steaming soup and waved back in acknowledgement.

'Thanks.' Tahira smiled towards Ruth. 'But I must phone Yasmeen's parents first, before anything else.' She turned to Imran. 'Is the office free?'

'Yes. Go ahead. Take as long as you like. But don't you think maybe you ought to give yourself a few minutes first, to ...?'

'No. I must do it right away. It's already been too long. They really ought to have been the first to know, not me. Aunty Marina will be so devastated, and Uncle Nadeem will … Oh poor Fatima! He'll never let her do anything after this, and nobody will be able to argue with him.'

'Fatima?' Bernie asked.

'Yasmeen's sister. She's only fifteen, but Uncle Nadeem's mother has already been suggesting the names of eligible young men who would make good husbands for her. She never approved of Yasmeen going to uni. She always said no good would come of it. And now she'll be convinced that she was right!'

Tahmina was on her feet too now. She put her arm around Tahira's shoulder and she and Ruth manoeuvred her firmly into Ruth's now vacant chair. Dominic returned with a glass of water, which he put down on the table in front of her while Ruth pressed a small packet of tissues into her hand.

'Just take a few minutes,' Imran urged again. 'This sort of thing is hard. Give yourself a bit of time. A few minutes won't make any difference to them. Really it won't.'

Nodding silently, Tahira pulled a tissue out of the packet and wiped her eyes. Then she took a few sips of water before blowing her nose and wiping them again. 'Thanks.' She looked round at the anxious faces watching her. 'Thanks, but I really do have to phone them now.'

She got up and walked, a little unsteadily, towards a door at the opposite side of the room. The others sat watching her progress. They saw her pause for a brief conversation with Khadija, who intercepted her just before she reached her goal. The two women embraced and Khadija held the door open for Tahira to go through then closed it firmly behind her.

For a few moments nobody spoke. Then Imran cleared his throat. 'I suggest that you all have lunch here,' he proposed. 'There are just a couple of more things I need to get straight about the wedding arrangements. We can talk those through while we eat.' He turned to Abdul and Tahmina, 'and then I know some of you need to get away. I'm so sorry it's all been such a rush for you.'

'It's hardly been your fault,' Abdul pointed out. 'No one could've known that this was going to happen.'

'I hope you're all staying to lunch.' Khadija was back holding a small notepad and a pencil in her hand. 'There's no charge, of course. What would you all like? I can recommend the soup of the day, which is watercress. It comes with a choice of white or wholemeal bread rolls baked on the premises. Or we have a range of freshly-made sandwiches, samosas – chicken or vegetable – onion bhajis, vegetable pakoras, pizza slices or if you want something more substantial, our main dish today is lamb scouse.'

'Oh!' Ruth gave an involuntary squeal. 'What a lot of choice! I thought it would all be curry and spicey things.'

'We try to have something for everybody,' Imran explained. 'A lot of the older people don't want to try anything new. So, we aim to always have something that will be familiar to them as well as the dishes that our regular volunteers are used to making. And some of the punters have started giving us recipes to try or are even offering to come in and help with the catering.'

'I think it makes them feel better about not paying much for the food,' Mariam put it. 'It makes it feel less like accepting charity.'

'We've got a wonderful lady called Ethel who helps in the kitchen,' Imran added. 'She's in her eighties now, but she used to be a school dinner lady and she knows all the old Liverpool favourites.'

'Her rhubarb ginger cake is really something,' Khadija agreed. 'Why not have some for afters? Or I could wrap some for you to take away with you.'

They gave their orders and sat back to wait while Khadija rallied a group of volunteers to serve them. Lucy was clearly keen to tell everyone about what she'd seen and heard at the mortuary, but Imran steered the conversation firmly back on to the subject of the wedding arrangements, conscious that Mariam's parents did not have a lot of time to spare, and also determined not to allow minds to dwell on the possibility that they might be being watched by a serial killer intent on picking off members of their community.

4. BACK TO SQUARE ONE

'I suppose, at least all the delay will have given the paint plenty of time to dry,' Peter observed as Lucy opened the door to the house in Knotty Ash that she and Ibrahim were preparing to move into. 'We'll be able to get another coat on the walls of the hall, staircase and landing this afternoon and then the carpet can go down tomorrow.'

'If you do that, Lucy and I can start stripping all that awful paper off the walls in the front room,' Bernie nodded.

'What do you want me to do?' asked Ibrahim. 'I don't seem to have made much of a contribution so far, with having been at work all week.'

'That was the whole point of us coming up to help,' Bernie pointed out. 'Us two elderly retired folk helping out all you busy young things with jobs and degrees to worry about.'

'You can make us cups of tea,' Lucy grinned, 'and tell us what a good job we're making of everything.'

'You can follow me round with a damp rag wiping off any drips that get on the skirting board,' Peter told him.

'And pick up all the bits of damp wallpaper and stuff them in this bin sack,' Bernie added, handing him a large black plastic bag.

Once they were settled into their respective jobs, Lucy returned to her account of her morning visit to the mortuary. 'There were definitely marks of strangulation on her neck,' she chattered eagerly. 'But they wouldn't let me close enough to tell for sure. I'm going to see Charles — Professor Mortimer — tomorrow morning, so I'll try to get him to tell me what he finds at the PM. He's doing it this afternoon. The reports in the Echo said that Rania was strangled with her own hijab. I wouldn't be at all surprised if Yasmeen was the same.'

'In which case, it might be a good idea if you and Mariam change your style of headgear,' suggested Ibrahim. 'There's no point going out of your way to attract the attention of this serial killer, if that's what he is, or to give him a weapon to use against you.'

'I'm not going to let him intimidate me!' Lucy protested. 'That's what terrorists want — to frighten people into changing how they live.'

'Who says he's a terrorist?' called Peter through the door leading from the front room into the hall. 'He could just have some sort of fetish about women with scarves over their heads. I think Ibrahim's right. There must be plenty of hats that Mariam could use to cover her scars without providing a handy length of fabric for a strangler to use.'

'And *you* don't actually need to wear *anything* on your head,' Ibrahim added, pleased to have the support of Lucy's stepfather. 'Well, except when you're painting the ceiling! Until we did that awkward bit over the stairs, I hadn't realised how much mess a paint roller could make!'

'I just don't want to give in and change my behaviour just because there's some nutter out there,' Lucy argued. 'Why shouldn't we wear what we like?'

'Of course you ought to be able to wear anything you choose, within reason,' Bernie agreed, 'but things just don't work that way. Obviously, it ought to be possible for anyone to be safe walking alone at night in any part of the city, and it ought not to be necessary to keep an eye out for people spiking your drink in a night club or to stand over the ATM when you're getting money out so that nobody else can see you enter your PIN. We all ought to be able to leave our doors unlocked and out windows wide open, but it's just not like that. We all have to take sensible precautions to keep ourselves and our valuables safe, because we know that there are people out there who will exploit our carelessness if we don't.'

'Exactly!' Ibrahim concurred. 'It really irritates me when I hear women going on about victim-blaming if anyone dares to suggest that they ought to take some responsibility for their own safety.'

'So, what should Rania and Yasmeen have done to stop whoever it was from attacking them?' demanded Lucy.

'Nothing! That wasn't what I meant,' Ibrahim protested. 'They didn't know there was someone targeting women in hijabs, did they? What I'm saying is that, now that we do know, it makes sense not to wear one – for the time being, until the police catch him.'

'Or her,' Bernie added. 'It doesn't have to be a man.'

'Statistically, it is more likely though, Mam.' Lucy scraped viciously at a last lingering piece of wallpaper that was obstinately clinging to the wall beneath the windowsill. 'And I don't see any way that Rania or Yasmeen put themselves at risk. They must've both been killed only a few yards from where they were living. It was as if the attacker was lying in wait for them.'

'You mean, it wasn't just a random attack on Muslim women?' Peter asked. 'It was more personal? It was someone who knew them?'

'Yes.' Lucy wiped the wallpaper scraper and put it down on the windowsill. 'They must've been caught off-guard, or they'd have been able to call out and attract attention. There must've been other students around so close to the halls.'

She pulled off the overall that she had been wearing over her jeans and tee-shirt. 'Now, we can't paint these walls until they've dried from all the water we've been putting on them to soak off the paper, so I'm going to go down to JMU and see if I can speak to some of the other students who're living in the same hall as Rania. They may know if she was seeing someone who could have turned against her or if anyone had been acting aggressively towards her or … And one of them found Rania's body the morning after she was killed. Maybe she'll remember something.'

'But the police will have asked all those questions already,' Peter protested. 'You really ought to leave it to them. Rania's friends won't want to go through it all again with you.'

'There could be something that they missed,' Lucy insisted. 'They didn't know it was a serial killer then, did they?'

'Sandra Latham knows her stuff. I'm sure she'll have thought of that. She'll go back and talk to them again if she thinks there might be anything else they can tell her.'

'And psychologists all say that it's good to talk about traumatic events,' Lucy went on. 'It will probably be cathartic for them to have someone whose interested in hearing about what happened.'

'I'm sure there won't have been any shortage of those,' Peter muttered. 'There are always plenty of vultures ready to gather around any suspicious death.'

'Well, I'm going to go down there and see what they can tell me,' Lucy insisted. 'I knew Rania. They'll think it's only natural that I would want to know all about what happened to her – especially now that she isn't the only one.'

'Well, if you must go, I'm coming with you,' Ibrahim sighed. 'I'm not having you wandering the streets on your own, especially if you're going to be asking people all sorts of awkward questions. What if the killer is one of the students in Rania's hall? They might not like you poking around, trying to find out more about what happened.'

'Lucy, love, I'm really not sure this is a good idea,' Bernie intervened. 'Peter's right. You really ought to leave all this to the police.'

Lucy, however, was already on her way to the door. 'Sorry Mam. I do see your point, but I simply *must* do *something*, and there are probably things that they'll tell me that they wouldn't tell the police. I'm a student too, remember, much closer to their age than DCI Latham.'

'I take it you won't want us coming with you then?'

'No, Mam, I don't.'

'You don't even want us to run you down there in the car?'

Lucy looked at her watch. 'I suppose that would save time. Thanks. If you could just drop us off by the Henry Cotton Building – it's down near the Queensway tunnel – and then we can get the bus back.'

'I think we'd better not come back,' Ibrahim said, looking at his watch. 'I must say goodbye to my parents before they go home. They said they had to leave by seven, because Mum's on an early shift tomorrow. We'd better have tea with them and come back to get on with the decorating tomorrow.'

'Good idea,' agreed Bernie. 'We'll make a start on the back bedroom, while the walls are drying in here, and then later maybe get a first coat on the walls down here. Can you just show me which colour it was you wanted?'

✳✳✳

'Poppy? Yes, her room's next to mine. Come up with me and we can see if she's in. I'm Lois, by the way – Lois Grainger.'

Lucy followed the tall student, whom she had accosted on her way into Fontenoy Apartments, through the glass doors into the reception area of the building, noting, as she did so, the CCTV camera on the wall above. Was there one round the corner, near the bins where Rania's body had been found? They must check that when they came back out.

'I'm Lucy Paige and this is Ibrahim Ali. We're friends of Rania Ansari.'

'Rania? Oh! Is that why you want to talk to Poppy?'

'Yes,' Lucy confirmed. 'It said in the Echo that she was the one who found her. It must've been awful for her.'

'Yes.' Lois led the way upstairs and along a carpeted landing. 'Rania was my mentor, so I knew her quite well. The Computer Science department assigns all first years someone in the final year to show them the ropes. It was terrible what happened to her.'

'Yes,' Lucy agreed, 'but we're not sure exactly what *did* happen. That's why we hoped …. I suppose Rania would probably have told you if anyone had been threatening her at all?'

'I'm sure they weren't.' Lois was emphatic. 'Everyone liked Rania.'

'Did she have a boyfriend at all?' Lucy asked, trying to sound casual.

'Not that she told me about, but then we mainly talked about work and where the best places to buy things are and that sort of thing – things to help me get settled in at uni.' Lois knocked on the door of a room on their left and stood with her ear close to it, listening for a response. At the sound of a voice from within, she opened it and stepped inside. 'Poppy, these are some friends of Rania. They'd like to talk to you.'

'If you don't mind,' Ibrahim added. 'We don't want to … I mean, if you don't want to talk about it …. We just want to try to understand why it happened.'

'And why it's happened again,' put in Lucy.

'Happened again?' echoed Lois.

'You mean, someone else …?' Poppy got up from the desk where she was sitting and gestured to them to come in. 'Sit down.'

Lucy and Ibrahim took seats at the tiny dining table next to the cooker, turning them round to face Poppy and Lois who sat down on the bed. Lucy stared round at the sink and wall cupboards. She had spent all five years of her student life sharing a house with Mariam, Ibrahim and Dominic. This studio apartment was very different from the attic room that she had there – and even from the rooms that her friends had had in university halls. They had ensuite bathrooms, but kitchen facilities were shared with other students on their floor, and most of them were much smaller than this.

'You said it's happened again,' Poppy prompted them.

'Yes,' Lucy nodded. 'Another student from our mosque was killed last night, in the grounds of Greenbank Student Village. I've just been with her cousin to identify the body.'

Poppy and Lois stared at Lucy in silence, eyes wide.

'Lucy's a final year medical student,' Ibrahim explained. 'So it wasn't quite such a shock for her – seeing a dead body, I mean.'

'Was she …? Did they know each other, Rania and this other girl?' Lois asked.

'Yes,' Ibrahim told her. 'They both volunteered in our internet café – helping people to fill in online forms to apply for Universal Credit and that sort of thing.'

'And they both belonged to a women's group at the mosque,' Lucy added.

'And you knew them both?' Poppy asked, looking from Lucy to Ibrahim and back again.

'Yes. Yasmeen's cousin is one of my best friends. I didn't know Yasmeen so well, because she only started at the university in September.'

'And it's Yasmeen who's been killed?' Lois asked.

'Yes.' Lucy nodded. 'And we'd like to know why.'

'Well, I don't know if I'll be able to help you much.' Poppy got up and started filling a kettle at the sink. 'I found Rania the morning after it happened, but that's about all I can tell you.'

She returned the kettle to its stand and depressed the switch to start it heating the water.

'I'm making coffee. Would you like some? Or I've got some teabags somewhere.'

'We'd prefer tea, if that's OK,' Ibrahim said quickly. He was not a great fan of instant coffee.

Poppy rummaged in a wall cupboard and brought out a cardboard box containing teabags. She dropped one into each of two mugs and then turned to Lois. 'How about you?'

'Coffee for me, please.'

Poppy poured the drinks and handed them round. Then she sat back on the bed, cradling her mug in her hands. 'I don't know what I can tell you. I went out early, like I always do, to get in two K before lectures.'

'Two K?' asked Ibrahim.

'Running,' Poppy explained. 'I do two K in the morning and then another three at lunchtime.'

'Poppy was in the London marathon last week,' Lois added. 'She did very well. I'm sure I wouldn't even have got to the end! And she raised a lot of money for charity – didn't you Poppy?'

'I ran for the Stroke Association,' Poppy told them. 'My gran had a stroke two years ago, and they've been great with her.'

'Poppy's training for the Great North Run now,' Lois put in. 'Would you like to sponsor her?

'Of course. We'd love to.' Lucy felt in her pocket for a pen. 'Do you have the form handy?'

A few more minutes passed as she and Ibrahim both added their names to the list of sponsors.

'I'll give you my mobile number,' Ibrahim offered. 'Give me a ring when you want the money.'

'Thanks,' Poppy looked down at the form. 'That's very generous of you – when you don't even know me.'

'Two of my grandparents died from strokes,' Ibrahim told her. 'We're always happy to support research to help improve treatments.'

'Now, could we get back to when you found Rania?' Lucy asked gently. 'You found her while you were out for your run. Where exactly was she?'

'Behind the big bins at the side of the apartments – by the wall next to the side entrance of the Henry Cotton Building. I nearly missed her, but her feet were sticking out from behind the last bin in the row. I thought at first it must be someone sleeping rough; so I nearly didn't bother to go up closer. But … I don't know! The shoes didn't look right somehow. They were quite new and clean.'

'So, then you went and looked closer,' Lucy prompted. 'How did you know she was dead?'

'I don't really know. She just looked all wrong somehow. Her hijab wasn't on her head; it was round her neck. I'd never seen her hair before; she always had it covered. I almost didn't recognise her, she looked so different. And her face looked a funny colour – sort of bluish and a bit puffy. I went and shook her to try to wake her up, but of course she didn't. And then I touched her cheek and it was cold. So, then I knew. I rang for an ambulance and the police right away.'

'And did you notice anything else?' Lucy pressed her gently. 'Anything else unusual or different from normal?'

'There was one thing,' Poppy answered slowly. 'I don't suppose it's anything really – probably nothing to do with … what happened.'

'What was it?' Lucy asked eagerly. 'You never know, it might be significant.'

'Well … OK. It's nothing much, but it was odd. There was a chess piece lying on the ground next to her.'

'Which piece?'

'Could she have dropped it?'

Ibrahim and Lucy asked at the same time.

'I don't think she plays chess,' Lois told them. 'In fact, I'm sure she doesn't. She told me that she finds – found – it annoying that people seem to think that anyone who's good at maths is bound to be good at chess too.'

'And why would she be carrying just one piece?' Poppy asked. 'It was a white knight. Of course, it could have been lying there for ages, but I did wonder if the person who killed her might have dropped it. Do you think it's significant?'

'It could be,' Lucy said cautiously. 'It could be the killer's calling card. Maybe he sees himself as some sort of white knight, ridding the land of the scourge of Islam.'

'The white knight in Alice through the Looking Glass was a bit of a bungler,' Ibrahim observed. 'I'm not sure I'd want to identify myself with him!'

'And it's a bit weird ruining a chess set just to leave a piece lying around for people to find, when they probably won't even realise what it means,' Lois pointed out.

'I suppose it could be a sort of message for someone who would understand,' Lucy mused. 'If it was a gang-related killing, I'd be thinking it was intended as a warning to someone, but …'

'But who could they be intending to get the message?' asked Ibrahim. 'Rania wasn't part of any gang, and anyway, the white knight wasn't reported on the news so nobody can have got the message, whatever it was.'

'Apart from the police,' Lois suggested. 'Maybe they didn't make it public because they do know what it means. Maybe whoever it is has done this before.'

'I don't know about that,' Lucy said grimly, 'but it certainly looks as if he's done it again now. Yasmeen's death sounds exactly the same: strangled and then left by the bins at a student residence.'

'It's as if they're saying that Muslim women belong with the rubbish,' Ibrahim added. 'If they *are* trying to send a message, that's what it is.'

'That's rather horrible,' Poppy declared. 'I hope they catch him soon.'

'So do we.' Lucy drained her cup. 'Thank you for talking to us. We'd better go now and leave you in peace.'

'I'm sorry I couldn't be more help,' Poppy apologised. 'I didn't see much at all really.'

'Just talking about it helps,' Lucy assured her. 'It makes it seem more real, somehow.'

'Thanks.' Ibrahim handed his mug back to Poppy as he got up to leave the room.

'And we're so sorry about the other girl,' Lois said as she walked with them as far as her own room. 'And it must be so awful for you,' she turned and looked at Lucy's green hijab, 'knowing there's someone out there who hates people like you so much.'

'Well, yes,' Lucy was unsure what to say to this. 'It does concentrate the mind rather. Oh! One other thing.'

Lois paused with her hand on the handle of the door of her room, and turned to look at Lucy.

'Did you go to the talks that night? You said you were studying computing too.'

'No. I thought they were really for second and third years. I'm only in my first year and I don't have any idea what I'm going to do after I finish at uni.'

Ibrahim refrained from pointing out the obvious flaw in this argument, which was that it was precisely those students who were unsure about their futures who were set to benefit most from hearing about the experiences of recent graduates. Instead, he asked, 'so, would Rania have been the only student from Fontenoy Apartments at the event?'

'Yes, I think she probably would. I can't think of any others.'

'Do you have a list of the speakers?' Lucy asked. 'Or the names of the organisers?'

'No, but you can find out all about it on the department website. They've got it splashed all across the front page, because this is the time of year when A' Level students start thinking about which unis they're going to apply to. It's an excuse to talk about the exciting things that you can do with a computer science degree.'

'Thanks. We'll have a look.'

Lois disappeared into her room, and Lucy and Ibrahim descended the stairs to the entrance hall.

'I want to have a look at the place where Rania was found,' Lucy told him. 'In particular, I want to see if it's in a blind spot for the CCTV.'

'Presumably it must be, or the police would have been circulating pictures of a suspect.'

'Well let's see for ourselves.' Lucy led the way round the side of the building, past a row of large bins: red-lidded ones filled with recycled materials and black-lidded ones piled high with bulging plastic bags of waste. A high redbrick wall separated the student accommodation block from the Henry Cotton Building. There was a tall metal gate to prevent trespassers from gaining access to the rear of the apartment block. In the secluded corner between the gate, the wall and the bins, crisp packets blew in the wind and beer cans lay scattered, having escaped from one of the over-full recycling bins. The floor was littered with cigarette butts.

'Yes!' Lucy exclaimed triumphantly, pointing up at the wall. 'That camera's facing the other way. It only catches people who get through to the other side of the gate. There's nothing to pick up what's going on out here.'

'And presumably the killer knew that,' Ibrahim agreed thoughtfully. 'So, he'd probably been here before and knew where the cameras were.'

'We'd already decided that Rania probably knew him,' Lucy nodded. 'Another computing student, d'you think?'

'One who'd been to the same careers event that Rania went to that evening?' Ibrahim queried. 'Yes, maybe. Or maybe someone who lived in one of these apartments. They could have met as he was going out and she was on her way in after the talks.'

'Or he could've been waiting for her to come out,' Lucy nodded. 'We need to talk to someone who was at the careers event. Someone who can tell us if she left alone or if she was with anyone, and if she met anyone she knew outside. Let's go home now and have a look at that website that Lois talked about.'

5. ROOK TAKES PAWN

'What's that gorgeous smell?' exclaimed Lucy as she and Ibrahim stepped inside the tall house in Kensington where the four friends had lived for almost five years.

'I recognise that,' Ibrahim smiled. 'It's my mum's special dahl.

He headed off down the hall to the kitchen, where sure enough, he found Tahmina standing over the gas cooker stirring something in a large pan. She looked up as he entered.

'I thought we all needed some comfort food after what happened today. I was hoping you'd be back in time to join us.'

'We wouldn't have let you go back home without saying goodbye,' her son protested. 'And we certainly wouldn't want to have missed out on this! Are those some of your garlic naans over there? I can't wait!'

'Well, you're going to have to because my Wet Nelly won't be ready for another twenty minutes or so,' Dominic told him, coming in from the garden carrying a handful of parsley. 'Is this enough for you?' he asked Tahmina.

'Oh yes! That's plenty,' she confirmed. 'It's just to sprinkle over the naans. She turned the gas down under the pan of dahl and took the parsley over to the sink to wash it. 'Do you have a chopping board I can use?'

The doorbell rang and Lucy went back out into the hall to answer it, almost colliding with Mariam who came out of the front room with the same intention. They opened the door together to reveal an extremely agitated-looking Tahira.

'Are you OK?' Mariam asked anxiously.

'Yes – well, not really.'

'Come in and sit down.' Lucy took charge. 'We're just about to have tea. You'd better eat with us. Tahmina's made loads.'

She led the way into the front room where Abdul was sitting on the sofa, watching a wildlife programme on the television. He switched it off when he saw Tahira.

'How are you?' he asked, getting to his feet. 'Can I get you a cup of tea – or a glass of water, perhaps?'

'No – no thank you. I'm fine.' Tahira shook her head.

'The tea's going to be ready in a minute or two,' Lucy added. 'Tahira's going to eat with us.'

'Good.' Abdul sat down again. 'You need to be with friends at a time like this.'

They all sat down. Abdul reached out and put his arm round his daughter's shoulders. Mariam responded by leaning her head so that it rested on his chest. Lucy looked expectantly towards Tahira, then down at her feet. Tahira appeared to be studying her fingernails in great detail. Nobody spoke for several minutes.

'How are Yasmeen's parents taking the news?' Abdul asked at last.

Tahira hesitated for what seemed to Lucy like an age, then the words came tumbling out in a rush.

'Her mum, my Aunty Marina, wants to come up here right away, but her dad, Uncle Nadeem, says they can't leave the shop.

They've got a shop in Handsworth. It's a convenience store; it stays open late. He doesn't trust anyone else to look after it. Aunty Marina's just been on the phone crying and saying she's coming up today whatever Uncle Nadeem says. He seems to be in denial. He won't step outside his routine for anything. Aunty Marina's going frantic, and poor Fatima's caught in the cross-fire and doesn't know what's going to happen to them!'

Lucy leaned across and put her hand on Tahira's shoulder. She didn't know what to say. She had never seen her friend like this. Tahira was usually the most completely together person that she knew.

'Perhaps there is no point in them coming today,' suggested Abdul, 'with it being the weekend. There won't be many staff on duty at the mortuary on a Sunday to make Yasmeen ready for them to see her.'

'That's a thought,' Lucy agreed. 'Why don't you ring them and suggest they wait a bit. That might give your uncle time for the news to sink in and then maybe he'd understand why your aunt needs to come.'

'And it'd give him time to find someone to look after the shop,' Mariam added. 'Surely, they must have someone who could take over? What do they do when they go on holiday?'

'I don't think Uncle Nadeem has ever had a holiday,' Tahira answered, smiling in spite of her distress. 'He and Aunty Marina never seemed to stop working. I think he's always been terrified of the business going bust and them all being out on the streets. I think maybe something like that happened to his parents before they came here from Pakistan, and it's made him a bit paranoid. We used to take Yasmeen and Fatima on holiday with us. Sometimes Aunty Marina would come too, but usually she said Nadeem needed her to look after him and help in the shop. It's completely ridiculous, really. Marina's a qualified teacher, like my mum. So, she'd earn far more if she got a job, but Uncle Nadeem

49

thinks women ought to stay at home and not go out to work. But you're right,' she went on, getting out her phone, 'it would make a lot more sense for them to come up tomorrow or even on Monday morning.'

But, before she had time to select her aunt's number, the phone began ringing. It was Marina. Tahira switched to loudspeaker so that the others could hear both sides of the conversation.

'Tahira? It's Aunty Marina. We're just getting packed. One of the neighbour's is going to give us a lift to New Street. Can you meet us at the station in Liverpool?'

'Yes, of course, but I've been thinking. It might be better if–'

'We don't know exactly what time yet. We'll ring you from New Street when we know which train we're on.'

'OK, but I was going to s–'

'And will you be able to put us up overnight? We don't mind sleeping on your sofa or even on the floor. It's just me and Yasmeen. Nadeem can't leave the shop.'

'Yes, of course. I'll sort something out.' Lucy could tell that Tahira was doing her best to sound more certain than she actually was about providing accommodation for her aunt and cousin. It was hardly surprising that she might be doubtful about having two guests to stay in the tiny studio apartment that she occupied above the Islamic Centre.

'Thank you so much! Now, I must go. I must prepare meals for your uncle for while we're away. If he has to cook for himself, I know he won't eat properly.'

'Can't Aunty Asma look after him?' Asma was Nadeem's widowed mother, who lived with them in the apartment over the shop.

'I don't like her to cook, now that her eyesight is so bad. I'm always afraid she'll scald herself or set the place on fire. Anyway, I must go. We'll ring you again from the station.'

'But–.' Tahira looked down at the screen and saw that her aunt had terminated the call. 'Well, that went well,' she muttered ironically. 'Does anyone have any good ideas for where they can stay tonight? I don't even have a sofa – or even much space on my floor!'

'Perhaps you'd better find them a hotel,' suggested Abdul.

'How much will that cost?' asked Tahira. 'Uncle Nadeem controls their bank account and I know Aunty Marina won't want to let me pay.'

'Lots of rooms will be booked already,' Ibrahim added. 'Liverpool are playing at home tomorrow and there are bound to be lots of Spurs fans making a weekend of it, especially with Monday being a bank holiday. Lucy and I were planning to take her Mam to the match, but with all this going on….' The Fazakerleys were loyal Everton supporters, but Bernie, ever the rebel, had given her allegiance to their Merseyside rival, the preferred team of her late mother's family.

'We've got plenty of room in our new house,' Lucy pointed out, 'just not enough beds to put them up. And they'd have Mam and Peter decorating and laying carpets and putting up curtains all around them.'

'I know Imran and Khadija would take them in if they could,' Tahira said, 'but their house is full to bursting as it is, especially now that Khadija's parents have moved in with them.'

'Perhaps an AirBnB?' Mariam got out her phone and began searching for accommodation. As they had surmised, vacancies were limited and those that were left were more expensive than she had hoped.

'I don't suppose they could stay in Yasmeen's room,' Tahira mused. 'Marina could have the bed and we must be able to find a li-lo or something for Fatima to sleep on, on the floor.'

'We've got two inflatable mattresses,' Lucy volunteered, 'but I don't think the police will have finished with Yasmeen's room yet, even if the university would allow them to stay there.'

'No,' agreed Tahira, 'I went up there this afternoon and it was all cordoned off. Her room and the ground by the bins where she was found. There were people searching for clues all round there, and I saw someone taking away Yasmeen's laptop in a plastic bag.'

'But that's an idea!' Mariam exclaimed triumphantly. 'The air mattresses, I mean. How's this for a plan: Lucy and I sleep on mattresses in the Knotty Ash house, and your aunt and cousin can have our rooms here?'

'Yes!' Lucy agreed enthusiastically. 'That would work. Dom and Ibrahim can look after them, and it'll hardly take you any time to cycle back here from your flat – ten minutes max.'

'It feels like a lot of trouble for you,' Tahira said doubtfully, 'when you're both supposed to be swotting hard for your exams.'

'It won't be for long.' Now that she had thought of it, Mariam was reluctant to give up on her idea. 'Just till the weekend's over and they can find somewhere else – or will they go back to Birmingham once they've been to the mortuary and spoken to the police?'

'Yes,' Lucy agreed. 'I expect the university will find them a guest room or something once the accommodation office is open again on Monday – no, bother! It's a bank holiday so make that Tuesday.'

'It still seems rather–.' Tahira broke off as Dominic entered the room.

'The food's all ready,' he announced. Then, looking round at them all, he sensed that all was not well. 'Is there something up? Something new, I mean?'

'Not really,' Lucy told him. 'We're just trying to work out where Yasmeen's mother and sister are going to stay tonight.'

'They're coming up on the train this evening,' Tahira explained. 'And they're expecting to stay with me, but …'

'Hmmm. Yes,' Dominic nodded. 'There's not a lot of floor space at your place for people to crash out on. Never mind. Come and eat and we'll talk it over. There must be something we can do.'

'Mariam's got a plan,' Lucy informed him as they settled down round the table in the dark little dining room at the back of the house. 'We two are going to sleep on air beds in the house in Knotty Ash, and Tahira's aunt and cousin can have our beds here. You won't mind having them, will you Dom – Ibrahim?'

'No, of course we don't mind,' Ibrahim said dubiously, 'but what about you and Mariam? It won't be very comfortable for you two – and what about all your books and stuff?'

'It's alright,' Tahira assured them. 'Forget it. I'm sure I'll find them a hotel or a B and B or something.'

Her phone buzzed and she hurried to check it. The others waited while she read something off the screen.

'That was a text from Yasmeen,' she told them. 'They're getting the 18.34 from New Street. They'll be in Liverpool at quarter past eight.'

'That gives us over two hours to sort something out,' Tahmina said calmly. Eat up before the food gets cold, and then we'll talk about it.'

'I think they should stay here, like Mariam said,' Lucy insisted. 'It's dead handy for Lime Street, so they won't have far to come. And Dom and Ibrahim will be here if they want someone to talk to – much better than being stuck on their own in a hotel room.'

'At least let's do that for tonight,' Mariam added. 'You'll sleep better too, knowing they're in safe hands – or relatively safe, anyway,' she added, grinning round at the two young men.

They continued to argue as they ate Tahmina's excellent dahl and home-made naan bread. Variations on Mariam's plan were discussed and cast aside. What if Tahira were to sleep on their sofa in the Kensington house, leaving her own studio flat for Yasmeen and Marina? But that would mean them sharing Tahira's none-too-large bed and catering for themselves alone in a strange city. Or perhaps space could be found somewhere in the Islamic Centre itself for the air mattresses that Lucy had suggested, and they could sleep there, with Tahira on hand in her flat above. But which room would be suitable? And could guests be expected to sleep on the floor in a semi-public space?

By the time that Dominic brought out from the oven the huge tin of that particular kind of bread pudding known locally as *Wet Nelly*, Tahira was beginning to waver in her insistence that Mariam's plan was too much trouble for her friends. Her cousin and aunt must be on their train by now, speeding (or, bearing in mind the usual state of the West Coast Mainline, especially at weekends, at very least moving) towards Liverpool. They had less than an hour in which to fix up accommodation for them, and at a price that would not give Uncle Nadeem apoplexy when he found out about it.

'OK,' she conceded, pouring custard over the fruit-filled pudding. 'Just for tonight. I'm sure I'll be able to find somewhere for them to stay tomorrow. Or, if they're able to see Yasmeen's body tomorrow, they may even go home. I'm sure Uncle Nadeem will be nagging them to get back, and Aunty Marina won't trust him to look after himself for long either.' She sighed. 'I know it's all down to him having such an insecure childhood, but it does drive me crazy the way he manipulates her and won't let her have a life of her own.'

'Well, that's settled then,' declared Lucy. 'We'll go up in the loft after we've finished tea and get down the air beds. I'll ring Mam now and ask her to bring the car to pick up Marina and Fatima from Lime Street and take us back to Knotty Ash with all our things.'

'Good.' Dominic finished serving the pudding and sat down in his chair. 'Now, tell us about your trip to Greenbank. What've the police found there? Did they tell you?'

'No. they didn't tell me anything. That plains clothes officer that you know, Lucy–'

'DCI Latham?'

'Yes. She was there. She took me up to Yasmeen's room and asked me if anything was different from normal. I couldn't see anything, but I don't go in her room all that often. I'm trying – I mean, I was trying – not to act like I was a spy for her father reporting on her every move. They took away her laptop and asked me if I knew her password. I told them that I would never have let her give it to me. I'd have told her not to share her passwords with anyone.'

'Does she think the two deaths *are* connected,' asked Dominic. 'Rania's and Yasmeen's?'

'She's not committing herself, but it seems perfectly obvious to me,' Tahira retorted. 'Two Muslim students, both wearing hijabs, both strangled with them and thrown away behind the bins. It's a clear message that whoever did it thinks that we're rubbish and belong there with the rest of the rubbish!'

For several moments no one spoke. There didn't seem to be anything to say to this.

'I did learn a few things, though,' Tahira went on at last. 'When I got there, the forensics people were all over the area round the bins, down on their knees picking up bits and pieces. I saw them bag up something that looked a bit odd.'

'What?' asked Lucy eagerly.

'A piece from a chess set – a white rook.'

'Really?' Lucy's eyes lit up with excitement. 'A white chess piece?'

'Which one is the rook?' asked Mariam. 'I always get confused. Is it the one that looks like a little castle?'

'That's right,' Tahira nodded. 'That's the one. I saw one of them pick it up and show it to her supervisor. She said something I didn't catch and then they put it in a plastic bag and wrote something on a label on the outside. I watched for a bit longer and then a uniformed police officer told me to move away.'

'This can't be a coincidence!' Lucy declared, looking towards Ibrahim. 'This *proves* that the two murders are linked!'

'What d'you mean?' asked Tahira. 'what's so significant about a white rook?'

'Only that there was a white chess piece left by Rania's body too!' Lucy announced triumphantly. 'Poppy, the student who found her, told us, didn't she, Ibrahim?'

Ibrahim nodded his assent.

'It must be the killer's calling card,' Lucy went on. 'I bet he's a chess enthusiast, and he leaves a piece by each of his victims, like a sort of signature.'

'But why?' asked Tahmina. 'Surely that just makes it more likely that he'll be caught?'

'That's all part of the game,' Lucy told her. 'Serial killers often have a subconscious desire to be caught – or else they're convinced that they're a lot cleverer than the police and this sort of thing is an act of defiance, a sort of, "Look, it's me again! Catch me if you can!"'

'I spoke to two of Yasmeen's friends,' Tahira continued. 'They were actually the people who found her this morning. One of them – Montana – had a birthday yesterday, and they went into town to celebrate. Yasmeen was with them, but she came home when the others decided to go on to a night club. They found her when they finally got home in the early hours of this morning.'

'So, Yasmeen was probably killed on her way home,' Lucy mused, 'the same as Rania. How did she get back? She can't have walked all that way.'

'The others thought she was going to get the bus,' Tahira informed her. 'I'd have told her to take a taxi. I wouldn't have wanted her waiting alone at the bus stop at that time of night. Oh dear! I sound just like a fussy parent, don't I?'

'There's no harm in parents wanting to keep their kids safe,' Abdul said firmly. 'You're quite right – especially after what happened to your other friend.'

'Anyway,' Tahira resumed, 'Montana and Lily were chucked out of the night club at four a.m. and came back in a taxi. So, it must've been sometime between four and five that they found her, which they only did because Lily went behind the bins to be sick and almost stepped on her.'

'Did they say whether she had her hijab on or if it was round her neck?' demanded Lucy.

'They said it was tight round her neck.'

'Just like Rania!' Lucy sounded pleased with this statement. 'It *must* be the same person! Someone who hates Muslim women who wear a hijab and uses it as a weapon against them.'

'And then leaves a chess piece behind to let people know that he did it,' added Ibrahim. 'I wonder if it's significant that the first one was a knight and the next was a castle.'

'And how many more murders there are going to be,' murmured Tahmina anxiously. 'There are still fourteen more white chess pieces left to go.'

'Or six at least,' agreed Lucy, 'if you don't count the pawns. I don't suppose someone like this killer would want to identify himself with a mere pawn!'

'If it had been two knights, I'd have said he was identifying himself as a crusader fighting the infidels that he thought were taking over his country,' Dominic said. 'But I don't see what a rook could have to do with that.'

'An Englishman's home is his castle?' suggested Lucy. 'Or, wouldn't the crusader knights have been based in castles?'

'Maybe the actual pieces aren't important,' said Ibrahim. 'Maybe he's just wanting to let people know that he sees himself as fighting for the white against the black – for the light against the forces of darkness.'

'Whatever it means,' Abdul intervened, 'your mother is right. This probably won't stop here, so you all need to be extra vigilant and not allow yourselves to be easy targets.' He turned to look Mariam in the face. 'I think you should stop wearing a hijab - you too, Lucy. We'd happily pay for a wig to cover where you've lost your hair – we've told you that before.'

'Yes, I know.' Mariam shifted uneasily in her chair. 'I just don't like the idea of false hair. It feels sort of dishonest, somehow.'

'I'll take her out tomorrow to buy some hats,' Dominic promised.

'And none of you girls ought to go out alone,' Abdul continued, 'especially not at night.'

'OK. We'll be careful,' Mariam assured him.

'The main thing is to make sure that whatever you wear on your head isn't long enough for someone to strangle you with,' Ibrahim pointed out. 'There must be plenty of things you could use – a bandana maybe?'

'It's OK, I've got the message. Dom and I will sort something tomorrow. Now, I want to hear what else Tahira found out at Greenbank this afternoon.'

'I think I've told you everything already. There were four of them who were going out: Montana and Lily from Greenbank and Montana's boyfriend and another girl who lives in rooms near the centre of town. Yasmeen made Montana a birthday cake, so they invited her to go as well. I got the impression that she was on the edge of their group rather. They thought she was a bit … well, not much fun, because she didn't drink or go to wild parties. But Montana seemed quite touched by her making the cake and very upset that she'd been killed. Maybe she felt responsible for her being out alone at night – especially after there had already been one student killed.'

'I suppose there had only been one,' Mariam wondered. 'Or could there have been others before Rania? If they were somewhere other than Liverpool, or if they weren't Muslims, we might not have heard about them.'

'Mmm,' Lucy agreed. 'You're right. What if these two aren't the first?'

$$***$$

'What if these two aren't the first?' DC Bryony Foster asked at the final team meeting of the day. 'What's to say this killer hasn't been active outside of Merseyside? Somewhere like Oldham, say, where half the population is Muslim, the pattern wouldn't be so obvious, would it?'

'Yes,' Sandra agreed. 'That's a good point. We ought to check with other police services if they've come across this sort of thing too. In particular, have they found chess pieces left beside any other victims? That's the most distinctive aspect of this killer. No need to rush with that, though. Monday morning will be fine. Can I leave that with you, Bryony?'

'Yes ma'am.' Bryony was pleased to have been entrusted with the task, even though it was not as exciting as going out to interview suspects or witnesses. Too often she felt that her superiors did not rate her ability and still, after six years in CID, thought of her as *the new girl*. 'I'll get on to it first thing.'

'Be sure to impress on anyone you speak to that we're not making the business with the chess pieces public,' Sandra warned her. 'We can do without any copycat killers jumping on the bandwagon. And that goes for all of you,' she added looking sternly round at the team. Don't mention that to *anyone*. Let's let the killer think we haven't noticed them. Apart from anything else, that will probably annoy him and then he'll be more likely to make mistakes.'

'I'd thought of doing the rounds of local chess clubs, but I suppose that would rather let the cat out of the bag.' Detective Sergeant Charlotte Simpson, although only two years older than Bryony, was Sandra's most trusted colleague, having worked with her for almost a decade and been her right-hand in tackling a good number of murder investigations. She was no longer the green newcomer that Lucy and Bernie had encountered on Lucy's first visit to her mother's home city[3].

'Mmm. That's a good idea,' Sandra mused, 'but you're right, it would have to be done discreetly. Not an official police enquiry, just a conversation to get to know people and see if there are any odd-bods harbouring Islamophobic intentions. Does anyone here play chess – seriously, I mean, good enough to be thinking of joining a club?'

'I represented Wirral Grammar in an inter-school match when I was sixteen,' Bryony said, after waiting long enough in the silence that followed Sandra's question that she wouldn't appear over-eager or a show-off. 'I wouldn't mind having a go.'

'OK.' Sandra thought for a few moments. 'This isn't an official undercover operation, just an informal thing. So, don't tell any lies, but don't mention that you're a police officer unless you're asked direct questions and can't avoid it. Just introduce yourself as a chess enthusiast who's looking for somewhere to find opponents who'll give them a decent game.'

---

[3] See Mystery over the Mersey © 2016 ISBN: 978-1-911083-19-1

'How about I wear a hijab?' Bryony suggested. 'That might flush out the Islamophobes.'

'Or it might blow your cover.' Charlotte sounded scathing. 'What if there are any real Muslims in the club? Or if someone asks you about why you converted to Islam? You'll be spotted as a fake right away.'

'We don't know for sure that it *is* Islamophobia rather than racism,' Sandra added more kindly. 'Or even just misogyny. And anyway, the last thing we want is for *you* to be the next victim! No, just be yourself and watch out for what crawls out of the woodwork.'

'OK.' Bryony's voice betrayed her disappointment, but she did not attempt to argue. 'I'll start by seeing if any of the clubs meet on a Sunday. With any luck, I'll be able to check out two or three tomorrow.'

'The other thing we mustn't lose sight of,' Sandra resumed, looking down at the notes that she had made on the back of a letter inviting her to subscribe to a new policing magazine, 'is the possibility that these killings aren't Islamophobic or racist but something more personal. The two women knew each other, and they both went to the same mosque. We found a travel chess set in Yasmeen Osmani's room. Could that be a link between her and her killer? That's something else you may be able to find out about, Bryony. Maybe ask if the clubs ever get students from the university wanting to join and then see if anyone mentions her. Her death is already out in the online newspapers and it'll probably make the national TV news tonight. I'm going straight from here to a press conference and we're expecting the BBC and Granada Reports to be there. So, if she was a member, people will probably be talking about it.'

Bryony nodded and smiled. 'What about the other one – Rania …?'

'Ansari,' Charlotte prompted smugly. 'We don't have any evidence that she played chess, but we haven't asked anyone about it ….' She looked enquiringly towards Sandra.

'Let's hold fire on that. As soon as we start asking questions about it, we'll let the cat out of the bag that chess could be the link between the two deaths, and I'd rather keep that to ourselves for the time being. It's about the only advantage we've got over the killer at the moment. Now, let's forget about chess and see if we can't fill in the gaps in Yasmeen's movements yesterday evening.' Sandra gazed round the room and caught the eye of the oldest member of her team. 'John, you were going to talk to the driver of the bus that Yasmeen's friends thought she went home on.'

'Yes.' DC John Fisher lumbered to his feet and looked round at his colleagues. He got out his notebook and thumbed laboriously through the pages. 'I talked to three of them,' he said at last. 'That covers all the buses that left the city centre between when the students said she left for home and midnight, when the buses stop running. They're only every 45 minutes at that time of night, so she may have had quite a wait. None of the drivers remembers her getting on. The company's going to let us have the CCTV recordings from the buses, in case she's on that, but I'm not convinced she ever made it to the bus. The driver of the 22.40, which is the most likely one, was certain that he'd have remembered her if she had, and I believed him. He was South Asian himself and he was sure there weren't any Asian women in hijabs.'

'If she was one of my daughters, I'd be hoping she'd give up the idea of the bus and take a taxi,' Sandra observed thoughtfully. 'I think we'd better check those out. She looked round the room, looking for likely victims for a bit of overtime. Her eyes lit on DC Oliver Ransom, a young officer with, as far as she knew, no partner or family responsibilities. 'Ollie! I'd like you to do the rounds of the taxi ranks in the city centre this evening. There's a good chance that the same drivers will be around tonight as were there when Yasmeen Osmani was trying to get home yesterday. See if you can find anyone who took a young Asian woman to Greenbank Student Village sometime between, let's say … half past nine to allow for her friends getting the time wrong, and midnight – no, make that one o'clock, just in case something happened to delay her setting off for home.'

'OK.' Ollie nodded eagerly. Sandra wished briefly that she still possessed his youthful enthusiasm for the job. Now that she was in her fifties, she found herself increasingly hoping for quiet periods when she could get home in time for a leisurely dinner and an evening in front of the television or a long relaxing bath. But this was not one of those times, she reminded herself quickly. She smiled round at the team. 'Now, before you all go, Charlotte will tell us all about the post-mortem, which Professor Mortimer very kindly came in specially to perform this afternoon.'

Charlotte got to her feet and stood holding her notebook in front of her, waiting until there was complete silence.

'Professor Mortimer says he won't be able to get the full report to us until towards the end of next week, but he pointed out the main findings as he went along. There was no sign of sexual assault, which is the same as for Rania Ansari. Cause of death is asphyxiation due to compression of the blood vessels in the neck, consistent with strangulation using the length of woven cotton fabric found round her neck.'

'Like Rania Ansari,' Bryony put in.

'Yes,' Charlotte agreed, with a touch of annoyance at having her flow interrupted. 'But Yasmeen was probably approached from behind, which is different from the assault on Rania, which the PM report said was more likely to have been face-to-face. Yasmeen's defensive wounds – and there weren't many – seem all to be associated with efforts to remove the ligature, rather than with trying to injure her attacker, and there was bruising and facial injuries consistent with her having been forced on to the ground, face downwards. The killer then probably knelt on her back in order to get better purchase on the ligature and prevent her from struggling. This is different from the attack on Rania, who appears to have been forced back against a wall to facilitate strangulation.'

'Was she killed in the same place she was found?' asked Bryony.

'Professor Mortimer said there's no evidence of her being dragged along the ground either before or after death and no signs that the body had been lying in more than one place.' Charlotte consulted her notes. 'And that's the same as for Rania.'

'In both cases,' Sandra said slowly, 'the victims were attacked in dark corners out of the range of CCTV cameras on the buildings that they were apparently heading for.'

'And next to the rubbish bins,' Ollie pointed out. 'Is that significant or is it just that the bins made a convenient place where they wouldn't be seen?'

'I think we'd better keep an open mind on that.' Sandra looked up at the clock on the wall. 'Now, I'd better get ready for that press conference, and you had all better get off home. It's been a long day, and some of you were supposed to have this weekend off. So, thank you all for coming in to get this investigation started.'

$$\text{✳✳✳}$$

'At a press conference, which ended a few minutes ago, DCI Sandra Latham from Merseyside Police, told reporters that she was keeping an open mind about whether or not the two murders were connected.' Sandra put out her hand to switch off the radio. Now that she was on her way home, she wanted to put the case out of her mind for a while, and she certainly could do without the torment of hearing a recording of her responses at the press conference. Whenever she heard her own voice across the airwaves is sounded to her very affected and unconvincing. And the broadcasters always seemed to choose the moments when some questioner had caught her unawares and she had had to improvise with stammering answers that conveyed the impression that the police were incompetent and out of their depth.

'But Olivia Akram, another young Muslim woman who knew both victims, is convinced that the same killer is responsible.' Sandra withdrew her hand and continued listening. 'Now, Olivia,' the presenter went on, 'you've also been the victim of anti-Islamic attacks in the past. Is that right?'

'Yes.' The voice was young but confident. 'Verbal abuse is a day-to-day occurrence. It's something you just get used to putting up with, but I think you're referring to an incident four years ago when a group of us had acid sprayed over us. One of my friends died as a result and another was seriously injured.'

'And what makes you think that these two deaths are related?'

'Of course, co-incidences do happen,' came the young voice again, 'but these two murders do seem to have more in common than you would expect if they were random attacks. Both victims were students; both were British women of South Asian appearance wearing hijabs – two characteristics that often attract Islamophobic abuse; both attended the same mosque and were members of a women's society there; and both were attacked late at night near where they were living and apparently strangled with their own hijab before being left by the bins with the rubbish. I'd say that it's obvious that there is someone out there who believes that Muslim women are trash who deserve to be killed and dumped with the rest of the waste.'

'And you think that they could be targeting members of your mosque specifically?'

'A sample of two is too small to say. We get a lot of students there, so that's probably a more likely link, especially with them being killed right by their student accommodation.'

'So, you would agree with DCI Latham that Muslim women should take precautions when they're out at night?'

'Yes. Of course, I'm not blaming the victims: these two students should have been safe walking the short distance home to their rooms, like thousands of other young female students. They were absolutely not acting in a reckless manner. But, until whoever it is that's targeting young Muslim women is caught, I'm not going to be out on the streets on my own after dark and I would advise other women – and not just Muslims – to be careful too.'

'Why not just Muslims?'

'Like I said, a sample of two isn't enough to go on. And who knows whether Muslims are the only group that this monster wants to consigns to the rubbish heap?'

'Well, I'll certainly be taking extra care when I'm out at night,' the interviewer agreed. 'Thank you, Olivia. That was Olivia Akram, a graduate of the University of Liverpool and now a trainee barrister at Mount Street Chambers. Now, on to other news. There is a row brewing in the Tory party after a senior MP blamed failures at the Home Office for the migrant crisis. Interviewed on GB News, Sir Bob Neill said….'

Sandra switched off the radio as she backed the car on to the drive of the mid-terraced ex-council house in Knotty Ash, where she lived with the younger of her two daughters. The house was in darkness. It being term-time, Philippa was away at university and her older sister, Sophie, had flown the family nest at the earliest opportunity to live with her boyfriend in a flat in Ormskirk.

Sandra was glad that there was no one there to complain at her late return or make demands on her for food or conversation or, as had so often been the case when the girls were at home, for transport to various venues across the city. She would make herself a reviving mug of tea while a ready-meal warmed up in the microwave. When the girls were both at home she had insisted on cooking "proper food" for them, determined not to allow her demanding job to get in the way of providing nutritious meals for her family. But now, with nobody around to notice and comment on the change, she was increasingly often taking the easy option, telling herself that cooking for one was wasteful as well as time-consuming.

She put the kettle on and selected a chili-con-carne meal for one from the freezer. She checked the instructions on the side of the packet and then dutifully removed the outer packaging and set the microwave timer. She got out her favourite mug and dropped a teabag into it. But when she went to the fridge for milk, she remembered that she had used the last of it on her breakfast cereal that morning. She had been intending to pick some up during the course of the day, but things had been so hectic that she had forgotten to do so.

Her first thought was to go round to her parents' house in the next street to "borrow" some milk from them. But her mother was sure to insist that she stayed to eat with them, even though they would probably have finished their "tea", as they persisted in calling their evening meal, and be happily settled together on the sofa watching TV while her mother knitted and her father wrestled with the crossword. And they would pity her for her failed marriage and her failure to cater adequately even now that she had only herself to think about.

She switched off the microwave and the kettle and picked up her purse from the table. The convenience store in the row of shops on Prescot Road would be open. It wouldn't take more than five minutes to walk. And she could pick up a few other essentials that she was running low on while she was there.

✳✳✳

On the way back from the shop, a car drove past her and then slowed down and stopped just ahead of her. As she continued to walk, the passenger window opened and someone leaned out. A stranger to the area asking for directions, perhaps. But no, it was Lucy Paige, her curly blond hair, no longer constrained, standing out like a halo around her head.

'Hi Sandra! Would you like a lift?'

'It's OK, thanks, I'm nearly home.'

'We must be going to be neighbours then. Ibrahim and I have got a house just round the corner. Mam and Peter are up here to help get it ready for us to move in. It was cheap because the old man who lived in it before hadn't done any maintenance or decorating for ages, so it's in a bit of a state.'

'There's something you probably need to know.' Bernie leaned across from the driver's seat.

'Oh?' Bending closer, to hear what Bernie was saying, Sandra saw Mariam in the back of the car. She too had abandoned her hijab, replacing it with a rather incongruous beanie hat in Everton colours.

'Yasmeen's mother and sister are here,' Bernie told her. 'They came up on the train this evening. They're staying with Dominic and Ibrahim overnight. Will they be able to see Yasmeen's body tomorrow, or will they have to wait until after the weekend? They're anxious to take her back to Birmingham for a funeral at home.'

'Aah! Tahira did say that the family would want the body released as soon as possible,' Sandra acknowledged. 'But the coroner certainly won't even look at the case before Monday – or probably Tuesday with the bank holiday. I'll see what I can do about them viewing the body tomorrow, but obviously Sunday isn't exactly the best day for it.'

'Thanks. I'm sure they'll appreciate that.'

'And I'll need to interview them,' Sandra went on. 'Yasmeen may have confided in them things she wouldn't have been comfortable about telling her friends. Shall I call in on them tomorrow morning? What time do you think would be best?'

'Probably best to give Tahira a ring first,' Bernie told her. 'She'll probably take them back to her flat above the Islamic centre in the morning. She's looking for somewhere better for them to stay. This is just a stop-gap.'

'OK.' Sandra looked at her watch. 'I'll give her a ring when I get home and fix up an appointment. Thank you for letting me know.'

'Have there been any developments?' Lucy asked quickly, seeing Sandra straightening up ready to resume her walk home. 'Do you have any idea what those chess pieces mean?'

'What do you know about chess pieces?' Sandra spoke sharply and bent down again to look Lucy in the eye.

'Poppy Venables told us about the white knight that she found next to Rania's body, and Tahira saw one of the SOCOs picking up a rook near where Yasmeen was found,' Lucy told her. 'We thought it must be more than just a coincidence.'

'Quite possibly it is,' Sandra agreed with a sigh, 'But for exactly that reason, it's not something that we want made public. So, I'd be grateful if you didn't spread it around. Who else knows about it?'

'Just us,' Lucy told her. 'That's me, Mariam, Dom and Ibrahim, and Tahira, and Mam and Peter, of course.'

'And my parents,' Mariam added.

'And Jonah,' Lucy remembered suddenly. 'He heard your press conference on the radio and rang us to know all about it.'

Sandra pulled a wry face. 'Well, I want you to tell them all that it mustn't go any further. Those chess pieces are the one definite thing that we've got to link the two murders, and we don't want the killer to know that we've noticed them. Do you understand?'

'Yes, of course.' Lucy sounded affronted at the suggestion that she might release confidential information. 'We wouldn't have told anyone anyway – not unless the police released the information officially.'

'Good.' Sandra straightened up again and swapped her bag of shopping into her other hand. 'I'd better get off home then and ring Tahira.'

'Mind you,' Bernie muttered darkly, 'if the killer is making a point with those chess pieces, they may not be that pleased not to hear them being mentioned on the news. Might they kill again just to get them noticed?'

6. QUEEN'S GAMBIT

'In death's dark vale I fear no ill,' Simon hummed as he pedalled through the bright but chilly morning air of Oxford. The chaplain of Lichfield College loved this time of the year, when the days were lengthening and the hope of Easter was still fresh and bright – despite some far from hopeful stories in the news, which he must remember to include in the intercessions this morning: people fleeing from fighting in Sudan, the ongoing war in Ukraine, strikes in schools and hospitals, desperate people still risking their lives crossing the channel in small boats....

'Thy unction grace bestoweth...,' he gently applied the brakes and dismounted a few yards away from the entrance of Lichfield College. 'And oh, what transport of–!'

He broke off as he found his way blocked by what at first appeared to be a pile of discarded clothes and other rubbish, but which he soon realised was a human form. It lay awkwardly alongside the wall of the college with one shoulder propped at a most uncomfortable-looking angle against the honey-coloured stone and its head lolling to one side against a cast-iron downspout.

He hastily propped up his bike on a nearby litter bin and bent down to look more closely. The nights were cold for rough sleeping and this young woman did not even seem to have a sleeping bag or blanket to shield her from the northerly breeze, which Simon could feel chilling his cheeks and hands as he removed his gloves and carefully pushed aside a greasy discarded chip paper that appeared to be stuck to her hair, partially hiding her face. She must be comatose from drink or drugs or she would surely have removed it herself.

As soon as he revealed her eyes, he knew that there was more wrong than that. They were wide open and slightly bulging. Her complexion, now that he could see more of her face, had a strange greyish look. Her cheek felt cold when his hand brushed against it.

Simon hastily sought the woman's wrist to confirm what he already knew. She had no gloves on and her hands were icy cold. Her arm was stiff and hard. Searching for a pulse would be pointless. She had clearly been dead for some time. What had happened? Had the cold killed her as she slept? But, in that case, why were her eyes open and staring as if in terror? He stood up, took out his mobile phone and dialled 999.

A quarter of an hour later neither police nor ambulance had yet arrived. Simon stared down at his watch and then peered up and down the road, willing them to come. How long were they going to be? He couldn't stay here all day, but nor could he leave the dead woman alone now that he had seen her. Her death would have to be investigated and evidence that might give a clue as to what had happened must not be disturbed. Besides, there might be rats or urban foxes around that would ….

He shuddered at the thoughts that came involuntarily to his mind and, turning his back on the corpse, gazed up and down the road again. Still no sign of the police, but there was the welcome sight of a pedestrian approaching. As she came closer, he recognised Julia Reeves, one of the team of college porters. She must be arriving to start her day in the lodge at the college entrance.

'Julia!' Simon stepped out into her path. 'I wonder if you could do something for me? Something rather … something dreadful has happened.' He half-turned and waved his hand towards the woman's body. 'When I got here this morning, I found …. It's a dead body – a young woman. I've rung for the police, but they haven't come yet and I need to go. The communion service in chapel's supposed to start in ten minutes. The chapel clerk will be having kittens. Could you … Would you mind? Someone needs to stay here until the police come.'

'A dead woman?' Fortunately, Julia had an unflappable nature and a wealth of experience of life – and death – which made her prepared for almost anything. She walked calmly over to check the veracity of Simon's statement.

'Do you recognise her?' he asked as they stood looking down at the dead woman.

'No.' Julia shook her head. 'She's not one of ours. Certainly not a student living in college, at any rate. I know them all by sight. OK. I'll stand guard while you do your stuff in the chapel, but come right back afterwards. With it being Sunday, I'm on my own today, and if I'm not there, some undergraduate is bound to have an emergency that needs my attention. They always choose the worst possible times for locking themselves out of their rooms or breaking their beds.'

'Thanks.' Simon picked up his bike and prepared to wheel it through the archway that led into the college. 'I'll come back the minute chapel's over.'

Julia stood staring down at the dead woman. She had been at the deaths of both of her parents and been called to identify her late husband's body after he was killed in a pile-up on the M4, but none of them had looked like this. Her mother, in particular, had experienced a lot of pain during her final days, and yet in death her features had appeared serene, as if she were at last at peace. That car crash must have been terrifying for Tom, but it did not show on his face, battered and bloody though it had been. But this young woman! Those staring eyes, so full of fear! And yet, there was something beautiful about her too.

It was a striking face. The skin was smooth and flawless, slightly tanned – or perhaps naturally darkish. Her black eyebrows were thick and gently arched over stunning blue-green eyes. Her hair, also black or a very dark brown, was coiled round her head in a long plait. No, she was definitely not a member of Lichfield College. Even if she lived out, she would have had to come into the porters' lodge occasionally to collect her mail or to send messages through the "pigeon post" internal university system. With a face like that, Julia would not have forgotten her.

At the sound of a vehicle approaching, she turned to see a police patrol car drawing up. It stopped and a female uniformed officer got out.

'Excuse me. I got a call to say that a body had been found in the street somewhere near here?'

'Yes. That's right. Over here.'

'Was it you who made the call?' The officer closed the door of the car and start to walk towards Julia.

'No. That was Reverend Sutcliffe. He had to go, so he asked me to wait with her. We've neither of us touched anything. This is how he found her.'

'I see.' The officer bent down to look more closely at the body. She pushed aside a length of fine purple fabric round the woman's neck and felt for a pulse in the carotid artery. Then she stood up again and turned to face Julia. 'It looks as if she's been dead some time. When was she found?'

'I'm not sure exactly. You'd have to ask Simon – Reverend Sutcliffe – when he's finished in chapel. He's college chaplain, you see, and he had to go to take the early service. He said he'd come straight back after that.'

I see,' the officer repeated. 'Well, I'll need to speak to him when he's free, but meanwhile, perhaps you can answer a few questions.' She took a small notebook out of her pocket and flipped it open. 'My name is PC Stella Gilbert – and you are…?'

'Julia Reeves. I'm a porter at Lichfield College.' Julia waved vaguely in the direction of the college entrance. 'Simon asked me to wait for you, to make sure nothing happened to ….' Her eyes moved towards the body that still lay at their feet.

'Yes. Thank you. The 999 call came through at 7.35. I assume he asked you to come out sometime after that?'

'Not exactly. I was due to start work at eight. He called me over as I was on my way in. It must've been about ten to eight. He was anxious to get away because his service was at eight.'

'I see,' Stella nodded. 'And you've had a look at the dead woman? Do you recognise her? Have you seen her before at all?'

'No. I'm sure I would remember if I'd met her. She's not a run-of-the-mill scruffy undergraduate.'

Stella looked down, appraising the neatly-braided hair and perfect complexion. Yes, there was something very remarkable about the young woman's appearance. That purple scarf was unusual too – it looked like expensive material and the intricate gold embroidery edging had an exotic feel to it. 'So, you've no idea at all who she might be or how she comes to be here?'

'None at all, I'm sorry.' Julia shook her head. 'Er … would it be OK if I went now? I'll be just over there in the porters' lodge if you need to ask me any more questions. It's just that I'm the only one on duty today, with it being Sunday….'

'Yes, of course. That's fine. And Simon Sutcliffe – what time do you think he'll be ready to…?'

'Oh, it's quite a short service. Half past eight, quarter to nine at latest. I'm sure he'll come straight back here as soon as he's free.'

Stella watched as the older woman made her way across the flagstones and disappeared into the archway at the entrance to the college. Then she put an urgent call through to the control centre, asking for a Crime Scene Investigation team and the duty Inspector to attend. She might be relatively newly-qualified, but she had enough experience to recognise a suspicious death when she encountered one. She had seen what looked like bruising on the victim's neck and the prominent eyes and tiny red spots beneath the skin on her cheeks also pointed towards the possibility that she had been strangled. Besides, what innocent explanation could there be for a young and apparently healthy woman to be found lying dead in an Oxford backstreet?

Her next job was to secure the scene. She returned to the car and took out a roll of blue-and-white tape and a pile of tall cones. What exactly constituted the crime scene? The SOCOs would no doubt prefer her to cordon off the entire street, but that would seriously inconvenience members of the colleges whose main entrances opened on to it. And, since the woman had clearly died several hours ago, there must have been plenty of traffic along the road since then. Just an area around the corpse large enough to provide room for the team to work must surely be sufficient.

She set to work arranging the cones in a rough rectangle around the place where the body lay. A grille over a small ground-floor window provided a convenient starting point to attach the tape. She tied it firmly and then walked backwards, allowing the reel to unwind in her hands as she went.

Suddenly her left foot slid from underneath her. She had stepped on something – some small object, round enough to roll when she trod on it. She bent down to see what it was. Then, with great care she pulled out a pair of latex gloves from her pocket and put them on. She picked up the object and studied it more closely. It was a white chess piece – a figure with a crown on its head. The white king? No, it was too dumpy for that. It must be the queen, the white queen. What a strange thing to find dropped in the street! Chess sets were expensive, not something to throw around casually. She sealed it carefully in a plastic evidence bag, labelling it meticulously with the date, time and location in neat handwriting.

She finished setting up the cordon and returned the unused tape to her car. There was no sign of the backup that she had called for. Neither had the chaplain returned. The street was empty and silent.

Stella went over to woman's body and stood gazing down, studying it thoughtfully. She was dressed in a long black coat over black trousers – nothing particularly unusual there; but that length of fine silky material around her neck was definitely not the sort of thing that most undergraduates were in the habit of wearing. It wasn't a college scarf. Nor would it have provided much protection against the cold night air. And it had been pulled tighter around her neck than could have been comfortable. It looked as if this might be the murder weapon. Did it belong to the killer, or …? Hadn't there been something on the news about women being killed by being strangled with their own … their own hijabs? Yes! That was what it was – not a scarf, a hijab!

Stella took out her phone and began flicking through her contacts. It was probably a coincidence, but perhaps it was not. She looked up and down the road as she waited for an answer to her call, now hoping that the duty inspector would not arrive until she had completed it. They might not approve of what she was doing.

'Hi Stella! How're you doing?' The voice was cheerful but also sounded surprised. Her friend had understandably not been expecting a call so early on a Sunday morning.

'Lucy! I'm so glad you answered. Are you OK to talk?'

'Sure. Go ahead.'

'That friend of yours who was killed – she was strangled with her own hijab, is that right?'

'Yes. At least, that's certainly how it looks. Why?'

'And there was another woman killed the same way?'

'Ye-es.' Lucy replied slowly, clearly wondering where this was leading.

'Well, right now I'm standing in Lichfield Street keeping guard over another victim until CID get here. It looks like she's been killed in just the same way!'

'A Muslim woman, strangled with her own hijab? In Oxford?' Lucy's voice rose in astonishment. 'I suppose it must be a copycat murder. But why?'

'And there was a funny thing I found lying on the ground near her,' Stella went on. 'Someone had dropped a piece from a chess set.'

'A chess piece!' Stella jumped at Lucy's squeal of excitement. 'A white one? Was it a white bishop by any chance?'

'No. It was the white queen. Why?'

'There were white chess pieces left beside both of the other two victims too!' Lucy could clearly hardly contain her excitement. 'A white knight and then a white rook. But the police haven't released that information publicly, so I don't see how anyone would have known.'

'So, you're saying it's not a copycat killing but the same killer? But that's weird! I mean, why two murders in Liverpool and now one in Oxford?'

'I don't know. But it can't be just a coincidence, can it?'

'No. I get that but – sorry! I've got to go. The SOCO van has just arrived. Speak to you later!' Stella ended the call and slipped her phone back into her pocket. 'Curiouser and curiouser,' she murmured to herself looking down at the plastic bag containing the small wooden chess piece.

She walked over to the van that had pulled up behind her patrol car. Scenes of Crime Officers were busily putting on their white disposable suits and taking out equipment from the back of the van. Their leader looked up as Stella approached and she recognised her as Ruby Mann, one of their most experienced Crime Scene Managers.

'I'm PC Stella Gilbert,' she told her. 'I've secured the scene as well as I could, but it looks as if the body could have been here for quite a long time before anyone found her, so …'

'Yes, I remember you, Stella. You were there when Kenny Hughes was killed[4], weren't you? I'm glad that didn't put you off finishing your training, but I couldn't have blamed you if it had. Now, can you talk me through what we've got here?'

'A young female,' Stella said, holding up the tape to allow Ruby to pass under the cordon. 'Of course, it's not for me to say, but I think she's probably been dead for a few hours at least. She's quite stiff and cold – and there are marks that suggest she's been strangled.'

'I see.' Ruby squatted down and peered at the body. 'Any idea who she is?'

'No. One of the Lichfield College porters was here when I arrived and she was confident it wasn't one of their students, but…. Oh! And there's something you ought to see.' Stella held out the evidence bag containing the chess queen. 'This was lying on the ground quite close to the body.'

Ruby took the bag and held it up in front of her face, turning it slowly round to view the contents from all sides. 'What makes you think this has something to do with the body? Anyone could have dropped it, couldn't they?'

---

[4] See *Weed Killers*, ISBN 978-1-911083-66-5, © Judy Ford 2020

'But there've been two other killings where chess pieces were found at the scene,' Stella told her, trying to speak in a calm, matter-of-fact way, not betraying the excitement that she felt at having uncovered this strange connection between crimes committed 180 miles apart. 'Not here – in Liverpool. I've got a friend who's at uni up there. She knew the victims. They were killed like this, by being strangled with–'

'We don't know for certain that this woman *was* strangled,' Ruby interrupted. 'Cause of death is for the pathologist to determine.'

'OK.' Stella conceded, rather crestfallen at having her assumptions questioned. 'But the thing is: there was a white chess piece left lying next to both of those other victims, and now this. What are the chances of that?'

'I suppose she does have this scarf thing tight round her neck,' Ruby admitted thoughtfully.

'And there's what could be petechial haemorrhages on her face,' Stella added, pointing downward.

Ruby bent forward to look at the body more closely. She put out her gloved hand and touched the woman's cheeks and chin gently. Then she carefully exposed her neck and studied the red marks indicative of strangulation. 'Mmm. Yes, I think you're probably right, but we'd better not make assumptions. There's supposed to be a pathologist on their way. Like I said, cause of death is their call.'

She stood up and looked round. 'Hi Janet! Over here please! I want some pictures of the corpse in situ.'

Forensic photographer Janet Kingman hurried over, camera in hand. Ruby moved aside to allow her to photograph the body full-length with the wall and drain pipe still supporting it.

'Now, some close-ups of the face and neck,' she ordered, 'and some of this stuff that she's got lying all over her.'

Stella watched as the photographer moved in to take pictures of various pieces of debris which were strewn over the surface of the victim's outer garments: crisp packets, cigarette ends, an apple core and two banana skins. It was as if the contents of the nearby litter bin had been emptied over her after she was killed – but why would someone do that? Stella went over to the bin and peered inside. It was empty. Turning round, she saw a black bin liner blowing against the wall of the college. There were empty drinks cans blowing around too. Had the murderer pulled the liner out from the bin and emptied it over their victim after killing her? If so, for what purpose?

'OK. Thanks Janet. I think you're done for the time being.'

Stella turned to see the photographer scrambling to her feet and stepping back to make room for Ruby to examine the body. She watched as the Crime Scene Manager knelt down and began feeling around in search of pockets. The coat yielded only a pair of woollen gloves, so next she carefully undid the buttons and opened it wide, revealing a loose-fitting mauve blouse, buttoned up to the neck. No pockets in that.

Proceeding methodically, Ruby felt down the sides of the trousers and drew out a bunch of keys from the right-hand pocket, which she held out towards Stella. 'Bag these up for me, please.'

'Excuse me!'

Stella jumped at the sound of a voice behind her. She turned to see a man in a clerical collar standing just outside the cordon, staring around apprehensively at the activities of the SOCO team. 'Good morning, sir,' she greeted him. 'You must be Reverend Sutcliffe.' The man nodded in affirmation. 'I'm PC Stella Gilbert. I need to ask you a few questions. Perhaps we'd be a bit more comfortable in my car?'

She led the way to the squad car and opened the door wide before remembering that she had not had time to clear away the rubbish left by the night-shift officers who had handed it over to her when she began work that morning.

'Sorry! Just a minute.' She leant inside and collected together empty coffee cups and cardboard takeaway containers from the front passenger seat and foot well. She stuffed them into the space behind the driver's seat and then brushed off the front seats with her hand before standing back to allow her interviewee to sit down inside. Then she walked round and got into the driving seat.

'Sorry about that sir. My colleagues had a busy night last night,' she apologised. 'Now, can I just check? You're Reverend Simon Sutcliffe, and you're the chaplain of Lichfield College, is that right?'

'Yes,' Simon nodded.

'And you were on your way to the college to take the morning service in the chapel when you found the body?'

'Yes. I cycled in from Summertown. I got here at about … er … half past seven, it must've been, and I almost trod on her. I thought she was drunk or stoned at first, but then… Well, I got up close to see if I could help her and… she was cold, quite cold, and stiff! I knew she was dead, even before I saw the way her eyes were staring. I didn't see them at first, because of all the rubbish there was all over her. I suppose the wind must have blown it.'

'Yes, I expect so,' Stella agreed encouragingly. 'And did you notice anything else – anything unexpected, perhaps? Or something that was out-of-place?'

'No, I don't think so, sorry.'

'And you didn't recognise her? You don't know who she is?'

'No – and I called one of the porters over and she didn't know her either. So, I don't think she can be a Lichfield student. The porters usually know everyone.'

'Yes, I spoke to her and she said,' Stella nodded. She looked down at her notes, trying to think of anything else that she ought to ask this witness before allowing him to go. Why wasn't the duty inspector here yet? They would know all the right questions. 'OK. I think that's all for now. Could you just write down your address and a phone number where we can get in touch with you if we need to speak to you again?'

She turned to a clean page in her notebook before handing it to Simon. He scribbled down an address in North Oxford and a mobile number then handed it back to her. 'I can go now?'

'Yes sir. Thank you, you've been very helpful.' Stella got out of the car and went round to open the passenger door, but Simon had already extracted himself from the vehicle and was standing looking round uncertainly as if he couldn't quite believe that he was free to go. 'We'll be in touch if we need anything else, but for the moment, it would be best if we can leave the area clear for the Scenes of Crime Officers to work,' she prompted him gently.

'Yes, of course, sorry,' Simon mumbled. 'Yes. I'll get off then.'

'PC Gilbert! I hear you have a corpse for me to look at!' Stella looked round to see forensic pathologist Michael Carson's smiling face. 'And a lovely morning it is for it too! What can you tell me about it?'

'Female, student age, I think, but almost certainly not from this college. Ruby was looking for ID. I don't know if she found any. I'll take you to have a look. She's got some marks on her face and neck that I thought looked like she'd been strangled, but…'

They found Ruby standing close to the body in conversation with one of her colleagues.

'Mike! I'm glad you're here. It looks as if she's been dead some time, but you're the expert. We've tried not to disturb anything, but we did have to turn her over a bit to get at her pockets. I found this in the back pocket of her trousers.' She held up a plastic card on which Stella could see a photograph of the young woman above a bar code and a name: Zahra Shahidi, undergraduate member of Holy Cross College.

'We think she was probably on her way back to Holy Cross when she was attacked,' Ruby went on. 'Probably late last night, so I'll be very interested to hear exactly what time you think she died. If it was before dark, it's odd that nobody noticed her earlier.'

'Now you know that *exactly* isn't in my vocabulary.' The pathologist put down his bag next to the young woman's body and pulled on a pair of disposable gloves before kneeling on the ground and peering closely at her face. Then he gently pushed aside the purple fabric and stared intently at the red marks beneath it. Using both hands, he gently palpated her neck, a frown of concentration on his face.

'I'm inclined to think that you may be right, Stella,' he said, briefly glancing round at her. 'Strangulation is a real possibility. I think that I can feel some damage to the larynx – and of course the petechial haemorrhages are indicative, but not conclusive. The post-mortem should confirm the extent of the injuries. There are also some scratches under the chin, which could be from the victim's own fingernails as she tried to loosen the ligature.'

'Was it her own hijab that was used?' Stella asked.

'Hijab? Is that what you think this is?' Ruby asked, pointing down at the length of purple fabric.

'I – I thought it might be.' Stella suddenly regretted having spoken. As the most junior and least experienced person there, it was hardly her place to be expressing an opinion. 'I mean… It's not the sort of scarf that students usually wear, and…'

'And her name sounds as if it could be Arabic,' Ruby said thoughtfully. 'But she doesn't *look* very much like a Muslim.'

'She could be of Middle-Eastern origin,' Mike suggested, 'or Bosnian – or a British convert.'

'That's right,' agreed Stella, plucking up courage to speak now that the pathologist seemed to be agreeing with her. 'Lucy knows quite a few white Muslims. Come to that, she often wears a hijab, even though she isn't one – for solidarity. And….' She hesitated, unsure whether to go on. 'And, the other victims were both Muslims,' she said at last. 'The ones in Liverpool, I mean.'

'Other victims?' asked Mike with raised eyebrows.

'PC Gilbert has a theory that this may be connected with two murder cases up in Liverpool,' Ruby old him.

'Really?' Mike smiled towards Stella. 'And would Lucy have anything to do with that?'

'Well, she was the one who told me about the chess pieces,' Stella confessed.

'Chess pieces? You've lost me there.'

'PC Gilbert found a chess piece near the victim,' Ruby explained, 'and apparently there were similar pieces left by the two Liverpool victims too.'

'But that hasn't been made public,' Stella added. 'So…'

'So, if it's not the same killer, it must be either a rather big coincidence or someone who knows more than the general public do,' Mike finished for her. 'Such as young Lucy Paige, I'm guessing. Where exactly does she come in?'

'She told me about the chess pieces – only after I told her about his one,' Stella added quickly. 'She knew both of the other victims and she's been talking to the people who found them. I – I rang her this morning, to… to sort of compare notes.' She could feel her cheeks becoming warm as she realised that she had shared information that should have remained confidential. 'I'd only just found the white queen and it seemed such a funny thing. And then, when I told Lucy about it, she said that there'd been chess pieces left at the other two crime scenes too.'

'What other two crime scenes?' They all looked up in surprise at this question. DI Andy Lepage had approached silently and was now standing behind them.

Mike was the first to recover. 'Andy!' he called out jovially. 'Are you the SIO?'

'It's looking a bit like it. Or, to put it another way, I'm the highest-ranking CID officer on duty this weekend, so I'll be in charge until tomorrow at least. Now what's this about other crime scenes?'

'Young Stella here thinks this could be linked to a couple of other killings up on Merseyside,' Mike told him. 'Apparently Lucy Paige is mixed up in those in some way and the two of them have been comparing notes. It sounded quite convincing to me, but of course, you're the detective. You'll have to make up your own mind. I just examine corpses.'

'And have you had time to examine this one?' Andy asked, jumping in to stem the flow of Mike's musical brogue.

'Just a brief preliminary. I think the rest can wait until we get her back to the mortuary. There are signs of possible strangulation, but whether that was how she died is another matter altogether. I can't see any indications that the body has been moved, so she's most likely lying where she fell. She's clearly been dead some hours. Rigor mortis is fully established, which means that death almost certainly occurred before midnight. I'll just take her temperature. Then I can do an independent time-of-death calculation to cross-reference with the rigor evidence. After that, I'm off home for my breakfast.'

'And the PM?'

'Would tomorrow afternoon suit you? Say, two-thirty?'

'Yes. That will be fine. I'm glad you can fit it in so soon; I'd heard you were run off your feet.'

'I always do my best to oblige,' Mike grinned back as he replaced his digital thermometer is his bag. 'Especially when I know that I'll have Lucy Paige on my back wanting results! How is she, by the way? It's a while since I've had her nosing round my lab.'

'Oh, she's fine – apart from having two of her friends murdered in the last three weeks, I suppose.' It suddenly dawned on Stella that Lucy's interest in finding the killer was more than simply an academic one motivated by her ambition to become a forensic pathologist and her close relationship with members of the police service. She hurried on to change the subject. 'Peter and Bernie are up there with her now, helping to get her new house ready. It's the wedding in a couple of months and there's a lot of work needs doing on it before they can move in.'

'Ah yes! The wedding. I'm looking forward to that. And a little bird tells me that you are going to be a bridesmaid.'

'Well, not exactly. Lucy didn't want to bother with all that sort of thing - dressing up all in white and bridesmaids and stuff, but then it turned out Peter's little granddaughter, Abigail had set her heart on being a bridesmaid. So Lucy said she could, and then she said she'd better have a grown-up bridesmaid to look after her. So that's me!'

Fascinating though this discussion is,' Andy interrupted, 'I think we ought to be concentrating on what the British public are paying us to do, which is to find out who killed this young woman. Do we know who she is?'

'Her name's Zahra Shahidi,' Ruby told him, holding out the student ID card, now sealed into an evidence bag. 'And she's a student at Holy Cross College. Assuming she was killed here last night, she was probably on her way back to her room when it happened.'

'OK.' Andy took the card and studied it briefly. 'I'd better get round there and find out who her next-of-kin is. And someone from the college should be able to confirm her identity. I'll leave you to finish processing the crime scene, Ruby. And can you get a few more uniforms here to keep back the spectators,' he added, looking round at the clusters of onlookers who had started to gather, many of them with mobile phones held up taking pictures of the forensics team at work. 'Stella! Come with me. You can fill me in on what you know about these Liverpool murders on the way.'

***

The College is Closed to Visitors, announced a notice outside the main entrance to Holy Cross College when they arrived there a few minutes later. Stella looked up at the huge oak door, strengthened with bands and studs of iron. It would have been a formidable barrier if there had not been a small wicket door-within-a-door standing open in apparent contradiction of the notice.

They stepped through into the dimness of a tunnel leading from the street into the main quadrangle and were immediately confronted by another notice, on an A-frame in the middle of their path: *All visitors must report to the Porters' Lodge*, with an arrow pointing to the right. Andy led the way up two steps into a room whose walls were lined with rows of pigeonholes labelled alphabetically. To his left, an opening that looked like the serving hatches that you might see in a school canteen gave a view into an anteroom where an elderly man was sitting reading a newspaper, a cup of tea on the desk in front of him.

'Excuse me!' Andy called, leaning his elbow on the counter and holding up his warrant card. 'Can I have a word?'

The porter jumped at the sound and the teacup rattled on its saucer. He whipped off his reading glasses, letting them drop down on a chain round his neck, put down the newspaper and hurried over to the hatch.

'I'm DI Lepage and this is PC Gilbert. I wonder if you can tell me anything about Zahra Shahidi. I believe she's a student here.' Andy held out the ID card.

Fumbling in his haste, the porter replaced the glasses on his nose and stood staring down at the card. 'Yes,' he confirmed. 'She's one of ours. Second year undergraduate – English. Thank you for returning the card. I'll put it in her pigeonhole.' He lifted a section of the counter with the intention of coming through into the main room of the lodge, but Andy put out his hand and took back the card.

'I'm afraid this isn't just a matter of a lost student ID card. We found this on the body of a young woman whom we believe to be Zahra Shahidi, and we're treating her death as suspicious.'

The porter took off his glasses again and stood staring at Andy without speaking.

'Now, I'm going to need to know the name and address of her next-of-kin. Presumably the college holds records of that sort of thing?'

'Er… yes! Yes, of course. The college secretary doesn't work weekends, but I'm sure someone will be able to look in the files for you. I think the best thing will be if I ring through to the principal. She ought to be told about this, and she'll know how to…. Yes. That's it! I'll ring the Principal's Lodgings.' He reached for the telephone, which lay on the counter a short way from the hatch, but Andy interrupted him.

'And we'll need someone who knew Ms Shahidi to confirm her identity – her tutor, perhaps?'

'Yes, yes. She was reading English, so she'll be one of Dr Usher's. He lives out, but I can ring him at home for you and ask him to come in, if you like?'

'Yes please, if you don't mind – Oh! And we'll need to see her room. Was she living in college?'

'I'd have to look that up. Why don't you take a seat and I'll make those phone calls and then find out for you.?'

'Thank you.'

Andy and Stella sat down on two easy chairs in a corner of the room next to a vending machine. A small table in front of them had a rack containing leaflets offering guidance on sexual health, the university counselling service, the Samaritans and various college and university societies.

Andy studied the photograph on Zahra Shahidi's ID card. It was too small to show much detail, but she was clearly wearing some sort of head covering. Stella was right: this was a third case of a Muslim woman being attacked and strangled with her own hijab. But what other link could there possibly be between this woman and the two in Liverpool? Why would a murderer travel all that way to find his third victim? Surely it must be a case of a second killer copying the first? But how then had they known about the chess pieces?

Stella had told him that the first two victims knew each other. They had attended the same mosque in Liverpool and had belonged to some sort of pressure group for feminist Muslims. Was Zahra Shahidi another member of their movement? Could they all have been targeted by someone who disagreed with what they were trying to achieve – a Muslim fundamentalist, perhaps?

'Professor Balachandran is on her way.' Andy looked up at the sound of the porter's voice. 'And Dr Usher will be in soon, but he's got to travel from Wolvercote. Now, I'll just check for you where Miss Shahidi was living.'

'Thank you.' Andy got to his feet and was about to walk back over to the counter when the outer door opened and he became aware of a Presence in the room. There was an aura about Professor Balachandran that somehow conveyed the feeling that she was the most significant person at any gathering.

'Good morning,' she greeted him, advancing across the room with hand outstretched. 'You must be Detective Inspector Lepage. I'm Veronica Balachandran. I'm the Principal here. Mr Palmer told me that you've found the body of one of our students – is that right?'

'Yes ma'am. According to the ID card she had in her pocket, her name's Zahra Shahidi. Do you know her?'

'I will have met her at her matriculation, and every undergraduate is invited to dine on High Table once each year, but I can't say that I remember her particularly. We have over 400 hundred undergraduates in the college, so I can't get to know them all personally. Her tutor would be the best person to help you.'

'Dr Usher is on his way,' the porter informed her. 'He said twenty minutes.'

'Thank you, Ernest. I knew you'd have everything under control.' The Principal flashed a benignant smile towards him and then turned back to Andy. 'What happened exactly? Was it a road accident?'

'No. I'm afraid that we're treating the death as suspicious.'

'In what way suspicious? Are you talking suicide? Murder? Or what?'

'We strongly suspect that someone killed her. I can't tell you any more than that at present. Meanwhile, we need someone to confirm her identity and we'll need to have a look in her room. And we were hoping that you would be able to provide us with contact details for her next-of-kin.'

'Yes, of course. Unfortunately, with it being the weekend, the college secretary isn't in, but I also have access to the database. It may just take me a bit longer to locate the information than if Julie were here. Would you like to come with me to the office?'

'Thank you.'

'Er, before you go, sir!' Palmer, the porter called. 'I've checked the accommodation file and Miss Shahidi does have a room in college. I've got the spare key here, if you want to have a look inside?'

'Thank you, yes.' Andy stood for a moment, undecided. Then he turned to Professor Balachandran. 'If you don't mind, I think I'd like to check out her room right away. Here's my card. It's got my mobile number on it. Perhaps you could give me a ring when you've got the information about next-of-kin?'

$$***$$

'I'll leave you to get on, Sir,' Palmer said as he stood back to allow Andy and Stella into the small first-floor room which had been home to Zahra Shahidi for the last six months. 'I'd be grateful if you could bring the keys back to the lodge when you've finished with them.'

Andy looked round at the narrow bed, which took up most of one wall, the mullioned window, and the bright red-and-yellow rug, which provided a splash of colour against the dull charcoal carpet tiles covering floor. The wall opposite the bed was fitted with a narrow wardrobe and a drawer unit, separated by a length of work surface with bookshelves and a mirror above it – a combined desk and dressing table, on which there lay a laptop computer, a pile of books, an A4 pad of paper with notes written on it, and a hair-brush.

'I'll bag up the computer. You have a look in the drawers,' Andy instructed Stella. 'We're looking for anything that can tell us more about what sort of person she was and why anyone might want to kill her. So, membership cards for societies, diary, address book – although those are probably all electronic these days.'

The top drawer was divided into two. In the left-hand one, Stella found two passports. At first, she thought they were both the familiar pre-Brexit burgundy British ones, but one of them lacked the royal coat of arms on the front. Turning it over, she read *Islamic Republic of Iran* in gold writing on what appeared to be the back. Intrigued, she attempted to open it. Of course! It opened on the left, which was why the title appeared to have been printed on the back.

Both passports had photographs of the young woman whose body lay in the street outside and confirmed her identity as Zahra Shahidi, a dual British-Iranian citizen, born in Southampton. The emergency contact in the back of her British passport was Dr Nasrin Shahidi with an address in Exeter.

'I think I've found her next-of-kin,' Stella told Andy. 'I'm guessing this is one of her parents.'

Andy took the passports and flicked through them. 'She visited Iran last year,' he murmured. 'I wonder if that's significant. OK, bag these up and we'll take them with us. Is there anything else you've found?'

'A purse with about ten pounds in it, and a wallet of plastic: credit card, debit card, library card… the usual things. The other drawer just has pens and pencils and stuff.'

'What about lower down?' Andy pulled out one of the full-size drawers to reveal a jumble of underwear. He pushed it closed again and reached for the drawer beneath.

'Hang on!' Stella pulled the drawer open again and started feeling around inside. 'If I had something I didn't want other people to find, this is where I'd keep it. If she kept a diary, for instance, I bet that's where it'd be.'

There was a knock at the door. Andy went to open it while Stella continued her search. Their visitor was a man whom Andy judged to be in his late sixties, with a thick grey beard and an almost completely bald head, giving the rather strange impression of his face being upside down. He blinked at Andy through black-rimmed glasses.

'Excuse me. You wanted to see me. I'm Gerald Usher – Zahra Shahidi's tutor.'

'Oh yes! Of course. Come in.' Andy closed the door behind their guest and gestured to him to sit down in one of two small easy chairs. 'It was good of you to come over so promptly. We're nearly finished in here and then, if you don't mind, I'd like you to come with me to confirm her identity. It's just a formality, but it is important that we're quite sure before we inform her parents.'

'Yes, of course. I quite understand.' Dr Usher sat looking nervously around, watching Stella as she turned out the remaining drawers, which disappointingly contained only clothes and makeup.

'What was Zahra like?' Andy asked him.

'Just a fairly typical undergraduate. She was a hard worker – got her essays in on time, didn't skip lectures. I didn't consider her first class material, but she was heading for a solid two-one.'

'Did she have many friends?' Before the don could answer, Andy's phone rang. 'Excuse me.'

It was Ruby wanting to know whether she could allow the body to be taken away.

'Ask them to wait just a few minutes. I've got her tutor here ready to identify her. Just hang on and we'll be right there.' Andy returned his phone to his pocket and looked towards Dr Usher. 'Ready to go now?'

'As ready as I'll ever be,' he nodded, getting to his feet.

Andy turned to Stella. 'Can I leave you to lock up and return the key? Then after that, come and join me outside Lichfield.'

$$***$$

'Yes, that's Zahra.' Dr Usher looked down at the black body bag on the trolley and then up at Andy's face. 'Do you know what happened to her?'

'As I said, we're treating her death as suspicious, but we're keeping an open mind on the details.' Andy watched as one of the crew zipped the bag back over the victim's face and began wheeling the trolley towards the waiting ambulance. 'When did you see her last?'

'On Tuesday afternoon at her tutorial.'

'And how did she seem?'

'The same as usual. Better prepared than her tutorial partner, but that was normal. She's – she was a very conscientious student. I think she was probably under pressure from her family to succeed – a lot of ethnic minority students are.'

'As her tutor, you would have been responsible for her general welfare as well as her academic progress; were you aware of her having any personal problems?'

'No, but students are often not very forthcoming to their tutors about that sort of thing.' Usher gave a little laugh. 'They think we're too old to understand.'

'But she didn't appear to be worried or depressed at all?' Andy pressed him.

'No. As I said, she was just the same as usual: quietly competent.'

'OK. And are you aware of anyone having threatened her at all?'

The tutor shook his head vigorously. Andy continued to probe. 'She hadn't fallen out with anyone recently?'

'Not that I know of, but she probably wouldn't have confided in me. You'd do better speaking to her friends. Her tutorial partner, for example, or the other students on her staircase.'

'Can you give me their names?'

'I can give you a list of the other English students in her year. The porters will be better placed to tell you about her neighbours.'

'Thank you.' Andy nodded towards Stella, who held out her notebook and a pencil.

Gerald Usher obediently took them and wrote down a list of seven names. 'Is that all now?'

'For the time being,' Andy confirmed. 'Thank you for your help.'

7. GRANDMASTER?

'What was all that about?' asked Bernie when Lucy put her phone down on the breakfast table after the call from Stella ended.

'It was Stella. There's been one in Oxford too now.'

'One what?' demanded Peter.

'A Muslim woman killed by someone who leaves chess pieces next to their victim. Stella's there now. She found it – the white queen.'

'But that doesn't make sense!' broke in Mariam. 'Why would a Liverpool killer go all the way down to Oxford just to kill someone?'

'And if it's not the same killer, how did they know to leave a chess piece by the body?' asked Peter. 'Sandra Latham will think someone leaked the information. Are we absolutely sure that none of us let it out accidentally?' he added, looking towards Lucy and Mariam. 'You haven't posted anything about it to your friends on social media?'

'No!' Lucy squealed indignantly. 'And Dom and Ibrahim would never do that either.'

'What about your friends at the mosque then? Did any of them know abou–'

'Anyway, we'd better hurry,' Bernie said, hoping to head off a row. 'Eat up everyone or we'll be late for mass. Joey and Ruth are expecting us at their house in about twenty minutes, so that we can all go together and demonstrate to Father Nat what good Catholics we all are.'

$$***$$

'Mariam! What a delight to see you this morning,' Father Nathaniel Milton greeted her as the family filed out of the little red-brick church where Bernie and her cousin Joey had attended Sunday School together more years ago than either of them cared to remember. 'I hope you haven't broken any rules by praying in a Catholic church.'

'The Qur'an instructs Muslims to protect churches,' Mariam told him. 'Because they're places where God is honoured.'

'Really? I never knew that! I am sorely ignorant of Islam I'm afraid. It's one of the many things that I feel I ought to learn more about, but there are always so many other demands on my time.'

'It's so good of you to agree to marry Dominic and Mariam,' Ruth broke in, taking the priest by the hand and shaking it fervently. 'I was afraid that it wouldn't be allowed. It used to be so difficult to get permission for mixed marriages.'

'Well, I admit that I did have a few … er, let's say *interesting* discussions with the bishop,' the priest smiled back at her. 'But I've got everything sorted out now, don't you worry.'

'For a while I thought they were going to make do with a registry office wedding,' Ruth went on. 'It's not that I'm set on a grand white wedding,' she hastened to add, 'but I do think marriage ought to be done in the sight of God and blessed by the church.'

'God is there in registry offices too,' Father Nathaniel pointed out gently. 'Everything that we do is in His sight. But I'm glad that Dominic and Lucy are allowing me to officiate. And I will be very interested to see what goes on at a Muslim wedding. It was very kind of you to invite me to come to that too.'

'We're off to the mosque now,' Bernie told him. 'You'll have heard that another Muslim student was attacked and killed on Friday night? She was the cousin of the assistant imam there.'

'Your friend?' Father Nat turned to Mariam. 'The female imam that you told me would be officiating at the wedding?'

'Yes. Yasmeen came here to uni because her parents thought Tahira would look after her,' Mariam answered. 'So now she feels responsible.'

'What a dreadful thing to happen! I will certainly keep the family in my prayers – if they won't mind, of course.'

'I'm sure they'll be pleased,' Mariam assured him. 'We're all praying to the same God, after all.'

✳✳✳

The community café was just opening when they arrived at the mosque.

'As-Salaamu-Alaykum,' a young man greeted them as they entered, putting away the pole that he had been using to wind up the shutters that protected the glass entrance doors at night. 'Breakfast is being served now, if you could just let the ladies know what you would like. There's free toast and tea or we can do you a cooked breakfast with frothy coffee for five pounds.'

'Wa-alaykumu-salaam,' Lucy responded, pronouncing the Arabic words carefully the way Mariam had taught her. 'We've already had breakfast, thanks. Is Tahira around? We wanted to see how she is.'

'I'm not sure.' The young man turned and looked across to the counter where a small group of women stood chatting over a large metal teapot. 'Mum! There're some people here for Tahira. Have you seen her?'

'She's upstairs in her flat.' A woman wearing an apron over a full-length dress hurried across to meet them. 'She's got poor Yasmeen's mother and sister with her. I don't know if she'll want to be– Oh! It's you Ibrahim – and Mariam. I'm so sorry, I didn't see you there. I don't know if you've met my son, Mohammed? He's living in Cardiff now and just up for the weekend.'

They exchanged greetings and introductions and then Mohammed was dispatched by his mother to let Tahmina know that her guests had arrived.

'I wouldn't say no to some toast,' Ibrahim said, as they stood in the centre of the room, surrounded by clinking sounds of crockery and the enticing smell of coffee brewing. 'And I know our Bernie can drink tea at any time of the day or night. Go and sit down over there and I'll and give the ladies a hand bringing some over.'

They had only just taken their places at the large table where they had eaten their lunch the day before when the front door opened to admit Sandra Latham. She allowed it to swing closed behind her and then stood looking around for any familiar faces. Mohammed's mother hurried across to greet her.

'Welcome to our community café! My name's Malika. We're just serving breakfast. What can I get you?'

'Just a coffee please – and I believe that Mrs Marina Osmani is here. I'd like to have a word with her. Do you know where she is?'

'They're in our assistant imam's flat upstairs. My son had just gone to– oh! Here they all are now. Tahmina! Your friends are here to see you and this lady is asking to speak to Marina. I'm sorry,' she added turning back to Sandra, 'I'm afraid I don't know your name.'

'I'm DCI Sandra Latham.' The inspector held up her warrant card. 'I'm leading the investigation into Yasmeen Osmani's death.'

'Do you have some news for us?' Marina pushed past her niece in her eagerness. 'Can we see her? Will we be able to take her home soon?'

'I'm afraid that I don't have any news on the investigation, but I have managed to arrange for you to see your daughter's body. As I said before, it's the coroner who will decide when she can be released for burial. Now the other thing is–'

'But we can see her? Can we go now?'

'No, I'm sorry. There isn't anyone at the mortuary today to prepare her for you to see, but I've organised for you to go at ten o'clock tomorrow morning. I am sorry about the delay. I know how important this is for you – for both of you,' Sandra added, looking towards Fatima. 'If you can tell me where you're staying tonight, I'll get someone to call for you and drive you over to the mortuary.'

'We're just trying to fix that up,' Tahira intervened. 'Can we let you know when we've found a hotel?'

'Yes, of course. And I've got your mobile number, so is it OK if I give you a ring in the morning, if you haven't been in touch before then?' Tahira nodded, so Sandra continued, 'and the other thing I wanted to let you know is that we have Yasmeen's laptop and phone. We need to have a look on them to see if there's anything that could throw any light on why someone might want to harm her. We should be able to let you have them back after any data that could be useful has been copied. I'm sorry that everything takes time, but we want to make sure that we don't miss anything that might help us to find out who did this.'

'Yes, of course,' Marina nodded. 'I'm sorry if I seemed… It's just rather difficult being away from home for so long, and…'

'And caring for the bodies of our loved-ones is very important in our culture,' Tahira added, as her aunt's voice trailed away into incoherence. 'But we do appreciate everything that you're doing — especially with this being a bank holiday weekend.'

'I'm afraid that doesn't help,' Sandra admitted. 'A lot of the mortuary staff are on annual leave this week. It was tremendously good of Professor Mortimer to fit the post mortem in yesterday.'

Malika returned with Sandra's coffee.

'Thank you, how much do I owe you?'

'Nothing. Tea and coffee are free, unless you want one of the fancy barista varieties.'

'That's very kind.' Sandra turned back to Marina. 'Why don't we all sit down? I know this isn't a good time, but I'm afraid I need to ask you some questions, Mrs Osmani.'

'Over here!' Tahira led the way to the table where Lucy and the others were sitting with the mugs of tea that Mohammed had brought them. 'And let's have tea and toast all round.'

They sat down. Lucy opened her mouth to speak, but Sandra got in first.

'Mrs Osmani,' she said gently, looking at Marina across the table and trying to make eye-contact. 'I am truly sorry for your loss. I have daughters of my own and I can't even imagine how I would be feeling if this were to happen to one of them. I know that this is a really difficult time for you, but it may help us to find out who did this to her if you can answer a few questions for me.'

Marina nodded. 'Yes, yes, of course. Ask anything you like.'

'Thank you. I'll try to take as little of your time as I can. First of all, did Yasmeen seem to you to be happy here? Was she enjoying her course?'

'Oh yes! It was everything that she'd dreamed of. It was hard work, but she knew what she wanted to do with her life and this was getting her there.'

'Is that how she seemed to you?' Sandra looked towards Fatima, thinking that a teenager might be more willing to confide in a sister of similar age than in her parents, especially if it meant admitting that she had made a mistake – and one that was perhaps an expensive one for them.

'Yes,' Fatima nodded in agreement. 'She was loving it all.'

'And she got on well with the other students on her course?'

'I think so,' Marina answered, less certainly. 'She didn't talk much about her social life. It was all more about her course. And about coming here – to the mosque. She … she made a big thing about this place and how much she was seeing of Tahira. I think she wanted to reassure us that she wasn't going to allow the student lifestyle to corrupt her morals.' She paused, as if wondering whether to go on. Sandra waited patiently. 'Her father wasn't keen on her going away from home. He's very protective of his girls.'

'So, if there was something wrong, maybe she would have been reluctant to tell you?' suggested Sandra. 'So as not to worry you.'

'I suppose so.' Marina looked perplexed. 'But–'

'I don't see why you're asking all these questions,' Lucy broke in. She had been longing to tell Sandra about the death in Oxford ever since she arrived, and now she felt that she could wait no longer. 'It's quite clear it's nothing to do with the victims! It's not personal! It's someone picking off Muslim women, just because of that. And there's been another one – last night, in Oxford – exactly the same: strangled with her own hijab and a chess piece left lying next to her. So, you're wasting your time asking about Yasmeen's friends and all that stuff, because it's a serial killer targeting Muslim women at random. You need to–'

She broke off as her mother placed her hand firmly on her arm, warning her that she had said more than enough.

'I'm sorry,' Peter apologised for her. 'Lucy can get a bit carried away sometimes. She had a phone call from one of her friends in Oxford this morning – a constable with Thames Valley Police. Apparently, a Muslim student was found dead there this morning, and it all looks very similar to the two deaths that you've had here – including a chess piece being left near the body.'

'It was a queen this time,' Lucy added. 'A white queen. So, now we've had a white knight, a white castle and a white queen. What are we doing to stop the next one – the white bishop?'

'Hold on there!' Sandra remonstrated. 'Remember, this is all new news to me. What exactly do you know about this death in Oxford?'

'Not a lot,' Lucy admitted. 'Only that it was probably a student, that she looked as if she'd been strangled by something that was probably her own hijab and there was a white chess queen lying on the ground next to her. But that's enough to tell you that it's connected with these deaths here in Liverpool, isn't it? How would anyone else know about the chess pieces?'

'How indeed!' replied Sandra. 'And I might ask how your friend from Thames Valley knew about it. I thought I'd told you to keep that aspect of the case confidential.'

'And I am!' Lucy insisted. 'I didn't tell Stella – or not until after she told me about finding the white queen. She rang me because she'd heard about the Liverpool murders in the news and she thought this looked like the same thing, and she told me about the chess piece because she thought it was a funny thing to find lying about in the street. I never said a word about it to anyone before that!'

'None of us have said anything to anyone about it,' Dominic backed her up. 'I didn't even tell my mum when she wanted to know all about what's been happening.'

'She invited us all to lunch,' Bernie added, with an impish grin, 'but we declined politely, in case she was going to pump us about it again.'

'So, it looks as if the death in Oxford is the third one in a series,' Lucy concluded.

'Or else someone else has leaked the information about the chess pieces,' Peter pointed out. 'It was one of the students who found the first one, wasn't it? They could've talked about it to their friends, and they could've passed it on to *their* friends and it wouldn't be long before it got round to friends of the second victim. And then it wouldn't take long for someone to put two and two together and start spreading the news that it's the killer's calling card.'

'But the students who found Yasmeen's body didn't notice the chess piece,' Tahira objected, 'or at least they didn't mention it when I talked to them. I think they were too drunk to notice much, to be fair.'

'See!' Lucy squealed triumphantly. 'The only people who knew about both chess pieces were us and the police – and the murderer, of course.'

'Well, it doesn't really matter what the connection is,' Sandra said firmly, with a warning look in Lucy's direction. This discussion was going nowhere and could not be helpful for the victim's mother and sister. 'I'll get on to Thames Valley and compare notes with them. Did your friend happen to mention the name of the SIO, by any chance?'

'No. I don't suppose anyone had been assigned to the case when she rang. She was at the scene waiting for CID to turn up. Would you like me to ring her and find out?'

'No thank you. I'll go through the official channels.' Sandra drained her mug and then stood up. 'I'll leave you all to your breakfast. Thank you for answering my questions, Mrs Osmani, and I really am very sorry for your loss.'

✳✳✳

After lunch in the community café, to which Imran insisted on treating them all, Peter and Bernie went back to the Knotty Ash house with Lucy and Ibrahim to get on with the decorating. Mariam and Dominic would have offered to help, had Khadija not taken them to one side and asked them to stay to keep Tahira company.

'She likes to think that she's strong enough never to need support from anyone,' she told them confidentially, 'but I can see that this has knocked her for six. She blames herself, which is nonsense, of course. And she's dreadfully worried about her aunt and especially her cousin.'

So, they sat in the community café, drinking coffee and carrying on a desultory conversation until suddenly Marina declared that she needed to see the place where her daughter had died. Mariam and Dominic offered to come with them, but Tahira shook her head.

'What would be really useful,' she told him, 'is if you could find a hotel room for Marina and Fatima. I've been getting nowhere. I just don't seem to be able to think straight at the moment. If possible, they want to book for one night, but with the option of staying longer if they need to.'

'We'll be happy to do that, but are you sure about only booking one night?' Mariam asked doubtfully. 'It'll be nearly lunch time by the time you've finished at the mortuary, and hotels usually expect you to check out before then unless you're staying on.'

'But Nadeem won't want us to stay away any longer than we need to,' Marina protested.

'If you pay for two nights, you can still leave tomorrow afternoon if you're ready,' Dominic told her, 'but you won't be under any pressure.'

'OK.' Marina conceded the point. 'Two nights then. Now, can we go?'

$$***$$

'Look at all those!' Fatima exclaimed as they crossed the courtyard that led to the place where her sister had been attacked. 'People must have left them there to remember Yasmeen.'

The others followed her pointing finger with their eyes and saw an array of soft toys and bunches of flowers lying on the ground in front of the police tape that surrounded the bin store at the back of the building where Yasmeen had been living. A single uniformed officer was standing next to them with his hands behind his back and eyes front, mounting guard over the crime scene.

Tahira greeted him boldly. 'Good afternoon, officer. I'm Tahira Siddiqui, and this is my aunt, Marina Osmani, and her daughter, Fatima. Marina is the mother of the student who was killed here on Friday night.'

'Good afternoon. I'm very sorry about your loss. I'm PC John O'Connor. Is there anything I can do for you?'

'No, not really.' Marina sounded nervous and unsure of herself. 'We just wanted to see where … where it happened.'

'You'll have to stay outside the cordon,' O'Connor told her. 'And there isn't really anything much to see – apart from the tributes from her friends, that is. She must have been very popular. There've been more of them coming all day.

Marina looked down at the piles of flowers. 'Yes. Yes, I'd like to have a look at those. Thank you.'

'There's no rush. Take as long as you like.'

'And this is where she was lying?' Marina asked, looking up again and gesturing towards the large waste bins.

'Yes, ma'am, I believe so.'

'Look Mum!' Fatima had bent down and was reading the small card attached to one of the bunches of flowers. '*To the best friend I ever had.* And this one here says, *Life will always be a little bit darker without you.* They must have all liked her a lot, mustn't they?'

'Of course they did!' Tahira agreed emphatically, suppressing the cynical thought that some of the tributes could have been prompted more from a desire to be part of something tragic and dramatic than from true affection for a dead acquaintance.

They walked slowly along the line of tributes, bending down to read the notes attached to each. Alongside the expressions of grief and loss were cries of disbelief and sometimes anger at the way that one of their number had been struck down in an apparently random way. Clearly some students were frightened that they could be next.

'This one's a bit odd,' Fatima said suddenly, holding up a small teddy bear dressed in a white coat with a toothbrush attached to one paw. 'Look what it says on the card.'

Tahira took the bear from her and read out loud,

'To my dearest Yasmeen. We thought that we would have a lifetime together, but you were snatched away before it even started. This was for your

birthday, but you'll never get to be 19 after all. Devastated to lose you, M.

'It sounds like a love letter, doesn't it?' said Fatima.

'Who's M?' asked Marina.

'I don't know,' Tahira confessed. 'Yasmeen never told me there was anyone special.'

'That was just what Nadeem was most worried about,' Marina murmured, so softly that Tahira could hardly catch the words. 'He thought that she would find a boy and they would want to ...'

'Just because this *M* talks as if he's her boyfriend, it doesn't mean that she felt the same way about him,' Tahira pointed out in an attempt to allay her aunt's fears. 'Maybe he was stalking her. She's – she was an attractive young woman. Lots of men must have fancied her, but that doesn't mean she encouraged them. In fact, I'm sure she didn't. She was too busy with her course.'

'And what if she *was* seeing someone?' Fatima added, 'why should you assume he wasn't a perfectly nice Muslim boy? Maybe *M* stands for Muhammad, and he's here studying to be a doctor – or a dentist, like Yasmeen was.'

'But then, why would she keep it secret?' demanded her mother.

'Because,' Fatima replied emphatically, 'however suitable he was, Dad would have found fault with him just because he wasn't the one *he'd* picked out for her. You know what he's like.'

$$***$$

'So, who do we think *M* is?' Bernie asked. She and Peter had driven Lucy back to the Kensington house, leaving the paint to dry on the walls of the bedroom where she and Mariam had spent the previous night. They were now sitting in the spacious lounge drinking tea and nibbling some of the biscuits, which Khadija had pressed on Marina when they left the Islamic Centre.

On the old-fashioned mantlepiece above the blocked-up fireplace sat the dentist teddy bear, which Fatima had brought back when they returned from the Student Village. She and Marina were now settling into their hotel, with Tahira and the other half of the biscuits. Fatima would have liked to take the bear with them, but changed her mind when she saw her mother reading the inscription on the card around its neck with tears in her eyes.

Bernie had driven them to the hotel where Tahira escorted them up to their room. The plan had been for Tahira to go back to her flat at the Islamic Centre after that, but when Marina saw that the room that Mariam had booked for them contained both a double and a single bed, she had instantly begged her to stay with them overnight.

'Fatima and I can share, can't we Fatima? And you can have the single. Please, Tahira. It's such a long time since I've stayed anywhere like this. You know we can't get away much, with having the shop. And then you'll be here when the police car comes to take us to see Yasmeen. I'd really like you to come with us.'

So, Bernie had returned in an empty car, and now she and Peter were spending the evening with the four friends in the house that they had shared for the past five years, but which they would soon be leaving behind. In less than three months, Lucy and Ibrahim would be living in their new home in Knotty Ash, while Mariam and Dominic settled into a house in West Derby, conveniently close to Alder Hey Children's Hospital where Mariam was to work after graduating, in pursuit of her ambition to become a consultant paediatrician. This should have been a happy time of remembering the past and looking towards the future, but it was now overshadowed by two – or should that be three? – deaths, and the worry that more could be about to follow.

'According to Tahira, none of Yasmeen's friends had any idea,' Mariam said in answer to Bernie's question. 'They saw a couple of them while they were out at Greenbank and asked them about it.'

'But I'm not sure how close they really were to Yasmeen,' Dominic added. 'I got the impression that there was a little group of them on her floor that did things together and she just tried to tag along with them.'

'Tahira said they all seem to be into drinking and partying in a big way, Mariam added. 'That wasn't Yasmeen's scene at all.'

'Maybe she would have liked it to be,' suggested Bernie. 'Students often go a bit wild in their first year, wanting to try new things they've never done before – maybe things their parents wouldn't have allowed them to do at home.'

'Yasmeen wasn't like that,' Mariam insisted. 'She was very serious about everything, and especially about her studies.'

'She was terrified that she might fail her exams,' Lucy added. 'And then her dad would've been proved right and she'd have ended up in an arranged marriage.'

Peter broke the silence that followed by holding up a cardamom-flavoured biscuit. 'These are good! Do you think Khadija would give you the recipe?'

'I think I like the cumin ones best,' Ibrahim contributed, realising that Peter was seeking to divert the conversation away from speculation on Yasmeen's relationship with her father.

'We met a lad called Mohammed at the community café this morning,' recalled Bernie. 'Could he have been M, do you think?'

'He doesn't live in Liverpool anymore.' Ibrahim shook his head. 'He was only visiting his mum. He's only been home for a week – ten days at most.'

'That'd be quick work for anyone!' Dominic agreed. 'But he's not the only Mohammed at the mosque, is he?'

'Well, there's little Mo Husseini,' Lucy laughed. 'He knew Yasmeen from the homework club, but he's only six.'

'What about Mohsin Iqbal?' suggested Mariam. 'He helps with the homework club too. He could've met Yasmeen there.'

'We have a club after school every Thursday,' Ibrahim explained for Bernie's benefit, 'for kids who need somewhere where they can be quiet to do their homework. And there are computers with internet access there too, for those who don't have it at home. We encourage students to volunteer to help. Mohsin's just finishing his degree and he wants to be a teacher–'

'A geography teacher!' Lucy put in, with a little giggle. 'I've threatened to buy him a tweed jacket with leather patches on the elbows so he looks the part.'

'So, this is perfect for him to get experience too,' finished Ibrahim, giving Lucy a friendly poke in the ribs.

'Yasmeen liked helping the young ones,' Mariam continued. 'So, I suppose Mo could have had a crush on her, but a six-year-old wouldn't be able to afford a posh teddy bear dressed up as a dentist like that.'

'And that note didn't sound like the sort of thing a six-year-old would write,' added Dominic. 'There are kids in my Year 10 class who'd struggle to think of something as sophisticated as that.'

'I think Mohsin is the most likely candidate,' Lucy asserted. 'There may be plenty of Mohammeds who could've known Yasmeen, but most of the ones that I can think of are too young, too old or already married!'

'But there's no reason to think it's someone from the mosque,' Peter pointed out. 'We only talked about that to stop Yasmeen's mother from worrying that she might have an unsuitable boyfriend. M could stand for Matthew or Miles or Max.'

'Or he could be Manuel from Barcelona!' joked Bernie.

'Yes,' responded Peter in a tone that made clear that he did not consider this to be a helpful suggestion. 'The point I was making was that it's far more likely that the bear would have been put there by a student living out there at Greenbank. If you want to know who M is, I'd start there.'

"Except that Tahira said that none of the people they talked to there could think who it was,' challenged Lucy.

'Or it could be Mary or Monica or Melissa,' continued Bernie, ignoring her husband's protests.

'That would certainly have worried her parents if they'd found out,' Ibrahim observed. 'The Pakistani diaspora are not noted for their empathy towards the LGBT community.'

'Montana begins with M,' Mariam murmured. 'Wasn't it her birthday that they were out celebrating on Friday night?'

'And Yasmeen made her a birthday cake,' added Lucy.

'But Yasmeen came home early and Montana went on to a nightclub,' Dominic pointed out. 'If they were a couple, surely they would have stayed together. I think we're wasting our time trying to work out who M is. It's not as if this murder was personal, is it? I've been researching that careers event at JMU the evening Rania was killed, and I've found out a bit more about one of the speakers.'

He paused dramatically and looked round at the others, who looked back expectantly but pointedly refused to offer encouragement by expressing interest.

'The penultimate presentation was given by a JMU alumnus called Guy Daniels,' Dominic continued. 'He did a degree in Computer Games Development and he set up his own gaming business while he was still a student. His talk was called, "From Drafts to Dragons: becoming a Gaming entrepreneur." And,' another pause for dramatic effect, 'he was chess champion at his school three years running, before he went to uni!'

Dominic looked round triumphantly, while the others sat nibbling their biscuits and digesting this new information.

'I've been on his LinkedIn profile,' Dominic resumed. 'He started writing computer games as a teenager, starting with a basic simulator to allow games of drafts to be played remotely. Then he moved on to an attempt at creating a programme that would play chess, but it wasn't long before he changed to creating fantasy games, initially based around the chess pieces. Players chose avatars like the white knight or the black queen and fought battles against each other.'

'And you're suggesting that he's started playing out his fantasies in real life?' queried Bernie. 'You think he followed Rania when she left the careers event, acting out the role of the white knight stalking an opponent?'

'Well, it does all fit, doesn't it?' Dominic replied excitedly, pleased to have caught the others' attention at last. 'He was there, on the spot. She wouldn't have been alarmed by him approaching her, so he could have got close without her screaming or running away. And he was into fantasy worlds and symbolism, so leaving a chess piece at the crime scene would have been just his style.'

'But why pick on Rania?' asked Mariam. 'What had she done to him?'

'Easy prey,' suggested Peter. 'A woman, on foot, alone. A perfect target for someone who gets a kick out of hurting people who can't fight back.'

'Or maybe she said something during his talk that annoyed him,' Bernie conjectured. 'These geeky types don't always take criticism very well.'

'If he's our serial killer, he presumably picked her because she was identifiable as a Muslim,' Ibrahim pointed out. 'Apart from the chess pieces, that's the only link between the murders.'

'Well, that and the fact that all the victims were students,' Bernie pointed out. 'But you're right Ibrahim. Whoever it was, it must be someone with a grudge against Muslims or Muslim women or Muslim women wearing hijabs.' She turned to Dominic. 'What else do we know about him?'

'Only what he's chosen to put on his LinkedIn profile,' Dominic admitted. 'Have a look if you like.'

He handed his smartphone over to Bernie, who began scrolling down to read what "Ambitious entrepreneur and online gaming expert" Guy Daniels had to say about himself. Lucy came over and stood behind her chair, leaning over to see the screen.

''Hang on! Go back up a bit. I want a look at his face. That's it! Mariam! Come and have a look. I'm sure I've seen him before somewhere. Does he look familiar to you?'

Her friend got up and came over. Bernie passed the phone across to her and she stood looking down intently at the face that filled the small screen.

'You're right,' she agreed. 'I'm sure we must've see– Oh!' She stopped suddenly and thrust the phone back into Bernie's hand. 'Yes. I do remember. He's that weirdo in the gardens at the back of St George's Hall. Remember Lucy? Last summer. I was sitting there waiting for you, and he came up and started talking to me.'

'Ye-es,' Lucy said slowly. 'Yes, that's it! That's where we've seen him before.'

'And he told me his name was Guy,' Mariam added softly. 'He was chatting me up. He seemed quite friendly – in a weird geeky sort of way – until I told him I wasn't interested. And then he suddenly got aggressive and tried to snatch my hijab off my head.'

'Just like he did with Rania and Yasmeen!' Dominic shouted out. 'Don't you see? It all fits.'

'No, it doesn't really,' Lucy contradicted. 'This was broad daylight with loads of people about. Rania and Yasmeen were both killed after dark in bin stores where there was nobody else around.'

'There may have been loads of people around when he assaulted Mariam,' her cousin retorted, 'but nobody apart from you did anything to stop him, did they?'

'Maybe they would've done if he'd tried to strangle me,' Mariam said. 'Lucy's right. 'He was an ignorant wally, but he never really tried to hurt me. I can't believe he wanted to kill me. He said something about my hijab being a symbol of male domination, and he was going to liberate me from the oppression of my family.'

'From what I remember,' Ibrahim chipped in, 'you said that he got angry when you told him you didn't need liberating. And don't forget how humiliating it must've been for him when Lucy grabbed him from behind and got him in an arm-lock!'

'That's right!' Dominic agreed jubilantly. 'There's nothing as embarrassing for a man who fancies himself as a knight in shining armour coming to the aid of a maiden in distress as being wrestled to the ground by a girl half his size!'

'I wasn't half his size,' Lucy objected. 'He was quite small, as far as I remember – and super-easy to over-power. He didn't know the first thing about self-defence.'

'All the more reason for him finding it demeaning,' Dominic insisted. 'He's probably always been sensitive about his size which would've made you beating him like that twice as bad, and so he goes away determined to get his own back on women in general and women wearing hijabs in particular.'

'It's still a big step from there to murder,' Bernie observed.

'But it all fits!' Dominic insisted. 'Here's this guy, a computer games geek, a bit of a loner, never had any luck with women, his only success in life is the gaming company he's set up for himself. He's feeling pleased with himself because he's been invited back to his old university to share that success with their current students. And, in the audience, he sees a woman wearing a hijab – just like that woman who humiliated him nine months earlier. And the resentment comes flooding back and he gets an urge to prove

116

to himself that he's stronger than any silly girl in a hijab. Maybe his talk went badly and he needs to convince himself he isn't a loser.'

'Or maybe it went really well,' Ibrahim broke in, 'and he thinks he can walk on water, and that's what makes him decide to face his old demons and start a campaign to destroy women in hijabs.'

'Either way,' Dominic resumed, 'he follows her out of the building and assaults her when they get to a deserted spot by the bins. And because he's a fantasist and fanatical about chess, he leaves one of his pieces by her body as an act of defiance – a sort of "catch me if you can" message to the police.'

'Why would he have chess pieces with him at the lecture?' asked the ever-practical Peter.

'Maybe he brought some along to illustrate his talk,' suggested Dominic after a brief pause. 'Remember the title? I bet he told them all about starting out writing online board games – chess and drafts and so on – and showed them an example of the difference between playing chess with real pieces and playing virtually.'

Peter continued to look sceptical. 'OK. I can just about buy the idea that this Guy Daniels committed the first murder, but what about the other one – or the other two, if we count the one down in Oxford? Let's start with Yasmeen. How did he pick on her for his next victim?'

'Saw her waiting for the bus and followed her home?' suggested Ibrahim.

'Do we know where he lives?' Peter asked. 'Would he be likely to be in the centre of Liverpool late at night?'

'His gaming company is registered on Companies House at an address in Meols,' Dominic told him. 'It looks like a private house, so my guess is that's where he lives and he works from home. I don't suppose you need much infrastructure to write games software.'

'And Meols is?' queried Peter, looking towards his wife.

'On the Wirral – the posh side,' Bernie answered. 'Life expectancy can be as much as ten years higher over there than in Birkenhead.'

'So, he could easily have been over in Liverpool for a night out and spotted Yasmeen at the bus stop!' Dominic crowed. 'See! I told you it all fits.'

'Until he produces an alibi that proves he was tucked up in bed over the water,' Bernie said crushingly. 'Peter's right, you really don't have the evidence to put him in the frame.'

'Then let's go and find it!' declared Dominic. 'Ask him where he was on Friday night. Take his DNA to see if it matches with anything at the crime scenes.'

'That's all for the police,' Peter told him seriously. 'On no account are you to try to make contact with him. Ring Sandra Latham in the morning if you like and tell what you've found out, but if you start taking things into your own hands all you'll do is to contaminate any evidence that you find and make a prosecution harder than it's going to be in any case.'

'Oh! Alright, I suppose you're right,' Dominic looked and sounded rather crestfallen.

'And Lucy and Mariam had better give her a proper statement about the incident last July,' Peter went on. 'And she ought to see the note on that teddy bear. That really could be evidence of something.'

8. MIDDLE GAME

The alarm went off and Andy reached his arm out from beneath the duvet to silence it. May Day! And one of the rare occasions when the Early May public holiday coincided with that traditional festival, which most people had forgotten about until 1978 when the Labour government declared a new bank holiday on the first Monday in May. Whether this was to honour the first day of Summer or International Workers' Day had been unclear.

It might be a public holiday, but for Oxford police it was always a busy time – even when they did not have a murder to solve. Uniformed officers would be out in greater numbers than usual keeping an eye on crowds that might gather to listen to the dawn chorus of choir boys on the top of Magdalen College tower or to watch the troupes of Morris dancers performing in the streets. Trouble could erupt among students fuelled with alcohol from all-night parties, and steps might need to be taken to prevent injuries to those foolhardy enough to climb the parapet and leap from Magdalen Bridge into the River Cherwell.

As he pulled on his clothes, Andy reflected that, as SIO on a murder enquiry he was at least spared the ordeal of walking the streets at first light trying to combine good humour and a light touch with strict enforcement of public order and an eagle eye out for pickpockets. He had the luxury of rising at the rather more civilised hour of seven thirty and would be spending much of his morning at his office computer in a video-link joint team meeting with the SIO from Merseyside Police who was charged with investigating those two murders in Liverpool which might be linked with his own case.

His mother was already sitting at the breakfast table when he got downstairs. She looked up as he entered the kitchen and reached out to pour him a mug of coffee.

'I put on some toast for you. Oh! There it is!' she said hearing the toaster pop up on the worksurface behind her. She made to get to her feet but Andy waved her back down.

'It's OK. I'll get it.'

'I suppose you'll probably be late back this evening,' Amanda Lepage observed as they munched their toast.

'I'm afraid I may be,' Andy nodded. 'But I'll make sure I let you know when I'm on my way.'

'I'll do something in the slow cooker.'

'Good,' Andy murmured absently. His mind was on the body in Lichfield Street and the need to brief whichever officers could be made available to him in advance of the joint briefing with the team from Merseyside. This DCI Latham had sounded on the phone like an experienced SIO with a good few successful murder convictions under her belt. He did not want his team to appear slipshod in front of her.

$$* * *$$

Breakfast was also underway in Liverpool. The bank holiday meant that the friends were all free to make a combined assault on a major piece of work in the Knotty Ash house: refitting the kitchen. While the four youngsters lingered over omelette and fried bread in the Kensington house, Bernie and Peter were already washing up the bowls from their muesli and filling buckets, jugs and kettles with water in readiness for disconnecting the sink.

'OK, I've turned the water off,' Bernie grunted, crawling out from inside the dilapidated old cupboard which housed the main stop tap. 'Let's just check.'

She turned the mixer tap over the sink full on and watched as a spurt of water diminished into a dribble and then a drip.

'Right! Now let's get these tap connectors off and the new one on before the others arrive. If all goes according to plan, we'll be able to get the water back on before they get here.'

'Then, what are all these buckets for?' asked Peter. 'You told me before that we might have no water all morning.'

'They're for if things *don't* go according to plan,' Bernie grinned back, 'which is quite normal with plumbing jobs. Now, I'll just disconnect the taps, and then we should be able to take the top off the sink unit, which will give us more room to work.'

She disappeared under the sink holding a large and very businesslike looking spanner. Peter stood by, watching and listening. Fumbling and soft banging accompanied by under-the-breath muttering from beneath the stainless-steel sink bowl suggested that his wife was struggling to turn the stiff nuts which connected the water supply to the taps. He watched as she twisted her body round, trying to attack the problem from a different angle.

'At last!' she gasped a few minutes later, crawling out and sitting on the floor looking up at him. 'One down, one to go! It's the usual story: everything's corroded on. And the water isn't as completely off as we thought. Where's the washing-up bowl – and those old towels we brought with us?'

Peter handed her the bowl and went in search of the towels. By the time he got back, Bernie was standing up tugging at the top of the sink unit. She turned round and brandished a lump hammer at him triumphantly.

'Don't force it, get a bigger hammer,' she declared. 'It's amazing what a few hard taps can do to shift reluctant nuts.'

'I'll bear that in mind for the future,' Peter replied, 'but meanwhile do you mind not waving it around in my face?'

'I've disconnected the waste pipe too,' she informed him, putting down the hammer and tugging at the stainless-steel sink top, 'so this ought to just come away. Give us a hand to pull it off.'

As they staggered out through the front door a few minutes later, carrying the sink top, with taps still attached, Ibrahim appeared in the front garden and ran to help. He was closely followed by Dominic and Mariam walking hand-in-hand.

'I thought you were going to leave the kitchen until we got here. Dom and I said we'd do the heavy stuff.'

'We're not too old for a bit of DIY,' Bernie retorted. 'And I thought it would be better if we could try to get the water back on before you arrived. As usual, the main stopcock has seized up and won't turn off completely, so I can't stand here talking. I need to swap the tap connectors for new ones with their own stop taps on them before we flood the kitchen.'

'She's exaggerating,' Peter confided to the others as they followed her inside. 'It's only a dribble, but *flood* sounds more dramatic. Where's Lucy?'

'She'll be along later,' Ibrahim told him. 'She's arranged to call in at Prof Mortimer's office to collect some old PM reports to have a look at.'

'On a bank holiday? And why does she want them, anyway?'

'Medics work all sorts of hours, even pathologists,' Mariam reminded him. 'As you'll know, people still keep dying in suspicious circumstances at weekends and on bank holidays.'

$$* * *$$

'I'm DI Andy Lepage,' Andy introduced himself via the video link with Sandra and her team. 'And I've got DC Josh Pitchfork with me. We're a bit depleted today, I'm afraid, because everyone else is either on leave or they've been diverted on to policing May Morning events. It's a big thing in Oxford.'

'Hi,' Sandra responded. 'I'm DCI Sandra Latham. I'm the SIO on these two murder cases. And I've got DS Charlie Simpson, DC Bryony Foster, DC Ollie Ransom and DC John Fisher with me. They've all been working on this for more than two weeks now, but until two days ago, we were assuming it was a one-off. So now we've got to re-evaluate everything in the light of it being a serial killer.'

'Have you spotted any patterns?' Andy asked.

'Well,' Sandra replied, 'there's the type of victim: both young Muslim women wearing a hijab; both students; both walking home alone after dark. And then there's the chess pieces.'

'I was wondering about them,' Bryony put in, eager to share a theory that she had come up with overnight, after hearing about the third death. 'Chess pieces all have a value assigned to them, based on how useful they are. Pawns are one, because they can only move one square at a time; knights and bishops are three, rooks are five and a queen is nine. We've had knight then rook and now queen. The pieces that the killer is leaving have been increasing in value.'

'What about the bishop?' Joshua Pitchfork asked. 'They've missed that one out. Or are you saying there must've been another murder that we don't know about?'

'That would explain the two-week gap between the first two and then another almost immediately,' Bryony agreed excitedly. 'Maybe between Rania Ansari and Yasmeen Osmani there was another one where the killer left a bishop.'

'And, if it is the same person who killed Zahra Shahidi, that could have been anywhere in the country,' Andy pointed out.

'Didn't you say bishops and knights are worth the same?' asked Oliver Ransom. 'Doesn't that mean that the sequence could have been either bishop, knight rook, queen or knight, bishop, rook, queen? It could be the *first* murder that we've missed.'

'Or this could all be idle speculation,' Sandra said in a warning tone. 'Let's stick to the facts, shall we? Bryony: as soon as we're done here, get on with sending out an alert to other forces to be on the lookout for attacks on young Muslim women, especially students. And ask them to review past cases as well. I don't know about this theory of yours about the values of the chess pieces, but I agree that these deaths may not have been the first.'

'Or the last,' Andy added. 'What if the killer is planning to use up a whole chess set? That's sixteen, even if we only count the white pieces. I agree, we need to review past cases to see if any of them fit the pattern. I'll get my team going through the Thames Valley files ASAP.'

'Good.' Sandra looked down at the notes that she'd jotted in her notebook before the meeting. 'Now, Ransom has been looking into our second victim's movements on the night that she died. Over to you, Ollie.'

'It turns out that Yasmeen didn't get the bus back to the student village, like her friends thought.' Ransom began. 'One of the taxi drivers that works the rank outside the back of Lime Street Station recognised her photo. He says he picked her up in Lord Nelson Street at just gone ten, and dropped her at Greenbank between twenty past and half past. He offered to walk her to her room, with it being dark and no one else around, but she declined. The last he saw of her, she was going into the student village at the entrance on Mossley Hill Road.'

'And you think he's a reliable witness?' asked Sandra.

'I would say so,' Ransom nodded. 'Not too cocky and sure of himself, as if he'd got his story off pat; and not too eager to please, like he just wanted to be in the limelight. I asked him if he saw anything suspicious when he dropped Yasmeen off, and he said definitely not. He said if he had he would've insisted on walking her to her room. He has nieces and he wouldn't want them wandering about alone at night. He seemed genuinely concerned.'

'But he must be our prime suspect, mustn't he?' Charlotte broke in forcefully. 'He was the last person to see the victim alive. He admits to having been only a few yards away from where she was killed at about the time she died. And no one is better placed than a taxi driver to approach young women in the street late at night. What's his name? Does he have an alibi for the night of Rania's murder?'

'His name is Max Barker,' Ransom answered. 'I've run his details through the computer and he doesn't have any previous. He's fifty-three and lives out Stanley way, near the meat and fish market. He's been registered as a cab driver since 2021. I don't know what he was doing before that, but I've got it in mind to keep digging. I did ask him about the evening Rania was killed – just casual like, so he wouldn't know he was under suspicion. He was working that night, driving all over the city. It was the opening day of the Grand National meeting, so it was a busy night with lots of people arriving. I was thinking of checking out the ANPR data to see if we can trace where his cab went that night.'

'Good work, Ollie,' Sandra commended him. 'Carry on with the background on Mr Max Barker. I agree with Charlie that he's a good match for the two Liverpool murders, but what on earth would he be doing in Oxford?'

'Perhaps that wasn't the same killer,' suggested Charlotte. 'Isn't it more likely to be a copycat?'

'Except that the chess pieces weren't made public,' Andy pointed out.

'Well, that's something we need to check on,' Sandra said with a sigh. 'It could have been leaked. And you know how fast things can spread on social media. All it takes is a few careless words and ….' She shrugged and pulled a face. 'But equally, it could be that it *was* a single killer who travelled to Oxford for the purpose of attacking his victim, or – much more likely in my opinion – he had some other reason for being down there and the killing was incidental to that.'

'I agree,' said Andy. 'These killings all appear opportunistic rather than targeted. The victims seem to have been chosen because they were available and low-risk – women on their own at night when nobody else was around – not as individuals.'

'How long does it take to get from here to Oxford?' Ollie asked.

'About four hours to drive,' Andy answered promptly, 'and much the same by train – which makes the timetable pretty tight for a single killer to have been responsible for murders two and three. We're not sure about time of death, but it couldn't have been later than the early hours of Sunday. The pathologist reckoned two a.m. is the absolute limit, and before midnight is more likely.'

'So, you're saying he'd have to have got to Oxford before midnight on Saturday?' Ollie asked anxiously. 'And it takes four hours?'

'That's right,' Andy nodded.

'I don't think Max Barker could've done it then.' Andy could hear Ollie's disappointment in his voice. 'I was talking to him round the back of Lime Street at 7.15. Add four hours to that and he'd have his work cut out to be lying in wait to kill that girl before midnight.'

'Hmm. I think you're right,' Andy nodded. 'We'd better check the traffic cameras on the route he'd have taken, just to be sure, but I agree it'd be incredibly tight. Just finding somewhere to park in Oxford can take hours!'

'He didn't need to have parked,' Joshua pointed out. 'He could've just been cruising along Lichfield Street when he spotted Zahra and just pulled up, got out and killed her.'

'Still a very tight schedule,' Andy said, and then immediately realised that it might appear that he was putting down his officer in front of Sandra's team. Josh Pitchfork was often lacking in self-confidence and would not benefit from feeling unsupported by his boss.

'DC Foster has been investigating local chess clubs,' Sandra said, breaking the uncomfortable silence that followed Andy's remark. 'Did you find anything useful, Bryony?'

'I went along to one that meets on a Sunday afternoon,' Bryony informed the meeting. 'They have a few student members, but none at all from ethnic minorities and not many women from any background. I played a game with one of the regulars, and then had a chat over coffee with some of the other members. I managed to bring the conversation round to the two killings – just casually; I didn't let on I was a police officer – and they all reacted perfectly normally: shocked that something like that could happen so close to home and concerned in case their own wives and daughters could be targeted.'

'So, they didn't see the attacks a racially-motivated?' asked Andy. 'If they thought their own relatives could be next?'

'No.' Bryony shook her head. 'But that may just have been their way of expressing their concern about the situation – placing themselves as potential victims. The main thing is, absolutely no one expressed any racist or Islamophobic views. There was one member who said that a lot of students bring things on themselves by their behaviour – drinking and taking drugs and causing a nuisance to ordinary people – but he was talking about students in general, not Muslims or even women in particular.'

'OK. Thanks Bryony.' Sandra looked round the room and then back at Andy's face on the screen, preparing to wind up the meeting.

'I've got another couple of clubs lined up for later in the week,' Bryony continued. 'They both have evening meetings. But the trouble is, chess isn't the sort of game where you chat while you play, so it's quite difficult to get to know people there.'

'Which probably means that chess clubs are full of the sort of lone wolf introverts who become serial killers,' Charlotte suggested.

'If I decide that we need a criminal profiler for this case, I'll call in a professional,' Sandra said warningly. 'At this stage, we need to keep an open mind. Serial killers aren't all stereotypical loners. Some of them have been life-and-soul-of-the-party types. Think of Harold Shipman, for instance. He was a respectable family man, loved by everyone who knew him, popular with his patients ....'

'I think a psychological profile might be useful,' Andy put in. 'But we'd need to get all the data together first, to give them something to work on. Why don't we go through the files, comparing everything we've got on the three cases to see if there are any other patterns emerging apart from just the chess pieces?'

'Good idea,' Sandra agreed. She looked round the room and spotted DC Fisher at the back. He was always happy to be given a desk job to do. 'John!' she called to him. 'Did you hear that? I'd like you to work through everything we've got on these three murders making lists of similarities and differences – anything that might give us a picture of the sort of person who did them, and anything that might suggest that it isn't a single killer after all. Remember,' she added, looking round at her team again, 'we're keeping an open mind and not jumping to conclusions, right?'

$$***$$

'They're anonymised,' Lucy said, taking the folders out of her bag and plonking them down on the kitchen table, now temporarily moved into the living room to make space for the assembly of new units in the kitchen. 'But it's easy to see that one of them is Rania's PM – unless there's been another very similar case that the prof looked at.'

'He's taking a big risk letting you look at that – if it really is Rania's PM report,' Peter observed. 'I thought he was giving you some old cases that had been closed by now.'

'He did hide it in the middle of a load of those,' Lucy grinned up at him, 'but I had a sort of feeling that I might find something a bit more interesting than that. And, under my skilful cross-examination, he admitted that he'd concluded that Yasmeen had been strangled by a thick ligature, such as the length of fabric that was found round her neck.'

'Well, now you're here, it's time you did some proper work for a change,' Bernie told her. 'Put those away somewhere safe and come and give us a hand with all these *packed flat for easy home assembly* kitchen units. It *is* your house, after all.'

'But first, you and Mariam had better ring Sandra Latham and tell her about that fellow who attacked Mariam last year,' Peter said seriously. 'That's going to be a lot more useful than interfering with the PM results.'

'I'm not interfering!' Lucy squealed indignantly.

'I wouldn't say that he attacked me exactly,' Mariam cut in at the same time. 'But it is odd that he turned out to be giving a talk at that careers event that Rania went to.'

'I'll ring her right away,' Lucy promised, picking up the pile of files and heading for the door. 'I hadn't forgotten. In fact, I did try to ring her earlier, but she was in a meeting. Come on Mariam. Let's go upstairs where it'll be quieter.'

'And there won't be any interfering parents,' Bernie added in an undertone, looking across at Peter who smiled back conspiratorially.

'I'll make us a brew,' Dominic announced. 'My back is complaining about humping so many heavy boxes around.'

'And I need a break from gently tapping in dowels 34b and 34c, and using the allen key supplied to tighten cam 31,' agreed Ibrahim.'

The tea was ready in a few minutes, but Lucy and Mariam had not returned. Bernie went upstairs to find out what the delay was. She found them kneeling on the floor by the bed, poring over an open file containing photocopied sheets of A4. At the sound of her approach, Lucy swung round and gave her a guilty smile.

'We just thought we'd have a read of Rania's PM report,' she admitted. 'Just in case there was anything interesting in it.'

'But there isn't,' Mariam added.

'Yes,' Lucy said regretfully. 'It only tells us what we knew already.'

'Which I suspect is why Professor Mortimer was willing to let you see it,' Bernie observed drily. 'Now are you going to come down and help us put your kitchen together or what?'

'OK. Sorry, Mam.' Lucy began collecting together the pieces of paper and putting them back in the folder. 'But I *was* hoping for more than just: she died not long after the end of that careers event; she was strangled with a ligature that might have been her own hijab; she hadn't eaten anything for some time – which she wouldn't have, because it was Ramadan and the careers event started well before sunset.'

'I'd forgotten that it was still Ramadan when she was killed,' Bernie said, becoming interested in spite of her disapproval. 'Doesn't that mean she might well have gone out again after she got back from the careers do – to go to an iftar event somewhere? Don't Muslims often get together to break their fast each evening during Ramadan?'

'She might have done,' Mariam agreed, 'or she might have been going to make her own iftar meal in the kitchen on her landing.'

'I was just thinking that might mean that she was killed on her way out of the hall, rather than on the way in,' Bernie explained. 'But that's all just speculation. Come on down! The others will be wondering what's happened to us. Did you ring DCI Latham, like you said you were going to?'

'Yes, of course. She's on her way over here to talk to us and so we can show her the picture we took of Guy Daniels when he attacked Mariam.'

As if on cue, there was a knock at the door followed by movement downstairs as Ibrahim came out into the hall to answer it. Lucy raced downstairs followed at only a slightly more sedate pace by her mother, with Mariam bringing up the rear.

'Come in, Inspector Latham,' Ibrahim greeted the visitors. 'And …?'

'DC Bryony Foster,' Sandra told him. 'We've come to see Lucy and Mariam.'

'Yes, of course. Come through here.' Ibrahim led the way into the living room. 'I'm afraid everything's in a bit of a mess at the moment. We're re-fitting the kitchen.'

'Oh, I know what a mess that makes!' Sandra grimaced in sympathy. 'After I did that a few years back, I vowed *never again*. Oh, Lucy,' she added, turning to see the others following her into the room. 'And Mariam. I gather you had a rather unpleasant experience in St John's Gardens last summer?'

'Well, it was a bit uncomfortable at the time,' Mariam smiled back, 'but nothing really happened – especially not after Lucy grabbed him from behind and pinned him to the wall!'

'Peter taught me some tricks of the trade,' Lucy grinned. 'And medical textbooks tend to be heavy in all senses of the word! I was afraid I might have broken his arm, but he didn't hang about long enough for me to check it was OK.'

'You said on the phone that you recognised him as Guy Daniels, one of the speakers at the careers event that Rania Ansari attended the day she died?'

'Yes,' Mariam answered, holding up her phone. 'I took this picture of him, before Lucy let him go. She wanted me to call the police, but I didn't want to make a fuss.'

'That's a pity,' Bryony commented, leaning across to see the photo. 'He looks like a nasty piece of work alright.'

'Nobody looks their best with their face scrunched up against a stone wall,' Bernie observed with a smile. 'I'd say he looks pretty much like Mr Average. No particularly striking distinguishing features.'

'And this is the photo he's got on his LinkedIn profile.' Lucy pushed her phone in front of Sandra's face.' See? It's definitely the same person.'

Sandra looked from one phone to the other. 'You're probably right, but it's hard to compare. You can't see the whole of his face in your picture, because of him being pushed up against that wall.'

'We had to take him like that. He'd have run off if Lucy'd let go of him.'

'Yes, I realise that, but it does make it harder to be sure it's the same man. You say he told you his name was Guy?'

'Yes,' Mariam confirmed. 'I was sitting on a bench, waiting for Lucy, and he came and sat down next to me. He told me he was called Guy and he asked me what my name was.'

'And you told him?'

'Yes, just my first name.'

'And then what happened? Did he go for your hijab right away?'

'Oh no! He tried to chat me up.'

'Just like that? What did he say?'

'The usual,' Mariam smiled. 'Where are you from? Where are you *really* from? Then he said something about having tickets for a concert and asked if I'd go to it with him. I told him my fiancé wouldn't like it and he went off on a rant about forced marriages.'

'And *then* he grabbed your hijab?' asked Bryony.

'Not right away,' Lucy intervened. 'When I got there, he was going on about male oppression and women being forced to wear what men wanted them to wear. *Then* he tried to grab Mariam's headscarf, and I belted him one with *Muir's Pathology*.'

'I see.' Bryony jotted all this down.

'Are you going to arrest him?' asked Dominic. 'You could arrest him for assaulting Mariam and then question him about the other attacks. It can't just be a coincidence that he was there when Rania was killed.'

'I'm afraid that's just what his lawyer will certainly argue that it was,' Sandra told him. 'I'll go and talk to him again, but we'll need a lot more evidence before we can charge him. And coincidences *do* happen sometimes.'

'And he didn't exactly assault me,' Mariam protested. 'Not as much as Lucy assaulted him, anyway!'

'Can you send us that photograph?' asked Bryony. 'It may not be good enough for a court of law, but it'll be useful for getting this Guy to start talking about his attitude towards Muslim women and Islamic head coverings.'

'Sure. I'll email it over now.'

'There's something else that might be useful to you,' Bernie said, while Mariam tapped busily on her phone. 'I've been looking further into Guy Daniels' company. It doesn't seem to have returned a profit in any year since it was set up. It's a limited company with him as CEO and a *Julie* Daniels as Company Secretary. I thought she must be his wife, but her date of birth is wrong. She's only ten years younger than me. So, my guess is she's his mother.'

'And I expect his parents are bankrolling him,' Peter added. 'Either they think it's an investment and they'll make a killing when he becomes the next Bill Gates, or they're just humouring him by letting him play with computers instead of getting a proper job.'

'The registered address is a private house in Meols,' Bernie went on. 'I've had a look at it on Google Street View. Very nice area, just off the Parade, sea view – everything! Not the sort of thing that a new-ish graduate would be able to afford. So, I should think that's his parents' house. Maybe he still lives with them.'

'Yes,' Sandra confirmed. 'That's the address that he gave us when we interviewed him after Rania's murder. He claimed he didn't remember seeing her in the audience. He didn't recognise her photo when we showed it to him. The other students that we talked to agreed that she didn't ask him any questions.'

'Well, she wouldn't have been likely to,' Lucy put in. 'She was interested in serious computing, not writing games!'

'There's probably more money in computer gaming than computer forensics,' Peter commented.

'Only if you can get enough people interested in playing your games,' Ibrahim pointed out. 'It's a crowded market out there. Half the teenage boys in the world are writing them. I've had a look at the things Guy Daniels produces. They're phantasy games where the players all choose an avatar from a cast of characters and work to achieve goals. Some of the other players are on your side and some of them are working to stop you reaching your goals. There's one in particular you might be interested in, Inspector. It's about a Utopian kingdom being threatened by mass immigration from an evil empire.'

'Supposed to be an allegory of Britain today, as perceived by the right-wing media?' murmured Sandra. 'Yes, I see what you mean. 'I'll get someone to look into that.'

9. KING EXPOSED?

'Concern continues about the apparent targeting of young Muslim women in Liverpool.' Dominic reached out and turned up the volume on the radio in the kitchen of the Kensington house so that he could hear it over the sound of the kettle as it approached boiling point. 'Some of them are choosing to change their dress in an attempt to make themselves less vulnerable. Our reporter, Freya Timms, spoke to some Muslim students outside the Guild of Students building yesterday afternoon.'

There followed a collage of snippets from conversations, between a very young-sounding reporter and some rather subdued students, whose views ranged from aggressively defiant to seriously scared.

'I'm not letting anyone tell me what I can and can't wear,' asserted a voice that reminded Mariam very much of a younger Tahira back when they first met. She smiled as she poured milk over her breakfast cereal.

'I've bought a different style of hijab,' came another voice. 'No one could strangle me in this!'

'That's interesting,' the reporter responded. 'I'll just describe it for the benefit of listeners. It looks a bit like a balaclava helmet, but in a much thinner material, and it covers your head and neck completely.' There was a short pause and then her voice resumed. 'Now your friend isn't wearing a hijab at all. Tell me, is that because you don't want to be identified as a Muslim in case it makes you a target?'

'No. I only cover my head when I pray or visit the mosque anyway. But I agree with Amina. We mustn't let this killer, whoever he is, dictate to us what we wear or where we go. If we do that, then he's won.'

'So, have these incidents not made you change your behaviour at all?'

'I try not to let it, but actually I think we're all being a lot more careful about never going out alone, especially at night.'

'We're getting all the Muslim students together,' a male voice cut in. 'We've created a WhatsApp group for us to keep in touch and provide escorts for female students if they need to be out after dark.'

'It's all very worrying,' came another voice. 'And I think it's worse in a way for people's parents, who aren't here and may be imagining all sorts of things. One of my friends was afraid her mother was going to make her give up her course and come home, but she managed to persuade her that she was overreacting.'

'And we're getting news that these attacks may not be confined to Merseyside,' the reporter added. 'That must give food for thought to anyone who was thinking of leaving Liverpool because of them.'

Dominic poured tea for the four friends and then sat down and looked round the table at Lucy, who was bare-headed with her hair tied back in an austere bun, and Mariam, now wearing a royal blue sun-hat, pulled well down to hide the bald patches on her head from the acid attack five years previously. Yes, their womenfolk had also changed their behaviour in response to the killings. Was that student on the radio right? Was this what the killer was hoping to achieve? Was this all about terrorising a portion of the population whom he wanted to scare away? Or …?

'Mariam?' he asked tentatively. 'Didn't you say that this Guy fellow who accosted you in the park told you that your hijab was a symbol of male domination?'

'Mmm. Something like that,' Mariam mumbled through a mouthful of bran flakes.

'So, he wanted you to take it off to assert your independence – to become more like … like British girls, or like his idea of what British girls ought to be.'

'To act more like white people,' Lucy amended. 'I bet that's how he was really thinking. That's how his sort does think: white is normal and it makes him uncomfortable when he has to be around anyone who's different from that.'

'He didn't need to come and sit next to me,' Mariam pointed out. 'There were plenty of other benches.'

'He'd still have known you were there,' Lucy argued. 'Being different and upsetting his idea of what the world ought to be like.'

'Maybe he genuinely believed you needed help,' suggested Ibrahim. 'Isn't it possible that he really thought someone else was forcing you to cover your head and to marry someone they'd chosen for you? And you've got to admit, that does happen sometimes, however much we'd like to deny it.'

'Then he should've listened when Mariam told him that wasn't true,' Lucy objected.

'But isn't that just what someone who was being subjected to coercive control would say?' Mariam pointed out. 'Ibrahim's got a point. Maybe he just needs educating.'

'What about that game he wrote?' retorted Lucy. 'It sounds from what Ibrahim said as if it's all about keeping immigrants out and sending them back if they do get in.'

'You don't know that. It could equally well have been inspired by Hitler's invasion of Poland or Russia's invasion of Ukraine,' countered Mariam.

'I don't really think so.' Ibrahim came to Lucy's defence. 'A key aspect of the game is the way that the invaders conceal themselves amongst the native population and then attack from within. It's not an invading army; it's mass migration.'

'There you are!' Lucy finished her cereal and got up to put her bowl in the sink. 'He thinks that anyone who wants to live here ought to behave just like the people he knows, and if they don't conform ... Well, he tried persuasion with you, and it didn't work, so now he's either trying to frighten Muslim women into taking off their hijabs and dressing like "normal" people, or he's trying to exterminate them. He thinks they're rubbish and that why, when he's killed them, he leaves them with the rubbish!'

'I agree with that.' Ibrahim drained his mug and joined Lucy at the sink. 'But Peter would say that we don't actually have any evidence that this Guy Daniels *is* the killer.'

'Then the police ought to get their finger out and *find* the evidence,' Lucy retorted. 'He was on the spot when Rania was killed. That can't be just coincidence.'

'It could be,' Dominic pointed out. 'Or ... or ... or he could've said something in his talk that encouraged someone else to do it! If he talked about that game of his, could that have triggered someone in the audience to try to play it out in real life?'

'I think you're getting into the realms of fantasy there,' Mariam smiled, putting her arm round him and kissing him on the cheek. 'Now, hadn't you to better be getting off? You'll be late for work if you don't hurry.'

✳✳✳

Dominic arrived at the school where he worked just as fellow teacher and Muslim convert, Emily Armstrong was getting off the bus outside. He waited for her, and they walked together to the staff room. She, too, was a member of the Feminist Sisterhood.

'Have you heard the news about Tahira's cousin?' he asked.

'Yes. I was away for the weekend, or I would have gone to see her. She must be devastated. Have *you* seen her? How is she?'

'Devastated, yes. And she feels responsible. Yasmeen's parents only let her go away to uni because she was here to look after her.'

'How awful for her! And how awful for Yasmeen's Mum and Dad. Are they here? Have you met them?'

'Her mum is, and her sister, but her dad couldn't get away from the family business. They own a shop and there's no one else to look after it.'

'Hmph!' Emily snorted. 'That sounds like a pretty feeble excuse to me! I'd have thought he'd want to come with his wife and daughter, especially with a serial killer on the loose, like they seem to be saying. And who carries on as normal when their daughter has been killed?'

'Perhaps he couldn't face the idea of seeing her there in the mortuary,' Dominic suggested. 'People show their grief in different ways. Maybe he wants to keep busy, and the shop gives him something to focus on.'

'My dad would've been here like a shot,' Emily continued, 'shouting at the police for not catching the killer after Rania was murdered. And accusing Tahira and the others of brainwashing me into reverting to Islam and putting myself at risk by dressing like a foreigner. He's already been on the phone telling me I ought to stop wearing a hijab.'

'Actually,' Dominic began cautiously, 'I think he might have a point about that. Mariam and Lucy have stopped, for the time being anyway – just 'til we know more about what the killer's motivation is. Maybe you ought to think abou–'

'Why should I?' Emily exploded. 'If we all start hiding our identity because we're scared to be seen as Muslims then he's won, hasn't he? Whoever he is. I'm not ashamed of my religion, and I'm not going to pretend to be something I'm not!'

'I only meant–'

'And what sort of message does it send out to the kids?' she went on, ignoring his attempts to calm her indignation. 'Give in to the bullies, you'll be safer that way? Throw away your principles if it gets too risky? I have every right to dress however I please, and I won't be intimidated by some Islamophobic thug!'

'There are other sorts of head covering that couldn't be used as a ligature to strangle you with,' Dominic cut in as soon as Emily paused for breath. 'There was a student on the radio this morning talking about one of them. That's the thing that's special about these attacks, in all three of them, it looks as if the killer pulled off the victim's hijab, put it round their neck and throttled them with it. You can still dress modestly, but hopefully without making yourself a target for this, this …'

'Why should I change?' Emily retorted stubbornly. 'And what do you mean, *all three of them*? Has someone else been killed? Is it someone we know?'

'No,' Dominic hastened to reassure her. 'It's nothing to do with us. It happened in Oxford – to a student down there. No connection with Liverpool at all, as far as I know. But it was the same thing – a Muslim student strangled with her own hijab.'

'And the police think it's the same person who did it? How do you know?'

'Er … Lucy knows someone down there – in the police. They told her about it.' Dominic suddenly wondered if he had divulged information that was not intended to be made public. 'It happened on Sunday night. It was on the radio this morning that the police think there could be a link; but I don't know how much of the details are in the public domain, so I'd better not say any more. The point is: it would be easy to wear a type of hijab that can't be used as a weapon to kill you.'

'I had to fight to get the school to include a hijab in the school uniform for anyone who wants to wear one,' Emily argued obstinately. 'Everyone knows that it's part of my religion. I'm not going to allow anyone to point the finger and say I was afraid to stand up for what I believe.'

'Maybe under the circumstances you ought to be advising the girls who wear hijabs to switch to something safer, instead of just indulging in religious grandstanding!' Dominic was beginning to lose patience with his young colleague. At times, Emily could be stubborn to the point of irrationality.

'You just don't understand, do you? It's what I believe! It's important to me! I'm not ashamed to be a Muslim, and I *want* people to know that I am.'

They walked on in silence. Just as they reached the staff room, an idea occurred to Dominic.

'How about,' he began as his pushed open the door, 'how about we buy a consignment of that other style of hijab – in the school colours – and give one to each of the girls in the school who normally wears a traditional hijab? I'm sure the head would be happy to add that to the uniform list. That way, you'd be helping them all to stay safe without compromising on modesty. You'd have to wear one too, of course, to set an example.'

'I suppose I could ….' Emily was reluctant but wavering.

'It'll be a lot better than risking them deciding not to come to school because they're frightened to go out of the house,' Dominic added, pressing his advantage now that he seemed to have found a chink in Emily's armour. 'Tell you what – I've got a free period, second lesson. I'll have a look on the internet and see what I can find.'

'OK. Yes. I suppose you're right. Thanks. Now, tell me about this student who's been killed in Oxford. Do you really think the same person did it?'

✳✳✳

'Do you really think it's the same killer?' Alice asked, as they waited for the Liverpool team to join their morning videoconference.

'Not necessarily,' Andy responded, leaning forward to un-mute his microphone as Sandra's face appeared on the screen in front of them. 'But there must be some connection. It's too much of a coincidence otherwise. Good morning, Chief Inspector, how are you?'

'Very well thank you. How about you?'

'I'm fine. Now let me introduce you to DC Alice Ray. She and Josh have been interviewing students who knew the victim. I'll let them tell you what they've found out later. How have you been getting on up there? Any progress?'

'We have had one new lead,' Sandra replied. 'I don't suppose you remember, but our first victim had been to some sort of symposium the evening she was killed. It turns out that one of the speakers has a bit of a history of approaching Muslim women and trying to get them to take off their hijabs.'

'Harassing them in the street?' asked Andy.

'Not exactly. And we've only actually got one report of him doing it. But it just so happened that the woman he approached was a friend of both of the victims, and–.' She broke off suddenly and then then continued in a slightly different tone, 'Of course! You know Lucy Paige, don't you? She was there. This man – Guy

Daniels – approached her friend Mariam and started talking to her. When she wouldn't take off her hijab, he tried to remove it by force.' Sandra paused for a moment and a smile crept across her face. 'And Our Lucy whacked him with a heavy medical textbook and then twisted his arm up his back and pinned him up against a wall.'

'That sounds like Lucy,' Andy grinned back. 'What happened next?'

'Mariam – her friend – took a photo of him on her phone, and then they let him go. Apparently, Lucy wanted to call the police and get him charged with assault, but her friend wouldn't.'

'And when was this?' Alice cut in.

'Months ago. Last July, I think. Anyway, with him having been with the first victim shortly before she died, we thought he warranted further investigation. So, Bryony's been digging into his background.'

'Turn up anything interesting?' asked Andy.

'Nothing you could use in court, but some of his social media posts were … suggestive. But better if Constable Foster tells you herself. Go ahead Bryony.'

Sandra's image disappeared from the centre of the screen and was replaced by that of a younger woman with short black hair that contrasted starkly with piercing blue eyes.

'He graduated from JMU in 2016,' she began.

'JMU?' Alice queried.

'Liverpool John Moores University,' Sandra explained. 'It's one of the new universities – not so new now, I suppose. It was Liverpool Poly back in the day.'

'I see. Sorry, go on. I didn't mean to interrupt.'

'He fancies himself as an entrepreneur,' Bryony resumed. 'He set up a business while he was still a student, writing computer games. He's making enough to pay himself a modest – a very modest – salary, but that's about all. As Sandra said, his social media activity is interesting. Nothing you can exactly put your finger on. I mean, not the sort of thing you could report as hate crime, but a sort of underlying misogyny and racism.'

'That does sound like the right sort of psychological profile,' Andy agreed. 'And you say he was on the spot when the first victim was killed?'

'That's right,' Sandra told him. 'We interviewed him at the time, but we didn't have any reason to suspect that he was any more than a witness at that stage. I had another look through the notes DC Ransom took yesterday. He showed him a photograph of the victim, and he claimed he didn't recognise her.'

'He said he didn't think she was even in the room when he gave his talk,' Charlotte interjected. 'He was very off-hand and dismissive altogether. He was confident that she didn't ask him any questions and he didn't see her after the event was over. He claimed that he didn't leave right away, because there were lots of students who wanted to talk to him about setting up their own gaming businesses. He obviously believed he'd been a great success and really wowed his audience.'

'If that's true,' Bryony observed, 'and if Rania went straight home after the lectures finished, then he wouldn't have been able to catch her before she got back. There's hardly any distance between the two buildings.'

'Maybe she stayed behind to talk to one of the speakers too,' suggested Andy. 'Or maybe she went home and then went out again.'

'Yes,' Sandra agreed. 'There are several possibilities.'

'He claims he went straight out to his car, after he'd finished talking to the students,' Charlotte went on. 'It was parked in one of the spaces on Fontenoy Street, just across from the Henry Cotton building where the talks were. He said he didn't see anyone hanging around outside. But he wouldn't have gone past the place where they found Rania's body; there's a footpath straight across to where he says he parked his car.'

'I'm planning to bring him in for a more formal interview later today,' Sandra told Andy. 'Mariam has given us permission to show him the photo she took of him. We'll start from that incident, and then spring our questions about the killings after he's already rattled.'

'Right,' Andy nodded. 'That all sounds rather promising. I'm afraid we don't have much in the way of progress to report at all. We've interviewed our victim's friends from her college, but we only got the usual things. She was well-liked – aren't all murder victims? – quiet, hard-working. The only useful piece of information they gave us was to tell us that she'd been with friends at Lincoln College on Saturday evening. That's almost certainly where she was coming back from when she was killed. Alice and Josh managed to speak to some of them yesterday. Did you get anything useful from them, Josh?'

'Er, not really.' DC Pitchfork sounded nervous at this unexpected summons to speak. 'The, er, host was a girl called Melanie Good. She's in the second year of an English degree. Her room isn't actually in Lincoln; it's in Bear Lane, on the other side of the High. She made dinner for a group of them – all English students – and then they sat in her room talking about their course. It all broke up shortly before ten, according to her.'

'I managed to speak to one of the others,' Alice added, coming to her colleague's rescue as he struggled to think of anything else to say. 'Keziah Cole confirmed that they all left at ten-ish. She walked with the fourth student, Milly Burton, as far as Magdalen, which is where she lives, and then Milly went on over Magdalen Bridge to St Hilda's. Zahra went the opposite way, so they didn't see anything of her after they turned out of the end of Bear Lane – where it meets Oriel Square.'

'Melanie came down to see her friends out,' Joshua Pitchfork came back in. 'I asked her if there was anyone hanging about in the road when they left. She said she didn't notice anyone, but as she was going back upstairs, one of the other students that lives there pushed past her and went out in a great rush, as if he was late for something. She ... she's probably just imagining things, sir, but ....'

'Yes?' Andy urged, suppressing his impatience with some difficulty, not wanting to undermine the young constable's confidence by showing him up in front of his colleagues and a senior officer from another force.

'Her room looks out over Bear Lane,' Joshua continued. 'When she got back to it, she looked out and she saw the same student going down the lane and turning into Oriel Square – the same way that Zahra went. She said she wasn't sure at the time, but she now thinks he was following her. Like I said, she's probably just imagining it after hearing what happened.'

'It's still worth following up on,' Andy told him. 'Did she give you his name? If he was going the same way as Zahra, he may have seen something, even if he wasn't following her.'

'Alfie Prescott. He's an English student too. In fact, he's Keziah's tutorial partner, but she said he keeps himself to himself and she hardly sees him outside of tutorials. I went and knocked on his room, but he wasn't in. I can go back and have another go today, if you like.'

'Yes,' Andy agreed. 'That's probably worth doing. In fact, it's probably worth talking to all the students that live there, in case any of the others were out in Bear Lane at around that time. And, now that we've got a pretty good idea of the route she'd have been taking, we can see if there are any CCTV cameras that may have picked her up as she went past.' He turned back to face the screen. 'I think that's about all we've got to report from our end. Zahra Shahidi's parents have arrived in Oxford. They weren't aware of any reason why anyone might want to hurt her. As far as they knew, she was happy in Oxford, had plenty of friends and was doing OK in her course. All the usual stuff.'

'Yes,' Sandra nodded. 'It's the same with the families of our victims. These killings definitely look random rather than personal. DC Fisher's been doing sterling work going through the files comparing the three incidents. There are the obvious common threads: the victims are all young Muslim students wearing head scarves long enough to be used to strangle them; the killer leaves a chess piece somewhere near the body; the bodies are left amongst rubbish – either next to the bins or with rubbish from a bin scattered over them.'

'It sounds like we're looking for a chess fanatic who thinks that Muslim women are trash,' Charlotte commented. 'I'd say this Guy Daniels fits that profile quite well.'

'The killings all took place late at night,' John Fisher continued, 'while the victim was walking alone close to where they were living.'

'That could imply that the killer had been watching them for some time and knew where they lived,' Andy mused. 'Which rather contradicts our assumption that the attacks were opportunistic and random.'

'Mmmm,' Sandra nodded. 'The chess pieces suggest a certain amount of pre-planning too. I wonder what their significance really is.'

'They're all white,' Bryony pointed out, 'and all valuable pieces – not pawns that don't pose much threat and are often sacrificed to protect other pieces. I'd say he believes he's some sort of white crusader driving out the forces of darkness. Isn't that what you said his computer games are all about?'

'Guy Daniels has certainly got some questions to answer,' Sandra agreed, 'but we mustn't lose sight of our other suspect. Max

Barker could so easily have killed Yasmeen Osmani, and he doesn't have an alibi for Rania Ansari's death either.'

'But we established that he couldn't have got to Oxford in time for the other murder,' Bryony argued.

'No,' Sandra admitted, 'but the only solid thing we've got to link that with the two up here is the chess pieces. They don't *prove* that it was the same killer. *Whoever* killed Yasmeen would've had his work cut out getting down to Oxford in time to find a suitable victim only a day later.'

'Are you suggesting a copycat? Andy asked. 'Or a conspiracy?'

'Either – neither – both!' Sandra sighed. 'I'm not sure I'm suggesting anything. I just want us all to keep an open mind.'

$$***$$

'Thank you for coming in to speak to us, Mr Daniels,' Sandra said as she entered the interview room and took a seat opposite the young man. 'I hope we won't need to keep you for long.'

Guy shifted uneasily in his seat and took a draft from a plastic bottle of water that he had brought with him. He put it back down on the table, but kept his fingers gripped tightly round it, the knuckles showing white with the effort.

'Is this about that girl that died after you say she'd been at my talk? I told you before: I don't even remember seeing her there. I can't help you.'

'We may come on to that later,' Sandra told him. 'But first, we'd like to ask you about another incident.'

She nodded towards Charlotte, who was sitting next to her. The constable turned round the tablet computer that she was holding, so that Guy could see the face displayed on the screen. 'Do you remember meeting this woman?'

'No?' Guy shook his head in bewilderment. 'Who is this? Oh! I get it! I suppose this is the girl who was killed on Friday night. Are you trying to pin that on me too? I told you – I never even noticed that Tanya girl, and I've never seen this one either!'

'I suppose they all look the same to you,' suggested Charlotte scornfully. 'Brown-skinned people, I mean. Look closer. We know you met this woman. It was in July, in St Johns Gardens – behind St George's Hall.'

'July?' Guy sounded incredulous. 'How d'you expect me to remember something that happened nearly a year ago? OK. Let's say I did bump into her there. What about it?'

'She was sitting on a bench waiting for a friend to join her,' Sandra told him. 'And you approached her. You sat down and started chatting. And then you tried to forcibly remove her hijab. Is it coming back to you now?'

'I don't know what you're talking about!' Guy's fist clenched so tightly around the bottle of water that the plastic began to deform with a cracking sound. 'I've never seen this girl before in my life. Either she's lying or you've got the wrong man.'

'Perhaps this other picture will jog your memory.' Charlotte showed him the photograph that Mariam had taken of Guy's face pressed up against the wall. 'Her friend arrived in time to prevent you doing her any harm. You're not going to try to deny that this is you in this picture, are you? Both women have positively identified you from your photograph on the JMU website. And you told them your name, too.'

Guy's mouth dropped open as he stared down at the screen. 'Wh-wh-where did you get this?' he demanded.

'The woman who took it gave it to me. The woman that you assaulted in St Johns Gardens last July.'

'Assaulted! You can't be serious! I never touched her. I was just helping her to take off that scarf thing she had round her head.'

'Did she ask for your help?' Charlotte's voice was cold and hard. Guy did not reply. 'I'll take that as a "no" then. She and her friend agree that you made a grab for her hijab and she moved away from you in an attempt to prevent you from taking hold of it. Do you deny that?'

'I – I – I never touched her!'

'Let me help you here,' Sandra intervened, speaking calmly and deliberately. '*Common Assault*, as defined in section 39 of the Criminal Justice Act 1988, includes not only the inflicting of violence on another person, but also acting in such a way as to make that person think that they are about to be attacked.'

'But – but ….' Guy stared round in disbelief.

'The maximum sentence for Common Assault is 6 months imprisonment,' Sandra went on inexorably. 'Unless it is racially or religiously aggravated, in which case perpetrators can be imprisoned for up to two years.'

'Wha – what about the way that girl assaulted me?' Guy's indignation rose above his fear and, letting go of the bottle in his hand, he slammed his fist on the table. 'She hit me with some great heavy book and she twisted my arm up my back and pushed me hard against a wall. You – you have the evidence right there! Why aren't you charging *her*?'

'At the moment, we're not charging anyone.' Sandra remained calm. 'We are merely asking you to tell us about your movements on a few dates when crimes took place that we're investigating. Shall we start with the day of the careers event? You were the last-but-one speaker on the programme. Did you leave as soon as you'd given your talk or did you wait until the end?'

Guy unclenched his fists and took a deep draught from the water bottle.

'I waited. I had some flyers for a new game I was just launching and I thought I might be able to give them to people as they went out.'

'Good. Now we're getting somewhere. So, after it all finished, you went round talking to people and trying to hand out flyers?'

'No. I was going to, but as soon as it was all over, this student came up to me and started telling me what a fan he was of my stuff. He kept me talking until everyone else had gone. So I never had a chance to connect with anyone else.'

'Did he tell you his name?'

'Oh yes! It was Tyson – Tyson Green. He's one of my beta-testers.'

'Beta-testers?' Sandra queried.

'I've got a group of players who try out new games for me before I launch them publicly,' Guy explained. 'They do it for nothing because it means they get to try them all out before anyone else.'

'So, you already knew him?'

'No. Well, only by his gaming name. I've never met any of them. I just reached out to a few players who were on my games a lot and asked them if they were interested, and he was one that said "yes".'

'And what *is* his gaming name?'

'Knight Crusader.'

Charlotte gave a sharp intake of breath and seemed about to speak, until Sandra shot her a warning look.

'I see,' Sandra said, her voice calm as if she attached no significance to this choice of alias. 'So, this Tyson Green kept you talking after the event was over. Does that mean you left the building together?'

'Yes, I suppose so.'

'And which way did he go then?'

'I'm not sure. I think he turned to the right.'

'Towards Fontenoy Apartments?'

'If you say so.'

'I'm asking you. When you say he went to the right, you do mean to the right as you come out of the building?'

'Yes. That's what I said. I'd left my car just across the grass. So, I went straight ahead and he turned right.'

'And was there anyone else around? No students hanging about outside? No passers-by?'

'I don't remember. I was trying to get away from him. He was being a nuisance.'

'Thank you.' Sandra smiled towards him, satisfied that they were making progress. 'Now, just for the record, I'd like the names of all your other beta-testers.'

'I told you – I don't know their names.'

'Their gaming names. The ones you use to communicate with them. You presumably do communicate with them or they wouldn't be much use for testing your new games.'

'Why do you want them?' Guy asked suspiciously.

'Just curiosity – indulge me.'

'But they might not like–'

'You won't be telling me anything they aren't happy for anyone else who plays the games to know, will you?' Sandra pressed him. 'Just their gaming aliases. That's all I'm asking for. If you need a bit of time to get it together you can email the list to me or you can print it out and I'll send someone round to your house to collect it.'

'OK. The others are Necromancer, Aragorn, Roadkill and Silver Bullet.'

'Only five altogether?' asked Charlotte. 'That's not many for beta-testing.'

'It's enough to iron out any major problems. Gamers send feedback all the time and I make updates. That's how online gaming works. You've got to be out there. You can't afford to wait until a game's perfect before it goes live.'

'And you really have no idea who these people are in real life?' Sandra pressed him.

'No,' Guy insisted. 'Why would I?'

'You don't need to take the names of the people who play your games when they buy them or take out a subscription or whatever?'

'They don't.' Guy's voice was scornful. 'That's not how I monetise my content. That's done through advertising.'

'So absolutely anyone could be playing your games and you wouldn't know?' Sandra asked.

'Why would I want to know who they are? The main thing is to grow my user base.'

'I see.' Not for the first time, Sandra wondered if she was becoming old. Her daughters would no doubt laugh at her ignorance of this new world of entertainment. 'Thank you. Now, I need you to tell me where you were on another couple of occasions.'

'Why?'

'Hopefully, so we can rule you out of our enquiries into another couple of incidents. Let's start with last Friday night from, say, nine pm.'

'Friday night? I was working late on fixing some bugs in the new game.'

'At home?'

'Er … yes.' Sandra got the impression that Guy was embarrassed to admit that his business premises were merely a loft conversion in his parents' house. 'In my development studio.'

'And your parents can vouch for that, presumably?'

'Do they need to?'

'It would make things simpler for us. All they need to say is they were there in the house with you.'

'Only they weren't,' Guy admitted at last. 'It was their anniversary. They went away for the weekend.'

'So, they went off on Saturday morning and got back – when?'

'They went on Friday night and came back Monday morning.'

'I see.' Sandra paused to give Guy time to elaborate on this, but he remained silent.

'Now, tell me about *your* weekend. What did you do on Saturday?'

'I got up about ten – ten-thirty. I had breakfast and then took the dog for a walk

'Where did you go?' Charlotte intervened.

'Just along the shore. We got as far as Leasowe lighthouse and then came back.

'Did you meet anyone while you were out?'

'I must've met loads of people.'

'Anyone you know, I meant. Anyone who can confirm you were there.'

'No.'

'OK.' Sandra stepped in, getting a feeling that Charlotte's questions were alienating their suspect and might cause him to clam up altogether. 'You're being very helpful. You got home, and then what?'

'I fed the dog. I put away a parcel that had arrived for Dad while we were out. Then I went upstairs and did some more work on the new game. I'd got some ideas for some new features.'

'That sounds exciting,' Sandra said encouragingly. 'I expect your beta-testers were keen to see those.'

'Well, they're not ready yet, but yeah, they told me they think they're great ideas.'

'What's the game about? Could you show me?'

'If you like.' Guy stared at Sandra as if he couldn't believe that she was interested. *Did she really look that old?*

He got out his phone and started tapping the screen. Eventually he turned it round so that Sandra could see it, resting his left hand on the table and pointing at the screen with his right. Sandra leaned forward to see better.

'This is a map of Thoria. It's a kingdom in the world that I've created.' Guy pointed at an irregular green shape that almost filled the screen. Peering closer, Sandra could just make out squiggly blue lines denoting rivers, a tiny image of a castle, a mountain range and several clusters of tiny houses denoting towns and villages, each with a name alongside it: Badgerthwaite, Redhaven, Raventhorpe. 'I got the name from Thor's stone – you know, on Thurstaston Common. The Thorians are mighty warriors, like the Norsemen, but their kingdom is under threat from hordes of invaders coming in from a vast evil empire just across the water.'

He swiped the screen and the map moved beneath is finger to reveal a narrow band of blue separating the green island of Thoria from a brown expanse that seemed to go on forever.

'The game is all about trying to keep the Sarcenians out of Thoria, but you can also convert them into Thorians by taking away the brainwashing helmets that they all wear.' Guy became more animated as he described his creation, pleased that he had a such willing audience. His mother always nodded and smiled when he tried to explain his games to her, but he knew that she wasn't really interested. And his dad! Well, he didn't try very hard to hide his opinion that Guy would be better employed learning the skills that he would need to take over the estate agent business that he had spent his working life building up.

'That's the dead subtle thing about this game. The actual Sarcenians aren't all evil. It's just that they've all been brainwashed by their leaders into thinking that it's their duty to exterminate the Thorian warriors and take over Thoria. *They* all think that the Thorians would be better off if they – the Sarcenians – were in charge; and the Thorians need to keep them out or else to get them to take off their helmets and become true Thorians. But here's the *really* like subtle thing.' He paused dramatically and looked up at

Sandra to make sure that she was paying full attention. 'You can't just rip the helmets off, because if you do the Sarcenians die, and Thorians aren't allowed to kill anyone – not even Sarcenians.'

'So, how *do* you get the helmets off?' Sandra asked.

'You have to find a way to get them to take them off themselves.'

'And you do that by …?'

'There's various ways, depending on how you're playing the game. If you're playing solo, then you need to earn special powers, which you do by completing tasks that the King of Thoria sets for his warriors. If you're playing as a team, then if three of you manage to surround a Sarcenian they'll do what you tell them. Or there's other more complicated ways. This is the King.' Guy swiped the screen and an image appeared of a stylised monarch with a gold crown on his head and a long red robe edged with white – ermine, Sandra supposed. 'He has to stay in his castle in Thorvik – that's the capital city of Thoria – and the Thorian warriors have to keep him safe. If the Sarcenians get into the royal palace and find the king, that's the end of the game and the Thorians have lost.'

'I see,' Sandra nodded. 'A bit like in chess?'

'That's right,' Guy agreed. 'I used to play a lot of chess when I was a kid, but I like computer games better. They're more, like … subtle. Or at least, the good ones are.'

'And you were working on this all day on Saturday?' Charlotte asked, keen to steer the conversation back on to the all-important subject of Guy's alibi – or lack thereof – for the three murders.

'Yes. At least, I took the dog out again in the evening.'

'And Sunday?'

'Yeah. I still had a lot to do to get the new features working. Apart from walking the dog, I was up in my studio all day Sunday and most of Monday. I'd got this dead clever idea for a dead cool new special power – really subtle.'

'Oh?' Sandra prompted.

'Yeah, I was dead chuffed with myself for thinking of it.' Guy smiled complacently. 'Most games are all about fighting your opponents. That's what's different about mine. But I was still using intimidation to frighten the Sarcenians into taking off their helmets. This new idea was a special power to talk to them and *persuade* them – convince them that they were being brainwashed and that they'd be free if they took them off!' He leaned back in his chair and looked round at Sandra and Charlotte with a smile of satisfaction.

Sandra smiled back. 'I think that's all we need to ask you – for now. Thank you for being so helpful and for showing us your game. It looks very good – and very subtle.'

$$*** $$

'Alfie Prescott?'

'Yeah, that's me.' It was almost noon, but the student was still in his pyjamas as he peered, bleary-eyed, at the warrant card that Josh was holding up towards him. 'What do you want?'

'We just want to talk with you,' Alice informed him. 'May we come in?'

'Suppose so.' Alfie turned and stumbled across the room to collapse into an easy chair leaving the door swinging open to admit the two police officers.

They came in and Alice closed it behind them. She looked round. It looked more comfortable than some student accommodation that she had seen. The bed was a small double – a far cry from the narrow one that she remembered from her own student days – and there was a two-seater settee in addition to the easy chair occupied by their interviewee, who was slumped there like a sack of potatoes with long legs stretched out in front of him and his chin lolling against his chest, as if he were having difficulty in supporting the weight of his head.

'Do you mind if we sit down?' Josh asked politely.

'Go ahead.' Alfie raised his head just enough to look Josh in the eye, pushing back a lock of black hair in order to do so. 'But first, are you going to tell me what this is all about?'

'A student from Holy Cross college was killed on Saturday night,' Alice began, perching uneasily in the edged of the sofa to avoid sitting on the discarded half of a pizza.

'Yeah, I heard. What's that go to do with me?'

'We're talking to all the students here,' Josh told him, bending down to move the half-pizza on to a small table, strewn with beer cans and crisp packets, before sitting down next to his colleague. 'The victim – her name was Zahra Shahidi – had been with friends in this building that evening, and she was killed on her way home. We're trying to re-create her journey, and we're talking to anyone who may have seen her.'

'Well, I didn't.' The lock of greasy black hair fell across Alfie's eyes but he didn't bother to push it away. 'I'm sorry, I can't help you,' he added, perhaps realising that his sullen replies were not creating a good impression.

'We have a witness who saw you leave this building just after Zahra did,' Alice said quietly. 'They told us that you went off in the same direction – to the end of the lane and then right, into Oriel Square.'

'It was about ten o'clock,' Josh added helpfully. 'Do you remember going out at around that time?'

'Maybe.'

'Where were you going?' Alice asked.

'What's that got to do with you?' Alfie glared towards Alice but did not make eye-contact. 'I can go where I like. It's a free country – or it's supposed to be!'

'It would be helpful to us to know where you and Zahra parted ways,' Josh explained patiently. 'In case you noticed anything that could help us. When you came out, did you see anyone hanging around in the street? Or was there anything unusual at all?'

'No and no. Look: all I did was go to the pub for a pint. I wasn't stalking this bird – or bashing her on the head or whatever happened to her – just a quiet pint. You can check if you like. They know me there. Ask Ron on the bar. He served me.'

Josh was about to ask which pub this was, but Alice got her question in first. This longer burst of speech from Alfie had enabled her to detect an accent that betrayed his origins.

'You're from Liverpool?' she asked, trying to keep the jubilation out of her voice at having established a link with the two earlier killings. 'Do you still live there – outside term-time, I mean?'

'What if I do?'

'I wondered if you ever go home for weekends. Last weekend, for instance?'

'No, I didn't. Of course not! You know I was here Saturday night; you've just been grilling me about it, haven't you?'

'What about Friday night? Where were you then?'

'Here of course! But what's that got to do with this bird getting topped on Saturday?'

'Just another line of enquiry that we're following,' Alice replied vaguely.

'Getting back to Saturday,' Josh cut in, sensing that their suspect was becoming increasingly hostile and might soon refuse to answer any further questions. 'Which pub was it that you said you went to?'

'The Raven in Lichfield Street. Like I said, Ron at the bar will *confirm my alibi* if you're thinking of trying to pin anything on me.'

'Zahra Shahidi must have walked past the Raven to get to her room in Holy Cross,' Alice observed. 'So, you must've been walking behind her all the way. Are you *sure* you didn't see her at all?'

'I may have *seen* her, but I didn't notice her in particular. Why would I? There are always lots of people about in Oxford at night.'

'She was quite distinctive.' Josh produced a photograph of Zahra from his pocket and handed it to Alfie. He stared down at the smooth skin and blue-green eyes beneath thick black brows, and the sky-blue hijab that concealed her hair and neck. 'She was wearing a different headscarf the day she died. It was purple with gold embroidery on it. Are you quite sure you didn't spot someone wearing a something like that walking ahead of you on Saturday night? It was a warm night. Not many people would have had anything on their head. I would've thought you might have noticed someone who did.'

'I might of, but I didn't.' Alfie put his head in his hands and rocked gently from side to side. Josh looked towards Alice, wondering what to do now. She started to get up, thinking to fetch a glass of water for the young man who seemed to be in some sort of distress. But before she could start looking for a clean glass among the jumble of crockery piled up next to the wash basin in the corner of the room, Alfie raised his head again.

'Look, I'm sorry,' he mumbled. 'I've got a migraine coming on and an essay crisis of gargantuan proportions and I really need you to go so I can do some work. I'd like to be able to help you find whoever killed this *Zahra* but I don't know anything about it and I didn't see anything. I'm sorry.'

'That's OK.' Josh got up, He put a small card down on the table next to the half-eaten pizza. 'There's a number on there for you to phone if you do remember anything that might help, but we'll go now and let you get on.'

✳✳✳

Outside in Bear Lane, Alice slapped Josh triumphantly on the back.

'We've established a link between the two locations, at last!' she crowed. 'When was that first murder? Just after Easter, wasn't it? Before the Oxford term started. He'd have been up in Liverpool then. And we've only got his word for it that he didn't go back home for a few days last week. He could've killed that second girl and then got the train down here in plenty of time to follow Zahra Shahidi from Bear Lane to Lichfield Street on Saturday night.'

'You could be right.' Josh was more cautious, 'but it's all just circumstantial. We'll need something a lot more solid before we can bring him in.'

'Then let's get it! Do you fancy a pub lunch? I hear they do a good one at the Raven in Lichfield Street.'

'No thanks. I've got sandwiches.'

'Of course,' Alice smiled. 'Your mum.'

'Yes,' Josh grinned back. 'She thinks I'll starve myself if she doesn't make them for me. You go ahead. I'll get back to the office and do some background checks on Mr Prescott.'

✳✳✳

The options for dining in the Raven were limited. This was not one of your gastro-pubs with fancy menus and a separate dining room. Half a dozen items were chalked up on a blackboard next to the bar, behind which what looked to Alice like a husband-and-wife team served drinks and took orders, while a bar maid – probably an undergraduate working part-time to supplement her student loan – went round collecting glasses and plates and delivering pies, burgers and sausages, each accompanied by chips, to punters who seemed to be mostly young and male.

Alice ordered pie and chips and then stood at the bar sipping a half pint of lager. 'Would you be Ron, by any chance?' she asked the man who had served her.

'Yes, that's me? Why?'

'I'm a police officer.' Alice got out her warrant card and laid it on the bar in front of her. 'A young woman was killed just down the road from here on Saturday night. We think she came past here between ten and eleven. Were you working here at that time?'

'Between ten and eleven on Saturday? Yes, sure; I was. Why? Do you think she came in here? What did she look like?'

'No. We don't think she came in, but another student, whom we think may have been following her, claims that he did. He said you'd remember him – Alfie Prescott? Tall, dark hair, Liverpool accent?'

'Yes, I know Alfie. Saturday, you say? Yes, he was in here. Not until late, though. It must've been gone half past ten. I was just about to call last orders.'

'He comes here regularly?'

'Yes. I suppose I see him here most weeks – mainly Friday and Saturday nights. He comes in, we have a chat at the bar and then he takes his pint and sits on his own and taps away on his phone. Funny kid. I think he's a bit lonely actually. A bit of a fish out of water down here with all these posh boys from public schools. He's from a comprehensive and nobody else in his family ever went to university, never mind Oxford.'

'Was he in here last Friday?'

'I'm not sure. He may have been. It was a busy night. It always is on Friday. Hey Joy!' Ron called out to his wife, who had just finished serving a customer at the other end of the bar. 'Do you remember if Alfie Prescott was in last Friday night?

'Alfie? He may have been, but I couldn't swear to it. it was a busy night. Fridays always are. Why?'

'This here's a police officer.' Ron lowered his voice and inclined his head towards Alice. 'She was asking about him.'

'He's not in trouble, is he? He's such a quiet boy. I wouldn't have thought …'

'No, no,' Alice cut in quickly. 'No trouble. It's just a student was killed near here on Saturday night, and we're doing checks on everyone who knew her.'

'Oh! If you meant *Saturday* night, yes, he was in here alright,' the woman said, coming closer and leaning across the bar towards Alice. 'He came in close to closing time and asked for a pint. He looked a bit out of sorts, don't you think so, Ron?'

'In what way?' Alice asked, taking another sip of her lager so as not to reveal her excitement.

'Like he'd seen the proverbial ghost. His hand was shaking as he paid for his pint.'

'Did he pay with cash?'

'No. None the youngsters carry cash with them these days. It's all contactless cards – or more often phone apps. Why?'

'I was just thinking, if we did need to know for certain whether he was here on Friday, and what time, you'd have records of when he paid, wouldn't you?'

'Yes, but …,' Ron began.

'We couldn't show them to you without a warrant,' his wife cut in. 'Data protection.'

'Of course, but it's useful to know – just in case we need it later. Now, I saw a camera over the door when I came in. Does it give a view of the street outside at all?'

'Only a few yards to either side of the entrance,' Ron told her. 'We don't want people to think we're spying on them. It's just to deter people from trying to break in, and it's sometimes useful for identifying people if we get any trouble – not that we do much, have trouble here, I mean.'

'But it would pick up someone walking past?' Alice asked.

'Only if they were on this side of the road. Like I said, we aren't spying on passers-by.'

'Could I see the footage from Saturday night? And Friday night too, if you don't mind?'

'I don't know about that,' Ron began, 'data protec–,' but his wife interrupted.

'We'll be happy to let you have it, but could it wait until we're less busy. It's lunchtime and we seem to have quite a full house. Could I download the files and send them to you?'

'Sure,' Alice nodded. 'That'd be great. Here's my email address.' She took out a business card and handed it to the helpful Joy. 'And there's a phone number there too, in case you think of anything else that might help us.'

10. CRITICAL POSITION

'We've got another suspect to add to our list,' Andy told Sandra in what had now become a daily update between the two Senior Investigating Officers. 'A student called Alfie Prescott appears to have been following Zahra Shahidi the night she was killed. *And* he's from Liverpool, so it's just possible he could've been responsible for the other two murders as well. We're working on placing him at the scene on Saturday night and checking where he was on Friday.'

'He certainly sounds promising for your Oxford case,' Sandra agreed, 'but how likely is it that he was in Liverpool last Friday? It's a bit early in the term to have gone home for the weekend, and anyway you're telling me he was back in Oxford on Saturday.'

'Some sort of crisis at home that made him rush back during the week?' Andy suggested.

'Something important enough to drag him away from his studies, but not important enough to stop him having time to cruise the streets on the look-out for a woman in a hijab to strangle?' Sandra sounded sceptical. 'Anyway, *we*'ve got a new suspect too. He's also a student. He was at the careers event at John Moores the evening Rania Ansari was killed. According to Guy Daniels – who, of course, is still a suspect in his own right – after the event he went off in the same direction as Rania. He could easily have caught up with her and attacked her. Charlotte and I had a little chat with him this morning. I would describe his attitude towards us as hostile and evasive.'

'And, if he and Rania were both Computer Science students, he could've known her and had a personal reason for wanting to harm her,' Andy agreed. 'And the same goes for Alfie Prescott and Zahra. They were both studying English. They'd presumably have met at lectures, even though they were at different colleges. She could've done something to upset him.'

'Do you think we could have more than one killer after all?' Sandra wondered. 'Could it be some sort of conspiracy between your Alfie and our Tyson? They must be about the same age, and you say Alfie is from Liverpool. They could've known each other – grown up together even. Whereabouts in Liverpool does this Alfie live?'

'I don't know. I've got someone doing background checks on him now.'

'We're doing the same for Tyson Green, as well as continuing to look into Guy Daniels. He still seems the most likely in my opinion. He's got all the hallmarks you associate with a serial killer: a loner, a bit obsessive, and one of the games he designed is all about evil invaders who can be disarmed by removing their headgear. It all fits rather neatly with pulling headscarves off women who look like foreigners and using them to strangle them. *And* there's that incident last year where he did actually try to pull off a woman's hijab.'

'Put like that, he does sound like a prime suspect,' Andy agreed.

'The trouble is, it's all circumstantial,' Sandra sighed. 'And we mustn't lose sight of our other suspect. Max Barker is by far the most likely person to have killed Yasmeen Osmani, but apart from the fact that he was on the spot and with her only minutes before she died, we've got nothing on him at all. And he definitely couldn't have got to Oxford in time to–'

'Sir!' the door of Andy's office opened and Jennifer Moorhouse's head appeared round it. She one of the civilian staff and a crucial member of the back-office team. 'Sorry to interrupt, but I think I've found something important on the CCTV.'

'Sorry, Sandra, but you might like to hear this. I'll put you on speaker phone.' Andy turned back to Jennifer. 'OK, go on, I'm all ears.'

Jennifer came into the room, closely followed by Alice.

'I was checking the video from the Raven pub,' she informed him. 'Alice asked me to find out what time Alfie Prescott got there on Saturday night. 'The camera got a clear picture of him entering the building at 10.36.'

'That sounds consistent with what we know about him leaving the Bear Lane student accommodation at around ten,' Andy observed, wondering what all the excitement was about.

'Yes, but we haven't come to the significant bit yet,' Alice cut in. 'The important thing isn't the time; it's the direction that he was coming from. I've seen the footage. He definitely came into the pub from the direction of Lichfield College – where Zahra Ansari's body was found!'

'You mean, he followed her down the road, past the pub, attacked and killed her out of sight of the camera, and then came back and established his alibi by going in an ordering a pint?'

'That's right,' Alice crowed. 'He and Zahra must both have walked past on the other side of the road, where the camera above the door of the Raven couldn't catch them, but then, when he came back …!'

'I'm sorry,' Sandra said, in the pause that followed as Alice left her words dangling in the air for dramatic effect. 'Remember, I don't know the geography the way you do. Are you saying that this places your Alfie Prescott at the crime scene during the window when your victim was killed?'

'That's a pretty good summary,' Andy agreed. 'He denied that he was following her. According to him, it was just a coincidence that they were both going that way. The pub that he habitually drinks in is en route between his lodgings and her college. But we now know that he walked *past* the pub – even though it was nearly closing time – and only crossed the road and turned back after he'd gone far enough down the road to be out of view from the camera on the door. Mind you, he must've been a quite a quick worker to manage to kill her, dump rubbish all over her from the bin, plant the chess queen and get back, all before 10.36.'

'Maybe they left Bear Lane earlier than we thought,' Alice suggested. 'Zahra's friend only said "about ten". If it was, say, ten to, he'd have had more time. And there's something else I've found out,' she continued excitedly. 'Everton were at home to Newcastle last Thursday. Alfie Prescott's an Everton supporter – I saw one of their magazines on the table in his room. What if he went up to Liverpool for the match, stayed over to Friday and come back Friday night or Saturday morning?'

'Well, it ought to be easy enough to check,' Sandra said. 'If you send me his details – full name, home address, mugshot and so on – I can probably find out if he was at the match. He'll have had his ticket scanned at the turnstile.'

'So, you do think he could be our killer?' Andy asked.

'Well, if there is just one killer, he does seem the least unlikely of our suspects.' Sandra was cautious in her reply. 'But, to be honest, I'm veering more towards wondering if it's more of a conspiracy – or maybe not even that. I get the feeling that maybe

Guy Daniels is in the background, pulling the strings, and we've got three different killers all doing what he tells them.'

'And the chess pieces are to let him know that they've completed their tasks?' suggested Alice.

'Something like that.'

✳✳✳

'Come in. I'm sure Guy won't be long.' Mrs Daniels opened the door wide and gestured to Sandra and Charlotte that they should step inside the large between-the-wars semi-detached house in a quiet road not far from the seafront. They followed her into a spacious hall with a durable cord carpet and clean cream-painted walls. Sandra looked around as she wiped her shoes carefully on the doormat.

'He's only taking the dog for a walk,' Guy's mother continued, leading the way into a light living room into which the sun was pouring through large patio doors looking over the back garden. 'Sit down, please! Make yourselves comfortable and I'll go and make us all a nice cup of tea – or would you prefer coffee?'

'Tea would be very nice,' Sandra assured her.

'Right you are then. I won't be a moment. I'll just pop out to the kitchen and put the kettle on.'

'Thank you very much, Mrs Daniels. Please don't go to any trouble.'

'Oh, it's no trouble! I was just about to have a cup myself anyway. And it's Julie. Mrs Daniels sounds so formal, and I like to think I treat everyone as my friend. I'm a carer. I deliver personal care to people in their own homes. And I always try to think of my clients as my friends and to treat them as if they were my own family. For some of them, I'm the only person they see from one day to the next. It's sad that, when someone doesn't have any family or friends who can just pop round for a chat. But that's what the world's like these days, isn't it? Children grow up and leave home, and the next thing you know they've moved to Australia or America! Of course, there's always Zoom, but it's not the same, is it? And a lot of my clients can't work the technology.' She sighed and shook her head at the thought of so many lonely people in the world. 'But I'd better get on and get that tea. Won't be a tick!'

She finally left the room, pulling the door closed behind her. Charlotte gave a low whistle. 'She can talk for England, can't she? I thought she was never going to stop.'

'Don't knock it,' Sandra murmured back. 'She may give us valuable information about Guy's psychology as well as his whereabouts at the relevant times.'

'According to him, she was away all weekend,' Charlotte pointed out.

'She may have rung him. I saw a phone in the hall. They must still have a landline. If she rang him here, it might establish whether he was at home or not.'

Sandra got up and wandered round the room. There were several photographs on the mantlepiece over a fireplace containing a wood-burning stove – family snaps of memorable past occasions. In one, a small boy grinned at the camera as he prepared to blow out the candles on a birthday cake. Another showed the same boy, a little older now, concentrating intently as he lined up his club to tackle a tricky hole at crazy golf. And then there he was again, as a teenager, self-consciously holding up a small silver trophy.

Sandra picked up this last picture and looked at it more closely. She could just about make out the words on the side of the cup: *Junior Chess Champion*.

'Ah! I see you've spotted Guy's big achievement.' Julie Daniels was back, carrying a tray laden with china cups and saucers, a teapot and a plate with slices of two different kinds of cake on it. She put it down on the large coffee table in the centre of the room and then reached out her hand to take the photograph from Sandra. She glanced down at it lovingly for a moment and then replaced it on the mantlepiece.

'He was Junior Champion at his chess club three years running,' she told them. 'We were so proud of him! Graham taught him when he was little and he took to it like a duck to water. I could never get the hang of chess myself. Graham used to ask me to play with him, but he always beat me, which was frustrating for both of us. That's why he joined the club, and then he took Guy along as soon as he was old enough. They used to have a great time together – until Guy got into all this computer games stuff. We're very proud of what he's doing in that too, but it does seem a bit weird, spending all day on his own in front of his computer, instead of getting out and meeting people.'

'Doesn't he have any mates he hangs round with?' Sandra suggested. 'Doesn't he ever kick a ball around with his old school friends or go to the match? Which football club does he support?'

'Guy was never interested in sports.' Julie poured a cup of tea and handed it to Sandra. 'Help yourself to milk and sugar. No, Guy's never been one for going out with his mates. He used to have them round here to play computer games sometimes, but then these games came out that you play over the internet and he got into that. So then he was playing with them, but his mates were in their own houses playing on their computers or on their phones. They can play anywhere these days. It's not at all like when he and his dad used to sit down here and spend whole evenings on a single chess game.'

'Does he have a girlfriend at all?' Sandra asked, trying to sound casual.

'Not at the moment. He did have a lovely girl until a few months back. Nicole, her name was. She was a bit young for him I thought at first, but a really nice girl. She's a student at the university. Really started to bring him out of himself she did. But then she broke it off with him. He wouldn't say why. Maybe she started to think he was too old for her. I don't know!' Julie shook her head in perplexity. 'Now, do please have some of this cake. The chocolate one I made myself. It's Graham's – my husband's – favourite. Lovely and moist, though I say it myself. The fruit cake's shop-bought I'm afraid, but still very good. One of my clients gave it to me.'

'How did they meet?' asked Sandra. 'Guy and Nicole.'

'You know, I'm not sure he ever told me. It was a while ago. He started bringing her over here back in …. You know, I think they may have met online, before the university re-opened after Lockdown, or … no! I think it was at a Computer Games fair. She was into all that too. She wrote a game based on one of Jane Austen's books. Guy helped her with it and put it up on his … his *platform* I think that's what he calls it. I don't think it was very popular. It's mainly boys who are into gaming isn't it? And they don't read books – not that sort of book anyway.'

'When did they split up?' asked Charlotte.

'Last summer. They were supposed to be going out to a concert in Liverpool one evening but he came back about tea-time and went straight up to his room and stayed there until breakfast the next morning. It was days before he would talk about it. He was furious with her. He'd bought the tickets, you see, for the concert, and then out of the blue she tells him she doesn't want to see him anymore.' Julie took a sip of her tea, shaking her head as she did so at the incomprehensible behaviour of her son's girlfriend. 'Since then, he's hardly been going out at all, apart from for his work – computer fairs, that sort of thing. Not that I used to like him stopping out to all hours at Night Clubs the way he used to when he was with her, but …. Well, he's not going to meet anyone stuck away in his room all day, is he? And I would like to have grandchildren one day – not that I'm pushing him into anything. I know better than to interfere in that sort of thing. Some of my friends have got kids who've never spoken to them after they interfered with their love lives. You've got to let your kids make their own choices, even if you disagree with what they choose.'

'That's very true,' Sandra agreed, thinking of futile arguments that she had had with her own daughters. 'Getting back to Nicole, do you happen to remember her other name?'

'I'm not sure she ever told me.' Julie took a bite of chocolate cake and chewed it slowly while she considered the matter. 'I think it began with a *D*,' she said at last. '*Dawson*, maybe or *Day*. No, I don't think either of those is right. I do remember she was from Hemel Hempstead – *Hemel Hempstead Herts*, she used to say, like that. Guy used to say it sounded like a made-up name, like somewhere in his games. And then Nicole wrote a funny poem about Henrietta Henderson from Hemel Hempstead Herts. That was the sort of thing they used to do together – making up stories and turning some of them into computer games. Guy loves creating worlds in his head. He always did. Even when he was a little boy, he was always making up stories – old-fashioned ones about knights fighting dragons and heroes rescuing maidens in distress. More tea? There's plenty in the pot.'

'Thanks.' Sandra held out her cup and Julie re-filled it. 'I gather it was your wedding anniversary at the weekend?'

'Yes. How did you know? We went back to the lovely little hotel in the Lake District where we had our honeymoon. Of course, it had all changed quite a bit since then – all ensuite bathrooms and free WiFi – but still very quiet and peaceful. Just what we needed. My job can be quite stressful sometimes and Graham has his own business, which is always demanding, isn't it?

And estate agents get such bad press, when they're only trying to do their job and make an honest living. It's not as if anyone gets rich selling other people's houses.'

'So, Guy was alone here over the weekend?' Sandra asked casually.

'Yes. I tried to get him to invite a friend to stay – for company – but he said he'd rather be on his own. He's always found it hard to make friends, even when he was a little boy. That's why it's such a pity that his relationship with Nicole didn't last. She was good for him – brought him out of himself. I left him meals in the freezer, so he'd eat properly and we rang a couple of times each day to check he was OK. Him and the dog – Graham was sure he'd forget to feed him and take him for walks, but Guy was fine about it.'

'Did you ring him on the landline or his mobile?'

'What a funny question!' For the first time, Julie Daniels appeared to wonder why the police were showing so much interest in her son's movements. 'We used the landline, as it happens, because then he'd have to come down out of his *studio* as he calls it. When he started up his gaming business, we converted the loft into an office for him. If I didn't call him down for meals, he'd probably stay up there all the time. So, I thought if he had to answer the phone – which is in the hall, with an extension in the kitchen for when I'm cooking – then he wouldn't forget to eat – and to feed the dog!'

'Very ingenious,' Sandra smiled. 'I'll bear that in mind for when my daughter's home alone. Now, I wonder if you can help me? We're particularly interested in whether your son was at home last Friday night. I suppose you'll have rung him to let him know you'd arrived at your hotel?'

'Oh yes! We left here at about eight. It should have been earlier, but Graham got detained at the office, checking that the staff were all set up to manage on their own on Saturday, so we ate later than we planned and, as I say, we didn't get away until eight-ish. It took us a bit over two hours to drive up there and then we had to check in, so I suppose we must've rung him at … say, half ten, quarter to eleven.'

'And he was here in the house then?'

'Yes. And then we rang him again at lunchtime on Saturday, because Graham wanted to check that he'd walked the dog. And talking of walking the dog, here they are! I knew Guy wouldn't be long.'

At the sound of a key in the front door, Mrs Daniels got up and went out into the hall, leaving the living room door open. Sandra and Charlotte could hear the conversation that ensued.

'There are two police officers here to see you. They're in the back room. You go on in. Give Bruno to me. I'll take him in the kitchen. You know how excited he gets when there are visitors.'

'What do they want?'

'Something about those girls who were killed in Liverpool. You know! The Asian students who were strangled. They said they thought you were a witness. Did you know them?'

'One of them was at that talk I gave at John Moores, but I've already told them I don't even remember seeing her there.'

'Well, there must be some reason they think you may have seen something. Go on in! The sooner you get in there, the sooner you'll find out, won't you?'

There was a scrabbling noise and some whines of protest. Presumably Bruno was making a bid for freedom. Then Julie Daniels passed the open door on her way to the kitchen, dragging a reluctant basset hound by the collar. The dog barked on catching sight of the visitors and strained to get free, but Julie held firm and they soon heard the kitchen door open and close. There was more barking, but muffled now and it soon stopped. Evidently Bruno knew when he was beaten.

'Er … you wanted to see me?' Guy entered the room, looking round nervously and avoiding eye-contact with Sandra and Charlotte.

'Yes.' Sandra got to her feet. 'We wanted to have a little chat with you.'

'About those girls who were killed? I told you: I don't know anything about them.'

'Yes. And about your computer games. One in particular. That one you were talking about last time – with the alien invaders that can only be disarmed by pulling off their helmets.'

'The Sarcenians, yeah. What about them?'

'Could you show us your studio?' Sandra suggested. 'And talk us through how you came up with the idea and how you turned it into a game.'

'I've given Bruno one of his chews and shut him in the kitchen.' Mrs Daniels was back. 'He'll be happy there while we finish our tea. Sit down, Guy, and I'll pour some for you.'

'We're going upstairs.' As Sandra had anticipated, Guy seemed relieved at the excuse to avoid his mother being present while he answered their questions. Not that there was much more that they could learn from him now that she had unwittingly confirmed his alibi for the second and third murders. 'They want to see the studio.'

'Oh! Yes, well up you go then. There's cake down here for you when you're finished.'

Sandra and Charlotte followed Guy up two flights of stairs and into a long room with a sloping ceiling and a large dormer window through which the sun was cascading, lighting up moats of dust that floated in the air above three large computer screens. Against one of the low walls of the room, there was a rather saggy-looking settee. Next to it, what looked like an old record cabinet provided a surface for an espresso machine. Evidence of its frequent use lay on a small table in front of the settee, in the form of five or six coffee-stained mugs.

'Quite a nice cosy den you've got up here,' she remarked. 'And this is where you write all your games?'

'Yeah.'

Sandra wandered over to the window and looked out. Between the roofs of the neighbouring houses, there was a view of the sea. Then, looking down, she could see the road. A red car stopped behind a row of parked cars and waited for a white van to come the other way. A woman pushed a child in a buggy while an older child followed, carrying a plastic lunchbox. A man came out of a house and got into a car parked on the drive. You could see everything that went on in the street from here. Did it give Guy a feeling of power, looking down on the world, watching people and knowing that they were unaware of his presence?

'Do you mind if we sit down?'

Guy shrugged. 'Be my guest.'

He sat down in the office chair by the desk, leaving the sofa for the two police officers.

'Your mother was telling us about what a whizz you were at chess when you were at school,' Sandra began. 'Do you still play at all?'

'Not really.'

'Do you still have a set?'

'Yeah, I do actually. But what's that got to do with you?'

'Could we see it?'

'See my chess set?'

'Yes.'

'But why?' He seemed genuinely bewildered. Did he really not know about the chess pieces that had been left by the murdered women? By now, it had well-and-truly leaked out and had become a hotly-debated topic in both the newspapers and social media.

'Just show us please,' Sandra repeated.

'OK. If you like.' Guy pulled open a drawer beneath the desk and started taking out piles of papers, some with scribbled notes in a mixture of pencil and ballpoint pen, others with intricate maps similar to the one that he had shown them on his phone at their previous interview, still others with family trees – or were they flow diagrams? At last, he seemed to reach the bottom of the drawer and, putting his hand in again, produced a chess board, which he unfolded and placed on the table in front to Sandra and Charlotte. Then, with exaggerated deliberation, he took out a small cardboard box, rather battered, and removing the lid, proceeded to set up the chess pieces that it contained on the board.

'Satisfied?' he asked as he set the final pawn in its place.

'Yes, thank you, Mr Daniels.'

'Of course, my dad's got his own set downstairs, and then there's our travel set. I think that's probably in his car. Do you want to see them too?'

'No thank you. That won't be necessary.' Of course, he knew that those would both be complete too. And there would be no point coming back with a warrant to search the house for other chess sets that might have pieces missing from them. Guy wasn't stupid. Odd and obsessive, perhaps, but not stupid. Writing those games of his took intelligence – and imagination, the sort of imagination that might plan a series of murders somehow linked to the pieces on a chess board. But the planning would be meticulous and would include ensuring that there would be no trail of evidence to link him to the crimes.

'We were wondering if you know either of these men.' Sandra took out photographs of Max Barker and Alfie Prescott and handed them to Guy.

He studied each of them carefully, then handed them back, shaking his head as he did so. 'Nope. Never seen them before. Who are they?'

'We think they may be players of your games – some of your beta-testers perhaps?'

'I told you: I don't know who any of them are, not even their names, never mind what they look like.'

'Alright.' Sandra got to her feet. 'Thank you, Mr Daniels. That's all for now. We'll be in touch again if we have any more questions – or if Ms Ali decides to press charges over that incident in St John's Gardens.'

11. BISHOP'S MOVE

'The children won't start arriving for a few minutes,' Tahira told her aunt and cousin later that afternoon as they entered the Islamic Centre. 'Why don't you sit down over here? Then you'll be able to join in if you want to or just sit and read or whatever, if you'd rather not.'

'I'd like to help,' Fatima said at once. 'Only my Arabic isn't really that good. I'm not sure I'll be much use.'

'Don't worry! This is a beginners' group. It's mostly quite young kids, plus a few adults who never got the chance to learn before or who are new to Islam.'

'Really?' Marina asked in surprise. 'Do you get a lot of people converting? There are hardly any in our mosque at home.'

'Not a lot, but we always get a few from the new intake of students – young people searching for more meaning in life. And then there are people like Dominic and Lucy, who aren't reverting, but want to know more about Islam. You may find other things about this mosque different too. Almost all our members are young British people looking for ways of expressing their faith in a way that fits in with twenty-first century western culture.'

'I suppose you're hoping that all the students who come along to look decide to become Muslims too, once they understand it properly,' Marina suggested.

'I don't know,' Tahira was hesitant. 'God's Messenger, peace be upon him, was very positive towards Christians and Jews. He called them *People of the Book* and recognised that they worship God, just as we do. He argued with them, of course, but then I argue about faith with lots of Muslims too and I don't think I need to convert them all to my way of thinking – even if that would be nice! I'm not sure that God wants us all to worship Him in exactly the same way.'

'But aren't you worried that Mariam and Ibrahim might convert the other way?' Marina asked. 'And what about their children? Will they be Muslims or Christians?'

'I expect if they have any kids, they'll show them both and let them choose for themselves,' Tahira laughed. 'Don't forget, the prophet, peace be upon him, said *there is no compulsion in religion*. But you're right. It would be a whole lot simpler if couples always had the same religion. But I'm sure marriage always involves compromises. They'll work something out.'

'I thought it was haram for a Muslim woman to marry a non-Muslim man,' Fatima said quietly. 'Did I get that wrong?'

'Well, you'll find plenty of scholars who would agree with that,' Tahira admitted. 'But there's nothing definitive in the holy Qur'an or the Hadith. Many scholars deduce it from a couple of texts in the Qur'an. There's one that prohibits both Muslim men and women from marrying "idolaters" – that is polytheists who worship false gods. And there's another that permits Muslim men to choose wives from among the People of the Book. It doesn't say anything about whether or not Muslim women have the same right. Some scholars claim that, if marriage between Muslim women and Jewish or Christian men was allowed it would have been stated explicitly in the same way that it is for Muslim men marrying Jewish or Christian women, but I think that's a rather weak argument. Personally, I think it's all down to the patriarchy. Historically most scholars have been men, and a lot of them use spurious arguments about the innate weakness of women to justify forbidding them to marry non-Muslims in case their husbands influence them to abandon their faith. I'm quite sure that Mariam can think for herself and won't allow Dom to browbeat her into becoming a Catholic. Whether Ibrahim might be seduced into Christianity by Lucy is a different matter,' she added mischievously.

'What's that about me?' Tahira swung round to see Lucy standing behind her, grinning. 'We've brought Mam and Peter with us. They're interested to sit in on the class. I hope that's OK?'

'Of course,' Tahira smiled back. 'We're always pleased to welcome visitors.'

'I've been doing an online Arabic course with Duolingo,' Bernie told her. 'But it's modern Arabic so a lot of the words won't be any use for studying the Qur'an. I think I've just about mastered the alphabet though – recognising the letters, I mean, not writing it.'

'We're going to be starting with practising a bit of Arabic writing,' Tahira told her. 'So, knowing the letters should help you to keep up with the kids. This is primarily an after-school class for children just starting out in Arabic. Unlike some mosques, it's a mixed class and we encourage parents to bring their girls as well as their boys.'

'Do you get many?' Peter asked, looking round at the low tables and child-sized chairs set out around the room. Most of the tables and chairs that had been in use for the community café were now stacked against the wall. 'It looks as if you're expecting a full house.'

'We usually get thirty or forty kids and half a dozen or so adults.'

'Impressive!' Bernie commented. 'I bet there aren't many churches with Sunday School classes that big.'

'And we have a more advanced class on Sunday mornings, before the café opens,' Tahira went on. 'That has more adults in it, which is why we have it at the weekend.'

'And you run both classes yourself?'

'Imran and I lead them together, and one of the older teenagers helps us with the little ones in this class. Here she is now! Nadia! Come over here and meet some friends of mine.'

A tall, brown-skinned girl entered at a run, letting the glass entrance door swing shut behind her as she headed towards the group of friends. She smiled nervously, allowing them to see that she had a brace on her front teeth. Then she turned and looked back as if checking that the door had indeed closed.

'Is something wrong?' Dominic asked anxiously. 'You came in as if the hounds of hell were after you.'

'No, not really.' Nadia shook her head and gave a nervous laugh. 'It's just this boy from school. I went out with him a couple of times and now he keeps following me around and trying to call me. I'm sure it's nothing really. He just doesn't seem to be able to take "no" for an answer.'

'That's harassment,' Tahira declared. 'You should report him to the police for stalking.'

'No,' Nadia answered at once. 'It's nothing like that. He's just a bit sore because I told him it was all over – not that it was ever more than just two friends having a laugh together as far as I was concerned. But last Thursday he made it clear that he thought we were dating and that, by the third date, he was expecting a bit more from me than my scintillating conversation! Don't worry; I can deal with it.'

'Well, if you want one of us to tell him where to get off, just say the word,' Dominic told her.

'Don't worry, I will. But I'm sure everything's fine. Now, Tahira, you were going to introduce me to some people.'

'Yes.' Tahira swallowed the good advice that she had just prepared in her head to give to her young friend and gestured towards Bernie and Peter. 'These are Lucy's mother and step-father, Bernie Fazakerley and Peter Johns.'

'Fazakerley?' Nadia looked from Bernie to Dominic and then back to Tahira.

'That's right,' Bernie laughed. 'Dom's father is my first cousin. In other words, Dom's grandfather was my father's brother. Dom is my first cousin once removed. So, Dom and Lucy are second cousins.'

'Wow! And I thought it was only South Asians who had these big extended families!'

'Well, the Fazakerleys aren't such a big family now,' Bernie laughed. My dad was one of thirteen kids, but COVID got the last of them in 2020. Most of his brothers emigrated in the seventies when there was no work in Liverpool and we've lost contact with their families – unless your Mam still writes to them,' Bernie added, turning to Dominic.

'I think she probably does. She's a great one for family.'

'And now this is Yasmeen's mother, Marina,' Tahira continued her introductions, 'and her sister, Fatima.'

'Oh!' Nadia's face changed to a mixture of concern and embarrassment. 'I'm so sorry! I hope you don't think we were being disrespectful just then. Chattering away like that. You must be devastated.'

'Thank you.' Marina gave Nadia a weak smile. 'Yes. I don't think we've quite taken it in yet. It's hard to believe that she … Even though we've been to say goodbye to her in the mortuary, I still keep expecting to see her walking in at the door. I thought I'd spotted her in the street this afternoon, but of course it was someone else entirely.'

A sudden clang prompted them all to swing round to face the entrance. One of the glass doors had been flung open with such force that it banged back against a pile of chairs, stacked against the wall next to it. Standing in the doorway was a young man. His red hair was dishevelled as if it had not been combed for several days and his chin bristled with what might be designer stubble, but Bernie judged was more likely to be the outcome of forgetfulness over shaving. Seeing them all looking at him, he blushed red and gave a sheepish half-smile.

'I'm sorry. I didn't mean to make such a noise coming in. I'm just a bit on edge, that's all.' He turned and closed the door carefully before advancing towards the group. 'Tahira. I'm so sorry about Yasmeen. I only heard yesterday. At least, I'd heard the news reports, but it never occurred to me it was her. Or at least … I sort of thought it must be because she wasn't … She doesn't usually miss lectures – but I didn't *know*, not until they named her on the radio. Is there any news? Do the police know who did it?'

'No, not yet.' Tahira stepped forward and put her hand on his arm, gently steering him towards her aunt. 'This is Yasmeen's mother, Marina, and her sister, Fatima. They're making the arrangements to take Yasmeen back to Birmingham for her funeral. The coroner released her body this morning. Marina, this is Morgan. He's doing dentistry, like Yasmeen and he's one of the regulars at our Beginners Arabic class. He's reverting to Islam and he's been working very hard to learn more about it. Yasmeen was helping him'

'Hello.' Smiling tentatively, the young man held out his hand towards Marina, who took it and shook it warmly.

'So, you were one of Yasmeen's friends?'

'Yes, Mrs Osmani. And I want you to know what a wonderful person she was!' Morgan looked earnestly into Marina's eyes. 'I can't tell you how much she means – meant – how good she was to me. I never knew anyone so kind and brave and ….' His face creased up and it was obvious that he was struggling to hold back tears.

'Here! Let's all sit down.' Tahira took charge. 'Morgan, you sit here with Marina and Fatima. I'm sure they'd like to have a chat with you. You must have got to know Yasmeen very well, going to all the same lectures and so on. Dom and Ibrahim, come with me and get tea and biscuits for everyone. Nadia, could you set up the whiteboard for me? And then, when the kids start arriving, get them settled in their places. Imran texted to say he's got a bit of a domestic crisis and may be late. Lucy, show your mum and dad to the adults' table and make sure there's enough pencils and paper for everyone.'

Morgan collapsed into the chair next to Fatima, who smiled uncertainly towards him. Marina sat in silence for perhaps half a minute, watching his face closely. Then she put out her arm and took one of his hands in hers. 'Yasmeen was more than just a friend, wasn't she?'

Morgan nodded, not trusting himself to speak. He wiped away tears with the back of his other hand and gave a loud sniff. Fatima silently pushed the box of tissues, which Tahira had thoughtfully placed in the centre of their table, towards him. Slipping his hand out of Marina's, he took one and blew his nose.

'I'm sorry. I didn't mean to …. We *were* going to tell you … I mean, I was going to ask for your permission – yours and her father's – but we thought …. We knew you couldn't allow your daughter to marry a non-Muslim. So, we were waiting while I …. I wanted to know as much as I could about it, so you'd know my conversion was real and you wouldn't worry about letting Yasmeen …'

Marina got up and came round behind Morgan. She put her hand on his shoulder. 'Thank you, Morgan. I'm really glad that Yasmeen had someone special. I can see you loved her very much. And I'm sorry that she didn't feel able to introduce you to us.'

'It's all Dad's fault!' Fatima burst out. 'Him and Daadi. She's so old-fashioned and set in her ways! And he does whatever she tells him. She wants us both to marry one of our cousins from Pakistan! She doesn't care what *we* thi–'

'That's enough, Fatima,' her mother cut in firmly. 'Be more respectful towards your grandmother. Remember that she's old and she grew up in a different culture. And what you say isn't true. Don't forget, we allowed Yasmeen to go away to university, didn't we? We haven't made her marry anyone, have we? Your father always listens to what your grandmother has to say, but he – we – make our own decisions. There was never any question of either of you being forced into an arranged marriage.'

'Can I hold you to that?' Fatima flashed back. 'Can I have it in writing? And will you *promise* me you'll let me go to uni after I've done my A' levels?'

'Now you're just being silly! Of course we'll let you go to university, if that's what you want, when the time comes. And I can't believe you don't trust us enough to know that. I've got a degree myself, remember?'

'Fat lot of good it's done you! Why don't you use it, instead of staying at home, cooking and cleaning and waiting on Daadi all day – oh! And helping in the shop, day *and* night.'

'Your grandfather opened that shop. Your grandmother brought up your father and all of your aunties there. It's their home, as well as the family business.'

'It's Dad's life! He cares a lot more about that shop than he did about Yasmeen – or me! Or you, come to that.' Now that she had started airing her grievances, Fatima was unable to stop. 'Why isn't he here? He ought to be here, talking to the police and the pathologist and making the arrangements for taking her body home. Why have *you* got to do it all? It's all because of that shop!'

'He's dealing with the funeral arrangements down there. It's nothing to do with not caring about Yasmeen. It's just a matter of–'

'I'd better go,' Morgan interrupted, getting to his feet. 'I'm sorry. I shouldn't be here. I'm only making trouble for you both.'

'No, don't go,' Marina said quickly. 'Please, we'd like you to stay – really we would. You're the only person here who really knew Yasmeen – knew how she was feeling, knew if she was really happy or just …. She wasn't *un*happy, was she?'

'No, not at all,' Morgan assured her. 'She was enjoying the course – although we were both finding it tougher than A' levels – and we were both … We were very much in love,' he muttered, his face flushing red again.

'But you were afraid to tell anyone, weren't you?' Fatima cut in. 'You couldn't risk Tahira telling Mum in one of her weekly reports, because she'd tell Dad and then he'd make her drop her course and come home, because his mother wouldn't like the thought of Yasmeen dating.'

'Fatima …,' her mother said warningly.

'No, but it's true! He only let her go because Tahira was here to spy on her.'

'He was only wanting what was best for her,' Marina insisted, leaning close to her daughter and speaking in a low voice. 'You've got to understand. His family were all very poor back in Pakistan. They came here looking for a better life. Your grandfather worked himself into an early grave building up that shop that you hate so much, so that he could provide for your dad and your aunties. Zainab and Aleena were still at school when he died, and your dad had to take over as the breadwinner. He never had a proper childhood. *He* never had the chance to go to university. In the early days of our marriage, he was always just a couple of weeks away from losing the shop, what with the rent going up all the time. He's still only trying to do what's best for us. Look, I know it's hard for us to understand, but he's always got at the back of his mind the way he and his cousin Waseem used to scour the rubbish heap for things they might be able to use or sell – and seeing two of his sisters dying because the family couldn't afford the medicine they needed. He can't help it. It's just the way he is, and it's because he loves us so much, not because he doesn't care!'

Fatima sat in stunned silence. Her mother had never spoken to her like this before. After a short pause, Morgan cleared his throat.

'Yasmeen knew her dad would be worried about her going out with a non-Muslim, so we decided to wait until I'd learnt enough to be able to do all the prayers and stuff properly before we told anyone. We didn't like keeping it secret; we just thought there was no point upsetting people if we could avoid it.'

'That was very thoughtful of you.' Marina smiled at him through tears and reached out for the box of tissues. 'I know that Nadeem would have come round in the end – and his mother too. They aren't either of them as hide-bound as Fatima paints them. They just need everyone to take it slowly and let things sink in gradually. You must come down to Birmingham so Nadeem can meet you. He'll like you, I'm sure of it. But of course, you'll be coming for the funeral, won't you? We're not sure when it'll be yet, but soon, very soon, I hope.'

'Are you sure you want me there?'

'Yes, yes. Absolutely. Quite sure.'

Tahira, paused in the act of setting down mugs of tea and a plate of biscuits on the table in front of Marina and stared at her aunt. She could not remember ever having heard her speaking so decisively before. Normally, she seemed always to feel the need to defer to her husband over everything.

'We're about ready to start,' she told them. 'Feel free to join in or just watch or you can go up to my flat if you'd rather have some time in private.'

'No thanks, we'll stay.' Marina still sounded uncharacteristically certain of herself. She looked round at the room, which seemed suddenly full of children, their ages ranging from pre-school up to nine or ten. Most of them were sitting at the tables that Tahira had prepared for them, but there was a cluster of girls standing over by the door, their heads close together, chattering and giggling, and two of the younger boys were chasing each other round the room, dodging between the tables with frequent changes of direction.

'I'm sorry we're late.' The door opened and Imran came in, leading his three-year-old son, Adam, by one hand. He was followed by Khadija and their two older children Noah and Lily. 'Sit down everyone, and we'll get started.'

The buzz of conversation dropped to a murmur and soon ceased altogether as Imran strode confidently to the front of the room. On his way, he deposited Adam on a small chair among a group of boys of similar age sitting around a table set a little apart from the others, under Nadia's supervision.

'Today,' Imran announced, 'we are going to learn one of the most important phrases in Islam. I expect a lot of you already know it: it is recited at the start every surah of the holy Qur'an except one; you have probably heard your parents or your grandparents saying it at prayer times or before they begin something important. But you may not know how it's written down. Today, we're going to learn how to say the words correctly and how to write them in Arabic. Does anyone know the words I mean?'

Several eager hands went up across the room. Imran smiled as he looked round at them deciding which child to choose.

'Safina,' he said eventually, catching the eye of a girl of about ten, 'go ahead.'

'Bismillah ir-Rahman ir-Rahim,' Safina recited promptly. 'And it means—'

'Thank you, Safina,' Imran interrupted. 'That's very good. And now, can someone else tell me what that means? Yes, Abdullah?'

'In the name of Allah, the most Gracious, the Most Merciful,' called out a small boy with an earnest expression on his face.

'That's right,' Imram nodded. 'Or, we might say, "In the name of God", because "Allah" is just the Arabic word for God. And we could use other English words when we translate "ir-rahman". Some people say "the most beneficent" instead of "the most gracious". Or sometimes, we might say, "the all-gracious" and "the all-merciful". There are lots of ways of saying these words in English. None of them quite capture exactly what the Arabic means, which is one reason why we use Arabic when we pray, and why we read the Qur'an in Arabic as well as in English translations. Another reason is that Arabic is the language that Allah, Subhanahu Wa Ta'ala, chose to use when he sent the angel Jibril to reveal his holy Qur'an to his Messenger, peace be upon him.'

He paused and looked round the class to check that he had not lost their attention before continuing. 'But the important thing to remember about these words is that we are declaring that God is like the best, most wonderful friend that we could ever have. And when we say, "bismillah" – in the name of Allah – we are saying that we are dedicating to Him whatever it is that we are about to do. We are doing it as a sort of *thank you* for everything that Allah, Subhanahu Wa Ta'ala has done for us and we are promising to do it to the best of our abilities, insha'allah. OK, now let's have a go at saying it together. Are you ready?'

He repeated the phrase several times. The whole class joined in, gradually becoming more confident as they repeated the words. Bernie tried her best, but she found it hard to persuade her tongue to roll the r's in the way that Imran did. Glancing towards Peter, she saw that he was remaining silent, unwilling to risk making a fool of himself.

'Very good,' Imran said at last. 'Now, Tahira will show us how we write it.'

Tahira stepped forward and began writing slowly on the white

board: بِسْمِ اللَّـهِ الرَّحْمَـٰنِ الرَّحِيمِ

'Remember that each letter looks different depending on whether it's at the beginning, the middle or the end of a word,' she said, stepping back so that they could see the whole phrase on the board. 'Now let's go through it, a letter at a time, and then after that, you can all have a go at writing it. Don't forget, we write from the right to the left. So, here we have baa, and it's joined on to the next letter, which is siin, and that's joined to miim. And underneath the baa and the miim, we have these little marks that tell us that these sounds are joined together with an "i" sound: bismi. Then next we have a word that you should all recognise: Allah.'

Bernie watched with interest as Tahira took the class carefully through the whole phrase, letter-by-letter. It all seemed very complicated, with vowels being represented by insignificant marks below or above the consonants that preceded them, and letters changing how they looked and how they were pronounced depending on the context. She soon began to feel out of her depth, and yet even the youngest of the children seemed to be following what their teacher was saying. Well, perhaps not quite *all* – little Adam had dropped his pencil on the floor and was crawling about under the table trying to retrieve it.

Then it was the turn of the students to try writing the phrase for themselves Bernie picked up her pencil and began. She

carefully shaped the first letter, ب, and joined it to the second,

س, and finally the third, making a whole word, but without any vowels. Now, what were the symbols that she needed to add so that *bsm* became pronounceable? She looked up at the board and then carefully added two small strokes beneath the *b* and the *m*. And what was that tiny circle above the *s* for? Tahira seemed to have been saying that it signified the *absence* of a vowel between the *s* and the *m*! How weird was that?

'That's not bad at all,' Tahira said over Bernie's shoulder, as she added the final diacritical mark to her first Arabic word. 'But try to relax and let the letters flow a bit more. Remember, Arabic script is always cursive; the letters melt into each other. Now, carry on. The next letter, *alif*, is easy: it's just a vertical line, and it's not joined on to the letters on either side.'

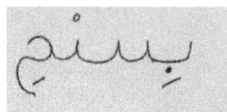

Bernie painstakingly copied the letters of the next word, casting surreptitious glances to either side to see how her husband and daughter were getting on. Peter seemed to be struggling with the unfamiliar script at least as much as she was, but Lucy had completed the phrase on the board and was intent on copying out more lines from a printed sheet that Tahira had left on their table.

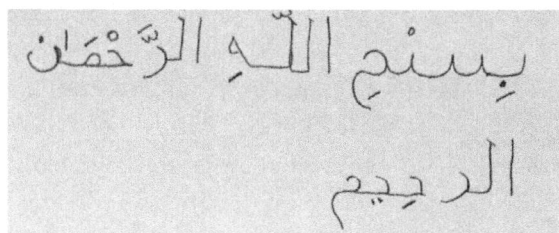

'What's that you've got there?' Bernie whispered.

'It's the rest of the first sura – that means chapter – of the Qur'an,' Lucy told her. 'Tahira always gives the adults and older kids some extra to do, so we don't get bored waiting for the little ones to catch up.'

'You mean the little ones and the OAPs,' Peter muttered. 'That little girl over there only looks about six and she's finished while I'm still trying to work out how to join an *l* to an *r*.'

Despite her struggles with the unfamiliar script, Bernie found that the time passed quickly. She had just begun an attempt at emulating Lucy by copying the lines from the printed sheet when Tahira, seeing that all but a few of the youngest children had managed passable copies of the verse, stood up and clapped her hands for attention. She recited the first sura of the Qur'an in its entirety, followed by an English translation, and then briefly expanded on its meaning.

'Now, for your homework this week,' she concluded, 'I want you all to try to memorise this sura.'

'All of it?' came a protesting voice from the back of the class.

'Yes, Yousef, all of it,' Tahira smiled back. 'You shouldn't find it too hard. It's the shortest sura in the Qur'an, and the most important. Many scholars say that the entire Qur'an is encompassed within it. So, it's worth making the effort to learn it. Have you been using the prayer app that I gave you? If you have then you'll have been hearing these verses five times a day for so long that you'll probably know them already.'

She looked round the room, waiting for a group of girls in a corner near the door to stop talking and giggling together. They had evidently found Yousef's intervention very funny.

'Now, Imran is going to close the class with a prayer – in English. We've got some Christian visitors with us today, so when he gets to the end and we all say *ameen*, they may say *amen*. Both words mean the same thing: we're just saying that we agree. OK? Let's all stand up, shall we? Put your pencils down on the table and stand up nice and straight.'

'Hang on! Could you wait a minute?' Morgan leapt to his feet, knocking the table at which he was sitting and sending pieces of paper fluttering to the floor. 'There's something I want to say.'

'Alright.' If Imran was surprised at this intervention, he didn't show it. 'Go ahead.'

The young man walked to the front of the room and turned to face the class. 'Ashadu an laa,' he began hesitantly, glancing down at a piece of paper that he was gripping in his hand. He cleared his throat and began again, blushing red and keeping his head bowed. 'Ashadu an laa ilaha illa llah.' He stumbled to a halt and stood studying the paper intently before continuing, 'wa ashadu … wa ashadu anna muhammadun rasulu llah.'

He stuffed the paper into his pocket and looked defiantly round the room. There was a moment's silence and then Mariam began clapping her hands. Ibrahim and Tahira joined in, followed by most of the children.

'What was that all about?' Peter asked in a low voice.

'It's the shahada,' Lucy whispered back. 'It means *I bear witness that there is no God but God, and Muhammad is God's Messenger.* He's declaring that he believes, and that means that he's now a Muslim.'

'Just like that?' Peter remembered all the meetings that he had had with their Parish Priest, Father Damien, when he was being instructed in the Catholic faith before his confirmation. And that had only been for a transition from a somewhat lukewarm Methodism to Rome.'

'Yup!' Lucy smiled. 'There's no baptism or confirmation or anything like that in Islam.'

'We believe that submission to God is the natural condition for people to be in,' Ibrahim explained. 'And everyone who truly submits to God is a Muslim. That's why we tend to talk about people *reverting* to Islam, rather than *converting*. They're getting back to the natural order of things, having drifted away for some reason.'

It sounds like the reverse of Original Sin,' Bernie observed. 'If I've got this right, you're saying that people are born good and they go bad. Or at least, that they're born in a right relationship with God and they go wrong?'

'Something like that,' Ibrahim agreed.

'Thank you, Morgan,' Imran stepped forward to take charge. 'It's great to hear you say that, and I know that Yasmeen would have been very pleased and proud to hear it too. Now we're going to have our prayers and of course we will be remembering Yasmeen and making dua for you and her family and everyone who knew her. Inna lillahi wa inna ilayhi raji'un: Indeed, we belong to God, and indeed to God we will return.'

Imran said a short prayer in English, finishing with Ameen, which was repeated by all present, including the non-Muslims who took the attitude of *when in Rome* …. This prompted a general movement from the children for whom this was the signal that the class was over. But Tahira held up her hand and called for everyone to go back to their seats.

'We have one more thing to do before you all go home,' she announced. 'Today is a special day for one of our friends. It's Lucy's birthday, and we mustn't let it pass without marking it in some way. Khadijah! Come and show us what you've made.'

All eyes followed Tahira's in the direction of the kitchen, from which Khadijah emerged carrying a large cake covered in candles. She walked forward slowly so that the air movement would not cause them to gutter and drip wax on the smooth iced surface. She placed it on the table in front of Lucy, who smiled up at her in surprise and delight.

'Are you all ready?' called out Tahira, waving her arm in the direction of the children like the conductor of an orchestra. 'Happy birthday to you!'

Everyone joined in, finishing with a round of applause as Lucy blew out all twenty-three candles in a single long breath.

'Speech! Speech!' called out a teenager from across the room.

'*I* wanted to blow out the candles!' piped up an aggrieved Adam, who came running up and started tugging at his mother's arm. 'Light them again, so that I can blow them out!'

'No, Adam,' Imran said firmly. 'It's not your birthday. You'll have candles to blow out when that comes round. But we're all going to have a piece of cake to eat. Go back and sit down and wait for us to bring you some.'

Adam looked from his father to his mother, screwing up his face in thought, as if pondering the likely outcome of further pleading. Then he walked slowly back to his seat, scuffing his feet along the floor as he went. Imran sighed. Why was it that other people's children always seemed so much better behaved than one's own?

Khadija cut up the cake and put slices of it on to paper plates, which Mariam and Dominic distributed around the class, while Tahira came round with a teapot and a jug of orange squash offering to top up everyone's mugs and glasses. When she came to the table where the smallest children were being supervised by Nadia, she noticed the student cancelling a sequence of phone calls in quick succession.

'Spam?' she asked.

'Well, sort of. It's that boy I was telling you about – Liam. He keeps calling and I keep not answering. I turned my phone off while the class was on and I've got about a million missed calls. It's dead annoying, especially when I'm busy.'

'Would you like me to talk to him?' suggested Tahira. 'I could point out that this is stalking and he's breaking the law.'

'No.' Nadia shook her head vigorously. 'I don't want to get him into trouble. I'm sure he doesn't mean anything. He's just upset because he thinks I'm rejecting him. And I'm not! I just don't want that sort of relationship. But he just doesn't get it.'

'Well, I'm going to walk you home this evening,' Imran said, looking up from cleaning Adam's hands before allowing him to touch his cake and joining in the conversation. 'Just in case he's waiting outside for you. I don't like the idea of him following you around.'

'There's no need, honestly!' Nadia protested. 'I can look after myself.'

'Better safe than sorry,' Imran insisted. 'Especially with this serial killer on the loose.'

'And you're a marked woman!' Tahira added, pointing to Nadia's pink and white hijab. 'All the victims so far have been female students walking home alone after dark. You definitely ought to have someone with you.'

'OK,' Nadia said reluctantly. 'But it's only just round the corner. I'm sure I'll be perfectly safe.'

'Rania was only going a few yards,' Tahira reminded her. 'The killer could be outside in the street right now, waiting for a victim to come out.'

'OK!' Nadia snapped back as her phone began to ring yet again. She glanced down at the screen and immediately cancelled the call. 'I've said I'll let Imran walk me home. Now can you just stop going on about it. You'll frighten the kids.'

'Why don't you block him?' Tahira persisted.

'I did – twice – but he got another phone.'

'Now that is seriously weird. I really think you ought to go to the police. That's not normal.'

'I'm dealing with it, OK?'

'OK. OK.' Tahira backed away with her hands raised. 'I get the message. I'll back off. But don't be afraid to tell one of us if you decide you could do with a bit of help after all.'

$$***$$

Half an hour later, the last of the children were leaving.

'Goodbye, see you next week!' Imran called out to two little girls and their mother who had come to collect them, holding open the glass doors for them to pass through. Then he turned round to look for Nadia. 'Are you ready? I'll walk you home now – or I could run you home in the car. That might be better.'

'Why don't you go home with Nadia, and I'll bring the kids in the car and pick you up from there?' suggested Khadija. 'We're nearly ready. I've just got to –'

There was a sudden crash followed by a loud wail. Everyone swung round to see what had happened. Adam, who had been helping Tahira to stack chairs at the side of the room, had taken it into his head to climb on one of the piles, which had toppled over, crashing to the floor. Adam lay on his back screaming, whether in pain or frustration was unclear.

'Oh Adam!' exclaimed Lily, in the superior tone that only an older sister can adopt.

Imran and Khadija both hurried to pick him up and assess his injuries, which proved to be more to his pride than his body. A bruise to his upper arm might well swell enough to be painful by the morning, but there were no broken limbs or damage to his head.

'Let's get you home, young man,' Khadija said as she picked him up. 'You're tired after working so hard at your Arabic lesson. It's time for your bath and then off to bed.' She looked round for her other children. 'Come along Noah! There's no more cake for you. Lucy's going to take the rest home with her.'

'I'll help you get the kids in the car and then ....' Imran's voice trailed off as he gazed round the room in confusion. 'Where's Nadia got to?'

Everyone looked back at him blankly. They had all been too concerned about Adam to notice what Nadia was doing.

'I think she must have slipped out,' Lucy said at last. 'She was just on her way through the door when the accident happened.'

'I'd better try and catch her up.' Imran was already halfway out of the door before he had finished speaking. 'She can't have got far.'

He turned to the left, knowing that this was the way that Nadia would have gone. Was that her up ahead? He wasn't sure. Should he call out to her to wait? Or would that just annoy her and make her go faster. He set off at a brisk pace, hoping to overtake her. Even if he failed in that, at least he would see if anything ... if anything happened to ... Was that a man following her?

He walked faster, but the woman that he thought must be Nadia seemed to speed up too. For a moment, a shaft of sunshine slanting between two houses picked out the bright pink of her headscarf as she turned left into a side street. Yes, that was Nadia alright! And the man behind her had turned left too. He *was* following her! Imran broke into a run, suddenly convinced that his young friend was in danger.

He rounded the corner and looked about for Nadia and her stalker. At first the street appeared deserted. Then he spotted movement in the gap between two houses, which formed the entrance to the lane that ran behind a long terrace of houses, giving access to their back yards. The evening sunlight did not reach into this narrow alley so it seemed dark, but, as his eyes adjusted, Imran could make out Nadia's slight form, pressed up against a tall brick wall, and a taller figure who seemed to be clutching at her hijab with one hand, while gripping her shoulder in the other.

'You shouldn't have dumped me,' Imran heard him say in a strange, almost despairing voice. 'Then I wouldn't have had to do this. Don't you see? It's all your fault! Why couldn't you of –'

Imran had heard enough. Hardly knowing what he was doing, he leapt forward and grabbed at Nadia's assailant from behind. Taken by surprise, the man let go of Nadia and Imran managed to pull him away. He dragged him, unresisting, out into the street and studied his face. He was surprised to see how young the attacker was – a boy, not a man. And he appeared frightened rather than aggressive. He certainly had no fight in him now!

'It's OK, Imran.' Nadia had followed them and was now standing at his side. 'It's only Liam.'

'Phone for the police,' Imran commanded. 'He assaulted you and I heard him threatening you.'

'No. He was just … you weren't really going to hurt me, were you Liam?'

'Course not!'

Imran was not convinced. He was not even convinced that the boy believed it himself or even that he wanted to be believed. Should he release his grip on Liam's arms and make the call himself? But it would make things much more difficult if he were to make a run for it. He stood considering the options. Nadia was clearly reluctant to get the police involved, but what if Liam were trying to pull off her hijab in order to strangle her with it, as it had appeared? He didn't look a very likely serial killer, but then what does a serial killer look like?

'Is everything OK?'

Imran jumped at the sound of a man's voice behind him. He looked round and saw Peter and Bernie approaching, followed by a small cluster of other people.

'We saw you rushing off after Nadia and we thought we'd just make sure she got home safely,' Bernie explained. 'It's not far out of our way, and it's a lovely evening for a walk. Who've you got here?'

'It's only Liam – the boy I was telling you about,' Nadia informed her. 'Everything's fine. Thanks for wanting to keep me safe, but you really needn't have bothered.'

Imran was not going to allow her to brush the incident off so lightly. 'When I got here, he'd got her pinned against the wall and he was trying to get her hijab off. And he was using some very threatening language. Help me to get him back to the Centre and someone call the police.'

$$* * *$$

'They're sending a car right away,' Peter reported a few minutes later, when they were all back in the big room in the Islamic Centre. He put his phone in his pocket and looked thoughtfully at Liam, who was slumped in a chair with Ibrahim and Dominic seated on either side of him poised to leap into action if their prisoner were to make any sudden movements. 'Turn out your pockets!' he ordered abruptly.

'What?' Liam raised his head and stared at Peter, who calmly pulled up a chair and sat down facing him.

'You heard me.' Peter's forty years in the police service showed in the tone of authority that his voice had taken on. 'Take everything out of your pockets and put it all down on that table there.'

'You're searching me? You've got no right!'

'I'm asking you to show me what you've got in your pockets. The police are bound to make you do it when they come, but I thought we might as well get it over with now. Don't worry, we're not going to steal any of your stuff. I'm just curious to know what you're carrying around with you, that's all.'

'I haven't got a knife or anything, if that's what you're worried about.'

'Good. But I'd still like to see for myself. Go on!'

Liam got up slowly and started to remove items from the pockets of his jeans: the inevitable mobile phone, a travel card, 72 pence in small change and … a white chess bishop.

Bernie, Ibrahim and Lucy all took in a sharp breath at the sight of this last item, while Dominic leapt to his feet and would have grabbed hold of Liam if Peter had not stepped between them and gently pushed him back into his seat, before turning round and picking up the bishop.

'What's this?' he asked quietly, moving almost imperceptibly closer to Liam and looking him steadily in the eye.

'It's a bishop,' Liam replied, looking down at the tiny wooden figure in Peter's hand. 'From a chess set.'

Out of the corner of his eye, Imran saw a sudden movement at the side of the room. He stepped forward to intercept Marina who, up until now, had been sitting with Fatima and Morgan, apparently taking no interest in the drama on the other side of the room, but was now striding across in Liam's direction with a murderous look in her eyes.

'Let me through to him!' she screamed as Imran put out his arms to bar her way. 'He did it, didn't he! He killed Yasmeen and he tried to kill Nadia! He's a monster! That's what he is, a monster!'

'I never!' Liam squealed in terror, looking round the room from one hostile face to another and finally resting on Nadia. 'You tell them, Nadia. I never hurt you. I never hurt anyone!'

'You still haven't answered my question,' Peter said calmly, while Nadia shook her head in silent confusion. 'I know it's a bishop from a chess set; what I want to know is why you're carrying it around with you and what you were planning to do with it. It's not much use on its own, is it? Where are the other pieces of the set?'

'We know where some of them are, don't we?' Marina shouted, trying to pull away from Imran and Tahira who were each gripping one of her arms and trying to guide her back to her seat. 'The police have got them, from where you left them when you killed all those other girls.'

'I never, I swear! I never killed anyone!' Liam looked desperately round at the accusing faces that surrounded him. 'I wasn't going to hurt you, Nadia! Not really. But I had to …. after the others went through with it, I couldn't …. Why couldn't you just …?'

'You can put the rest of your stuff back now.' Peter told him calmly. 'And then sit down.' He held up the chess piece. 'The police will want to have this. And they'll be getting a warrant to search your house. Presumably they'll find a chess set there that this came from. How many pieces will there be missing from it?'

'Only this one. I told you! I never killed those other girls! And I wasn't going to hurt Nadia, just take off that headscarf thing she wears and leave the bishop to show I'd done it. I had to do it! It was a group quest. I couldn't let the others down.'

'You mean it was all a game?' Morgan gasped, coming over and taking a seat next to Peter. He leaned forward until his face was almost touching Liam's. 'A stupid game? You were killing people for fun?'

'I *told* you – I never killed anyone!' Liam's face turned very white as the blood drained away from his cheeks. His blue eyes were wide in terror and sweat began to form on his forehead.

'But you knew these other people had – the others who were involved in this *group quest*, didn't you?' Peter pressed him remorselessly. 'You knew it wasn't just a computer game. Real people were being killed, and you didn't try to stop it.'

'I couldn't. I never knew who they were. I don't know who any of them are. And I never knew they *had* really killed anyone. Are you saying *they* killed that girl at JMU? And that one out at Greenbank?'

'You tell me,' Peter replied, clearly in the driving seat now. 'Let's start by you telling us about this *quest* of yours. What is a *group quest* exactly?'

207

'It's when you all – that's everyone in the group – have to complete a task. If anyone fails then the whole group fails.'

'Like, for example, you might each have to find a Sarcenian and get them to take off their helmet?' Peter suggested.

'You've played *Thoria*?' Liam stared at Peter in palpable amazement.

'No, but I've heard a lot about it. Ibrahim here has played it. He tells me that, if you just rip the helmets off them, the Sarcenians die, but if you can persuade them to take them off, they come over to your side. Is that right?'

'Yeah,' Liam nodded. 'But if you're on a group quest then they become part of the group and they have to do the task too.'

'So, killing them might make it easier to complete the quest than persuading them to come over to your side?'

'Yeah, but in the long run it's better to have more Thorians, so ....'

'So, it's not a clear-cut decision which is better?'

'No. That's what makes it such a great game.'

'But this wasn't just a game, was it?' Peter's voice remained calm but implacable. Morgan opened his mouth to add something and then changed his mind and shut it again. 'People died – real people.'

'That's what you keep saying, but I don't know anything about that.'

'Not even after your friends had killed three people?'

'*You're* saying that, but how do you know it was them? It could've been anyone. Lots of Muslims get attacked in the street. That's one reason I wanted Nadia to stop wearing that thing on her head.'

'But just anyone doesn't leave chess pieces next to their victims, do they?'

Liam raised his head and stared Peter in the face. It was clear to everyone present that he had not heard the news reports about this aspect of the sequence of murders.

'Ch-chess pieces?' he stammered weakly.

'That's right – like the tokens that Thorians leave when they kill a Sarcenian – lying on the ground next to each victim.'

'And that's what …? You mean they really did kill those girls?' Liam appeared to be genuinely taken aback – or was he just an extremely good actor?

'Well, *somebody* did – somebody who wanted people to know that it was them – somebody who left their token behind to prove it. So, tell me: who are those other people who are doing this *group quest*?'

'How would I know? I only know their gaming names. They could be anyone!'

Peter paused to consider his next move, but he was saved the trouble by the arrival of two uniformed police officers accompanied by Sandra.

'We asked DCI Latham to come with us,' PC Janet Morecambe explained, 'because it sounded like another of those attacks we've been seeing on Muslim students.'

'And it looks as if you were right.' Peter held up the bishop for Sandra to see. 'Liam here has been telling me about a game he's been playing with some online friends of his. It's been extremely interesting.'

'You've got to arrest him!' Morgan was on his feet and striding across the room. 'He killed Yasmeen and he was trying to kill Nadia!'

'Actually, it's a bit more complicated than that,' Peter told Sandra, while Ibrahim and Imran stepped in front of Morgan and held him back. He glared at them for a few seconds and then resumed his seat next to Marina. 'I think you need to take him in for questioning, but it's quite possible that there's been more than one killer responsible for these attacks.'

'He *did* assault Nadia,' Imran intervened. 'I was there. I saw it. He grabbed her and tried to pull off her hijab. Look at her face: you can see the marks where he pushed her up against a brick wall.'

Sandra looked towards Nadia, who appeared at first to be about to protest, but saw Imran looking at her and nodded instead. 'Yes. That's right.'

'And he's been stalking her for days,' Tahira added. 'She can show you the texts and voicemail messages.'

Sandra nodded towards Janet and her companion, who stepped forward and pulled Liam to his feet.

'Liam Casey, I'm arresting you on suspicion of Common Assault ....'

12. END GAME – OR STALEMATE?

'My son's not saying another word until his lawyer gets here.' Paul Casey paced the floor of the reception area, waving his arms in frustration as the desk sergeant spoke urgently on the phone to Sandra in the interview room where Liam was currently being questioned under the watchful gaze of the duty solicitor. Liam had initially declined legal representation, but in view of his youth, Sandra had insisted.

'I ought to be there with him,' Clarissa Casey added, leaning on the desk and taking hold of Sergeant Wharton's arm. 'He's only a boy. He needs his mother. You shouldn't be talking to him without me there.'

'Technically, he isn't a boy any longer,' the officer told her, putting down the phone and looking up. 'He's eighteen, which makes him an adult.'

'But he's still at school!' Mrs Casey protested. 'And he's done nothing wrong.'

'We have several reliable witnesses who have given statements confirming that he has been harassing one of his fellow-students for some time and that he assaulted her this evening, and we have reason to believe that he may be involved in the recent murders of three women.'

'Murder? What absolute poppycock!' Liam's father strode over to the desk and slammed his fist down on it. 'Liam wouldn't say boo to a goose! You're barking up the wrong tree there and I'm going to see that you pay for it. Just wait until my lawyer gets here. He'll soon sort you lot out. Arresting innocent boys and accusing them of murder. I want to speak to whoever's in charge here – now!'

'As I was about to tell you, DCI Latham has agreed to speak to you. If you'd just like to go with Constable O'Connor, he'll show you through to somewhere a bit more private.'

A tall, dark-haired man in police uniform emerged from the room behind her, smiling benevolently towards them. 'I'll come round and take you there now, sir – madam.'

He disappeared and then re-appeared through a door at the side of the room. 'If you'd just like to follow me?'

He led them to a small room with half a dozen plastic chairs ranged against the walls and a small table in the centre.

'If you'd like to sit down here, Inspector Latham will be with you shortly.' O'Connor turned to go, but Mr Casey called him back abruptly.

'Oh no you don't! You said we were going to get to speak to the officer in charge and I'm not letting you go until he comes.'

'That's right!' His wife agreed. 'We don't want to be stuck in here for hours while you lot bully our son into confessing to something he didn't do.'

'I can assure you that DCI Latham is on her way. Please, sit down. Would you like me to bring you some tea?'

'No, young man.' The menacing tone of Mr Casey's voice as he stepped forward to prevent the officer from leaving the room would have been more convincing if he had not been several inches shorter than PC O'Connor and considerably less muscular.

'We do not require tea. We want to speak to the officer in charge of this shambles and to take our son home where he belongs.'

'Mr and Mrs Casey?' Sandra Latham appeared in the doorway, smiling brightly. 'I gather you wanted to speak to me?'

'If you're responsible for arresting our son on a load of trumped-up charges.' Casey swiftly switched his vitriol from O'Connor to this new target.

'Yes,' his wife cut in. 'Where is he? And what have you done with him?'

'He's quite safe.' Sandra continued to smile amiably. 'He's currently writing a statement for us about an incident that he was involved in this evening. Once he's finished that, he'll be released on police bail, which means that we'll be wanting to speak to him again – probably tomorrow. You'll be able to take him home shortly. Would you like a cup of tea while you're waiting? Or coffee, if you'd prefer?'

'For the last time,' Casey exploded, 'we do not want tea! We want an explanation! Why did you arrest our son? What's all this nonsense about him being involved in a string of murders?'

'Your son assaulted a young woman in the street this evening,' Sandra told him patiently. 'She has given us a statement confirming that this was the culmination of a pattern of stalking behaviour and harassment that has been going on for some time. We also have a statement from an eye-witness who saw him pinning her against a wall and attempting to remove her headcovering. He has admitted to doing these things, for which he can expect to be charged in due course.'

'But what's all that got to do with murder?' demanded Mrs O'Connor.

'Exactly what I was going to ask,' her husband backed her up. 'I can see what's going on. You haven't been able to find who's responsible so you're fitting our Liam up for them just because his girlfriend's a – a – a whatcha-ma-call-it – Muslim, the same as those dead girls. Well, it won't wash! Liam's innocent and you won't prove otherwise.'

'In that case, he has nothing to fear,' Sandra told them calmly. 'And neither do you. However, we do have reason to believe that he may be able to provide us with information that could lead us to the person – or group of people – who killed three young women, which is why we will be needing to speak to him again. Now, are you quite sure that you wouldn't like something to drink while you wait for Liam to finish his statement?'

$$*** $$

'It's looking very much like some sort of conspiracy,' Sandra told Andy the next morning at their regular video-call case conference. 'Liam Casey's parents have confirmed that he was at home last weekend – shut up in his room most of the time, studying hard for his A' levels, according to them. My guess is that a good part of that time was spent on that fantasy computer game that Guy Daniels wrote – when he wasn't texting or ringing Nadia trying to get her to go out with him again.'

'He's one of Guy's beta-testers I assume?'

'Yes, he admitted that, but he insists he has no idea who the other testers are. I've given his phone to Ollie Ransom, who knows how to play this sort of game. He's having a go at impersonating Liam and infiltrating the group that way. I'll let you know if he gets anywhere with that.'

'Are you suggesting that Guy incited the others to murder Muslim women through his game?'

'It would fit. It's about the only thing that makes sense of that one killing in Oxford when all the other murders and the attempted murder were in Liverpool. None of *our* suspects could have got down to Oxford and back in time to kill … Zahra, was it? But your Alfie was on the spot. What if they're all in on it, and the point of the chess pieces is to identify which of them it was that committed each of the murders – for the benefit of the others in the group. Liam is the bishop, your Alfie is the queen, either Tyson Green or Guy himself is the knight, seeing as they were both at the crime scene when the first murder took place. That just leaves the rook.'

'I suppose that could be the taxi driver who dropped Yasmeen off at her hall of residence,' Andy suggested.

'Max Barker? Yes, I suppose it could. We ruled him out because he couldn't possibly have got down to Oxford in time, and we couldn't place him near the Henry Cotton Building when Rania was killed. If we hadn't been looking for a serial killer, he probably would have been near the top of our list for Yasmeen's murder. He's a lot older than the others, though – not really the right profile for a gamer.'

'Taxi drivers have a lot of down-time, don't they,' Andy pointed out. 'Maybe that's what he did when he was hanging around waiting for his next job.'

'I suppose so. Yes! And wasn't one of their gaming names something to do with …?' Sandra fumbled on her desk for the notes she had made following the interview with Guy Daniels. 'Yes! Here it is: *Roadkill*. Isn't that the sort of name someone who made their living by driving might choose?'

'Yes, it could be. So, what about the others?'

'Knight Crusader – Guy told us that was Tyson Green, and it fits with him leaving the white knight at the scene of the first murder – Necromancer, Aragorn, Roadkill and Silver Bullet.'

'Aragorn comes from *The Lord of the Rings*,' Andy mused. 'Do we know if any of our suspects are interested in that?'

'Probably they all are – it's all fantasy, after all.'

'The Necromancer could be Tolkien-related too.'

'Or Harry Potter,' Sandra put in. 'I read all the books with my kids. I'm sure there's stuff about necromancy in those.'

'What about Silver Bullet?' Andy wondered, 'Silver bullets are what you're supposed to use to kill vampires, aren't they?'

'No, that's a stake through the heart. I think silver bullets are for werewolves.'

'Sauron, the Necromancer in the Lord of the Rings lived in a fortress in Mordor,' Andy thought out loud. 'So maybe his chess piece would be the castle.'

'Which would mean he was Max Barker, whom we've just said might be Roadkill,' Sandra pointed out.

Andy sighed. 'I don't think we're going to get anywhere trying to match our suspects to their gaming names. After all, the names are going to be the way they think they are, not what they're really like.'

'Mmm,' Sandra nodded. 'Or what they'd *like* to think they are.'

'Actually, the main thing we ought to be worrying about is that there are five beta-testers and there've only been four murders or attempted murders,' Andy observed grimly.

'You mean there's going to be another?'

'Unless there's already been one and we've missed it.'

'We need to get Guy Daniels back in for questioning,' Sandra declared decisively. 'He's at the centre of all this. Even if he isn't controlling the whole thing, he's the one who brought these people together. And there must be some way of finding out who they all are in real life. I'll get our IT people on to it – see if they can locate the devices that the beta-testers are using to play the game.'

'And we'll see what else we can find out about Alfie Prescott. You asked whereabouts in Liverpool he lives: his address is Churchdown Road.'

'Churchdown Road?' Sandra repeated. 'That sounds familiar! Hang on a minute.'

Her face vanished from Andy's screen and was replaced by the Merseyside Police logo. He waited patiently for her to return to the call, mulling over in his mind what his next steps should be. Alfie Prescott certainly looked as if he must be Zahra Shahidi's killer, but did they have enough evidence to arrest and charge him?

'Yes! I was right.' Sandra was back and smiling with satisfaction. 'Tyson Green, AKA Knight Crusader, also lives in Churchdown Road. And did you say that Alfie was a second-year student?'

'Yes. That's right.'

'So's Tyson. They're the same age. They live in the same road. They may well have been to school together. They *must* know each other!'

'Alfie swore blind he didn't know who any of the others are.'

'So did Tyson. So did Guy. He claimed he didn't know anything about his beta-testers, but if they're random players of the game who just happened to volunteer to give him feedback in exchange for early access to new games, how come they all live so close together? Liam Casey, for example. His home is in Old Swan, which is only a mile or so from Dovecote, where Tyson and Alfie live. And Max Barker – his address is just another mile further on from there.'

'You said Liam's still at school?' asked Andy. 'Would that be the same school that Tyson and Alfie went to?'

'Difficult to be sure. Tyson and Alfie are well within the catchment area for the high school that Nadia and Liam go to, but it's a Catholic one, so if their families aren't Catholic, they mightn't have wanted them to go there or they mightn't have got in.'

'I see. Maybe it's worth checking. Alfie's college will be bound to have a record of which school he was at. I'll check it out. And maybe you could do the same for Tyson. If they were both at Liam's school, they could easily have met him there. They're only a couple of years apart. Maybe they were all three in the chess club, or something.'

✳✳✳

'Lucy!' Nicole Siddaway pushed her way through the throng in the Guild of Students building, lifting the tray that she was carrying high over the heads of those still waiting to be served. 'You know about police procedure and stuff, don't you?'

'A bit, why?'

'Can I ask you something? I've been asked to do something and I'm not sure about it.'

'Intriguing! Let's find somewhere to sit and you can tell me about it.' Lucy led the way to one of the few empty tables in the crowded room and set her own tray down on it. Nicole unloaded a cup of decaffeinated coffee and a plate containing a falafel wrap, propped the empty tray against the leg of the table and sat down opposite her.

'There's this guy I was going out with,' she told Lucy. 'I gave him the push ages ago, but this morning I got this call from his mum out of the blue. He's been arrested and she wants me to go to the police and tell them he couldn't have done it.'

'Be his alibi, you mean?'

'No, I don't think so. More a sort of character witness.'

'I don't see how that would work – especially if you haven't been seeing him for ages. Why did she pick on you?'

'No idea! Probably she couldn't think of anyone else. He's not exactly the sociable kind. He's more what you might call a loner. I met him at a computer gaming fair. That's what he does. He's got his own company. I think he's more at home in the fantasy worlds he creates than in real life.'

'What's he accused of?' Lucy asked, trying hard to conceal the excitement that she was feeling at Nicole's description of her ex-boyfriend.

'His mum was a bit incoherent, but I think she was saying that they're going to charge him for harassing a Muslim woman sometime last summer. But the big thing is that they're saying he's got something to do with those two students who were strangled. She said something about the police searching their house and confiscating his computer equipment and … Oh! Of course! She knows I'm in the Interfaith Society. That must be why she wants me to speak up for him. She said they've been accusing him of being racist and attacking Muslims.'

'And is he – racist, I mean?' Lucy asked bluntly.

'No, not really.'

'That doesn't exactly sound like a ringing endorsement.'

'What I mean is, he doesn't mean to be. It's just ….' Nicole sighed. 'He's very immature in many ways. His mum was worried about the age difference between us. She thought I was too young for him, but honestly, it often felt to me like it was the other way round – *he* was too young for *me*.' She gave a little laugh. 'Maybe that's what attracted me to him. Maybe it was my maternal instinct making me want to mother this little boy who never grew up!'

'Do you mean he was childish? He did silly things?' suggested Lucy

'No, I don't think *childish* is the right word – *child-like* is probably nearer the mark. He tended to see things in black-and-white – as if the real world was one of his games, where you knew for certain who were the good guys and who were the villains. I tried to show him that it was more complicated than that. I did think he was starting to get it, but then ….'

'Go on,' Lucy urged.'

Nicole sighed. 'That was what we split up about in the end – his attitude towards multiculturalism. He was always banging on about his Nan in Bolton who was the only white person left on her street because all her friends had moved out when it started filling up with Pakistanis. His mantra was, "She feels like a foreigner in her own country." He claimed she couldn't chat to her neighbours anymore because none of the women spoke English, and she was frightened to go out in case one of the men attacked her in the street. He couldn't seem to grasp the fact that it must be far more frightening for her neighbours being uprooted from their homes and brought over to a strange country.' She sighed again and brought her wrap up to her lips ready to take a bite. 'But he'd never have the nerve to approach a woman in the street, never mind grabbing hold of her and trying to pull off her hijab. Like I said, he was a loner.'

'Isn't that what they usually say about serial killers?' Lucy pointed out. 'After the event, killers always seem to be sad losers with no friends, and victims are always kind, popular and destined for future greatness.'

'If Guy wanted to kill someone, he'd make them into one of the characters in one of his games and do it virtually. He wouldn't need to do it in real life.'

'Is that his name – Guy?'

'Yes – why?'

'Guy Daniels?'

'Yes. Do you know him?'

'Not exactly.' Lucy took a bite from her pizza and sat silently chewing it while she thought out how to break the news to her friend. Then she swallowed and looked Nicole directly in the eye. 'I'm afraid he *did* approach a Muslim woman in the street – or rather in those gardens round the back of St George's Hall – and try to snatch her hijab. I was there. I saw it happen. And … the woman in question was Mariam Ali, which made it all the more dreadful, because …'

'Are you sure?' Nicole's eyes widened in horror and surprise.

'Completely,' Lucy affirmed. 'I made Mariam take a picture of him on her phone, so she could report it to the police, but she didn't want the hassle. But then, after Rania and Yasmeen were killed, we started to wonder …'

'And it was him? You're sure?'

'The police confirmed it. And Rania was killed on her way home from a talk he was giving at JMU. I'm sorry, Nicole, I really do think he must be involved in some way, even if he didn't actually kill anyone.'

'But it doesn't make sense!' Nicole shook her head in disbelief. 'He really isn't that sort of person, not when he was with me. He was … gentle. And he did always want to do the right thing. He just wasn't great at working out what that was!'

'He said Mariam ought to take off her hijab because she shouldn't let her family dictate what she had to wear,' Lucy told her. 'He wouldn't listen when she tried to tell him it was her choice.'

'That sounds like Guy,' Nicole admitted. 'Trying to make the facts fit his view of the world, instead of changing his views when the facts prove them wrong.'

'He was determined to believe that she'd been brainwashed by her upbringing,' Lucy went on. 'She told him she was engaged, thinking that might make him leave her alone, and he assumed that it was an arranged marriage. So, he told her that she didn't need to go through with it, now she was in Britain, because we had laws against that sort of thing. I don't think he ever got that she was born here and so were her parents. She had brown skin and was wearing a hijab, so she must be an immigrant. And she was a woman, so she must be being oppressed by her male relatives.'

'Yes,' Nicole nodded, 'I can believe all that, but *killing* someone! That doesn't sound like the Guy I knew at all.'

✳✳✳

'Thanks. Yes, he's in Interview Room two. You might as well take him straight there. We'll come down right away.' Sandra put down the phone and looked at her sergeant across her desk. 'OK Charlie, that was the duty sergeant at reception. Guy Daniel's lawyer has arrived. Let's get down there and see if we can persuade him to co-operate.'

When Charlotte opened the door of the interview room a few minutes later they found a rather subdued-looking Guy in a blue jogging suit slumped in his chair with his arms resting on the table in front of him and his head bowed. Alongside him was a man in his forties with dark brown hair and beard, both neatly trimmed. He got up when Sandra entered the room and extended his hand across the table in greeting.

'George Fawcett from Harrison Young. I'm here to represent Mr Daniels.'

Sandra recognised the name of one of the leading law firms in Birkenhead. Of course, Guy's father, being an estate agent, would know all the local solicitors. She shook his hand, noting as she did so his smart grey three-piece suit, spotless white shirt and dark red bow tie. There was even a silk handkerchief visible in the top pocket of his jacket. What a contrast with his slovenly client!

'My client has provided you with a statement about the incident last July,' he said smoothly. 'And the alleged offence clearly does not warrant his detention. So, I suggest that you release him immediately.'

'I'm sorry Mr Fawcett, but we have other things that we need to talk to Mr Daniels about.' Sandra turned her attention from the lawyer to his client. 'We believe that your computer game, Thoria, has been the inspiration behind three murders and an attempted murder. We need you to te–'

'No!' Guy leapt to his feet, grabbing hold of the table with both hands to steady himself. 'I never had anything to do with killing them girls! I never went anywhere near them!'

Fawcett put a perfectly manicured hand on Guy's arm and pulled him gently back into his seat. 'Sit down. I'll deal with this.'

Guy looked round, as if noticing the lawyer for the first time, hesitated for a moment and then subsided back into his chair. Fawcett eyed Sandra across the table. 'Do you have any evidence at all to connect my client with the deaths of those unfortunate women?'

Ignoring his intervention, Sandra continued to address Guy. 'Actually, I believe you,' she said quietly. 'I don't think you followed those vulnerable young women as they walked home alone. I don't think you seized them from behind, snatched off their hijabs and brutally strangled them. I don't think you left them lying like rubbish next to the bins.'

Guy's eyes opened wide as he listened in silence to this litany of assaults. Fawcett watched Sandra closely, ready to respond the moment she stopped talking.

'But I do believe that the people who did those things were instigated to do them by one of your computer games. Whether this was a deliberate intention on your part, I don't know, but–'

'No!' Guy shouted out. Then, more quietly, 'No, that's all wrong. Thoria's just a game. It's got nothing to do with killing real people.'

'But the Sarcenians, the wicked invaders, are all dark-skinned,' Charlotte pointed out, laying down a tablet computer on the table in front of Guy, who looked down and saw a scene from the game displayed on it. 'And the helmets that they wear – the ones that the Thorians have to try to take off – bear a striking resemblance to hijabs.'

Guy shrugged. 'So what?'

'And the Thorians – the heroes – are all fair-skinned and blond-haired,' Charlotte continued. 'It doesn't take much imagination to work out that this game is an allegory of the far-right picture of Britain today – the one in which white, Anglo-Saxons are being swamped by swarms of Muslim migrants.'

'Thor's a Norse god,' Guy retorted scornfully. 'Of course his people are white and fair-haired! And you've got to have the Sarcenians looking different, so you can tell who's who.'

'But the brainwashing helmets?' Sandra persisted. 'That's what you think of women who wear hijabs, isn't it? That they've been brainwashed by their families – or their religion? That's what you told Mariam Ali, back in July, wasn't it?'

'No! Well, sort of.' Guy looked round in confusion. 'I told you! I never meant her any harm. I just thought …. I wanted to help her.'

'By forcing her to take off an item of clothing that she'd chosen to wear?' Charlotte demanded scornfully. 'The women in some African tribes go round stripped to the waist. What would you think of them if they came over here and started pulling off women's shirts and bras, because they thought they needed liberating from our decency conventions?'

'I think we are straying into the realms of fantasy here,' Fawcett intervened. 'Rather than exchanging opinions on dress codes across the world, perhaps you could explain exactly what my client is being accused of?'

'Mr Daniels.' Sandra addressed Guy very clearly and calmly. 'Whether or not you intended players of your game to interpret it as a call to attack Muslim women, it is clear to us that a group of them have been inspired to do just that. We think that your group of beta-testers are playing a game of their own, in which they are each required to kill a Muslim woman by strangling her with her own hijab. And they leave a token, in the form of a chess piece, at the crime scene, so that the other players know that they've completed their task.'

'And what evidence do you have for that preposterous assertion?' demanded Fawcett.

'One of the beta-testers was caught in the act of attempting to remove a young girl's hijab yesterday evening,' Charlotte told him. 'He was carrying a white chess bishop, which he admits he was going to leave at the scene to let the others know that he'd done what he had to do.'

'The thing that we're most concerned about at the moment,' Sandra went on, 'is that you told us that there were five beta-testers, which makes me worried that there's still one of them who hasn't killed or attempted to kill yet. We need you to help us identify them all, so that we can prevent whoever it is from attacking another woman.'

'I told you – I only know their gaming names,' Guy insisted.

'And you told us that they are Knight Crusader, Necromancer, Aragorn, Roadkill and Silver Bullet,' Charlotte recapped. '*Knight Crusader* is Tyson Green and the lad who attacked the girl last night has told us that his gaming name is *Necromancer*, which leaves us wondering about *Aragorn*, *Roadkill* and *Silver Bullet*. Do you have any ideas?'

'No! I told you.'

'Tell us a bit more about how you selected your beta-testers,' Sandra resumed, hoping that this more oblique approached would jog Guy's memory. 'Did you put out a message of some sort asking for volunteers?'

'No. Actually they asked me if they could do it.'

'Each individually, or as a group?'

'Aragorn came up with the idea, and he said he'd got some friends who'd do it too.'

'Friends?' queried Charlotte. 'People he knew? In real life?'

'No, I don't think so. It was just a group of them who'd been playing some of my games together. You can do that if you want. You can ask to be allocated some other players to be, like, in your team. And then they're your friends and you can choose to play other games with them if you want to.'

'So, basically, they met online through playing your games?'

'Yeah.' Guy nodded. 'They'd all been playing them right from the start, from when I wrote my first game.'

'And you've really got no idea who any of them are?' Charlotte asked sceptically. 'How do you tell them about new games you want them to test for you? And how do they give you their feedback?'

'There's a fully encrypted messaging service included within the gaming platform. You can message anyone who's accepted a friend request, and as Admin, I can message any player and receive messages from anyone.'

'And can you see what the players are saying to each other?' Sandra jumped in. 'Do you monitor their conversations?'

'No. Like I said, it's a private messaging service, fully encrypted.'

'But you could send a message to a player and ask them to get in touch outside of the platform?' Sandra suggested.

'Yeah,' Guy nodded. 'But it'd be up to them whether they did.'

'OK,' Sandra said slowly. She felt in her pocket and took out a business card, which she placed on the table in front of Guy. 'OK. Now this is what I want you to do. I want you to send a message to each of your beta-testers asking them to ring this number. Don't tell them why; just say it's important that they do it as soon as possible. Have you got that?'

Guy nodded and reached for his phone, which Charlotte pushed across the table towards him, but his lawyer was quicker. He put his hand over the phone and gave Sandra a hard stare.

'What exactly are you asking my client to do? Is this some sort of entrapment operation?'

'Not at all.' Sandra's voice was calm and even, and she smiled benignly across the table at the lawyer. 'I'm merely asking him to help me to get to speak with a few of his acquaintances whom we have reason to believe may be able to help us with our enquiries.'

'It's OK,' Guy mumbled. 'I don't mind. I've got nothing to hide.'

The lawyer relinquished the phone and sat back in his seat. Guy immediately picked it up and began tapping away rapidly on the screen. Charlotte got up and came round to the other side of the table so that she could watch over his shoulder to check that he confined his activities to the messages that Sandra had instructed him to send. He was just on the point of sending a note to *Roadkill* when there was a knock and Oliver Ransome put his head round the door.

'Sorry to interrupt, but I've got something I think you'll want to know about.'

'Excuse me.' Sandra got up and left the room, closing the door firmly behind her. 'What is it, Ollie?'

'I've found out who *Silver Bullet* is. You see, the gaming platform has this private messaging facility, which—'

'Fully encrypted,' Sandra nodded with a grin. 'I've been hearing about it. But sorry, I interrupted. Go on.'

'I managed to get him chatting on it and he told me his real name and quite a bit about himself. He doesn't sound a very likely murderer, but …'

'Believe me, they come in all shapes and sizes. Well, go on! Put me out of my misery. What *is* his name and where does he live?'

'His name is Corey Macdonald and he's a primary school teacher from Formby – newly-qualified; he graduated from Liverpool Hope last summer.'

'He didn't happen to mention which secondary school he attended by any chance?'

'No. That topic didn't come up. Why?'

'It's just that three of our four suspects all went to the same high school, and if he's a new graduate, his time would've overlapped with two of them. But never mind. You've done well to identify him.'

'And I've managed to find out which school he's working at,' Ollie continued eagerly. 'I trawled through the websites of every primary school in Merseyside and I found a newsletter from last September, in which they were welcoming a Mr Macdonald as a new member of staff. I was wondering about going over there at chucking out time this afternoon and picking him up as he's leaving.'

'Good idea,' Sandra nodded. 'But try to keep it low-key. We don't want all the parents panicking and thinking that one of the teachers at their kids' school is being arrested. Don't forget, at the moment we've got no reason to assume that he's anything more than a potential witness who might be able to fill us in a bit on the other beta-testers.'

'I thought of that. There was a photo of all the staff on the website, so I'll be able to recognise him when he comes out and approach him discretely. All the other teachers are women, so he'll be easy enough to spot.'

'OK. Take Bryony with you. Then, if any of the parents notice you talking to him, they'll probably assume you're parents too, come to ask why little Johnny isn't doing as well at his reading as he should be.'

Sandra went back into the interview room, where Charlotte was now holding Guy's phone and staring down at the screen.

'Come and have a look at this message from *Roadkill*. You were right – it *is* Max Barker. It must be. It'd be too much of a coincidence for it to be another taxi driver.'

'If you want to meet, tell me where you'll be at 6 tonight and I'll pick you up in my cab,' Sandra read out. She turned to Guy. 'Does he know what you look like? Would he recognise you?'

'Maybe.' Guy shrugged. 'My picture's been in the Post a couple of times – local entrepreneur, Wirral man leads Games Design revolution, that sort of thing.'

'OK.' Sandra thought for a moment. 'In that case, we're going to need you to help us. Tell him you'll be … in William Brown Street, outside the museum at six this evening. You'll wait there for him to come. DC Simpson and I will be there too, but keeping out of the way until he identifies himself. Then we'll step in and have a word with him, and you'll be free to go. How does that sound?'

'Fine by me.'

'Just one moment,' Fawcett interjected. 'Do we have your assurance that my client is no longer under suspicion in respect of these appalling murders? And that he is helping you voluntarily and is free to leave at any time?'

Sandra looked him full in the face. 'I can confirm that we are not at present actively pursuing Mr Daniels over his involvement in three murders and one attempted murder. I have decided, for the time being, to accept his statement that he was unaware that his gaming platform was being used to plan a reign of terror against Muslim women. *However*, I cannot guarantee that evidence won't turn up that will cause us to re-evaluate that position, and if he *was* directly involved in this campaign, he may face a charge of conspiracy or incitement.'

'I tell you, I didn't know anything about it!' Guy burst out. 'I'll do what you say. I want to catch them bastards just as much as you do! I never put them up to it. It's just a game. Don't you see? It's supposed to be about that thing Abraham Lincoln said, "do I not destroy my enemies when I make them my friends?" The way to win the game is for the Thorians to persuade all the Sarcenians to take off their helmets and become Thorians themselves.'

'In other words,' Charlotte observed coldly, 'they have to deny their Sarcenian identity.'

'Let's not get into all that,' Sandra intervened hastily. 'The important thing is that we're now well on the way to finding out who all five beta-testers are. Mr Daniels, you can go home now, but I'd like DC Simpson to accompany you in case you get a response to your messages from any of the others. She'll also brief you on what to do this evening when you keep your appointment with *Roadkill*. Thank you for your co-operation.'

13. CHECK MATE

'I tested out the new oven by doing some baking,' Peter said, holding out a plastic carrier bag towards Marina. 'There are some chocolate chip shortcake biscuits for the journey and some Jamaican patties and a Bakewell tart for when you get home – I hope none of you has a nut allergy. I've only just thought of that.'

'You're alright,' Fatima assured him, taking hold of the bag. 'We don't have any allergies – my grandmother would never allow us to indulge in that sort of thing! She believes in children eating whatever's put on their plate and being grateful for it.'

'It's very kind of you,' her mother added quickly. 'There was really no need.'

'We've both been there,' Bernie put in. 'You'll be busy with the funeral, and you'll have lots of people coming round, I'm sure. And you may not feel like cooking – or eating – but you need to keep your strength up.'

'Besides, Peter loves cooking,' Lucy added.

'And I did want to test out that new oven.'

'You're all very kind.' Marina smiled round at the party of well-wishers who had come with them to the station to see them off. Yasmeen's body had been dispatched by road in the care of a Muslim funeral director the day before. Now Marina, Fatima and Tahira were returning to Birmingham where Yasmeen would be laid to rest in the same municipal cemetery in which her grandfather had been buried a quarter of a century before.

'And you're right about people coming round,' Fatima added. 'We've got my aunty Zainab flying in from Pakistan later today with a load of cousins that I've never even met before.'

'And your other aunty, Aleena,' Marina added. 'She's promised to come.'

'The one we never talk about?' Fatima asked in surprise. 'I thought she'd been cast out and told never to darken our door again.'

'Don't be silly, Fatima. She's your dad's youngest sister and Daadi's youngest daughter. There's never been any question of her not being welcome in our house. She's the one who decided to cut herself off from the family. But I rang her husband – while you were out shopping with Tahira yesterday – and he persuaded her to come to Yasmeen's funeral. He said he'd come too and maybe even their two girls – or they must both be grown up by now, I suppose. They're a bit older than Yasmeen.'

'You mean I'm actually going to get to meet our family apostate?' Fatima asked in mock astonishment. 'What if she corrupts my mind and gives me dangerous ideas?'

'I just told you,' Marina said testily, 'Nobody drove Aleena away. And we've tried over and over to get her to come for a visit. When her Angharad was born, I hoped that she and Yasmeen would be playmates. They were only a few weeks apart in age. But Aleena had married a Welsh farmer, and she was determined that she was going to be a Welsh farmer's wife and forget all about her own roots.'

'Not much chance of that in rural Wales!' Bernie joked, hoping to lighten the mood and remove the hostile atmosphere that was building between mother and daughter. 'They're sure to see her as a wicked English incomer!'

Apparently, she's learnt Welsh and that's all they speak at home,' Marina told her, returning her smile. 'She has great determination. I'm sure that she will have done it very well. But her great problem is that she doesn't understand the idea of compromise. It has always been all or nothing with her.'

'She'll probably have mellowed if she's been through the terrible teens with two daughters,' Peter joked. Then more seriously, 'I wouldn't be surprised if she's been itching for an opportunity to hold out an olive branch.'

'I suppose so,' Marina sounded doubtful. 'Anyway, I'm glad she's coming. Her mother's not in the best of health and I wouldn't have wanted her to die with one of her children still not speaking to her.'

'The train's ready.' Tahira had been watching the departure board. 'Platform 10. We'd better be going. Thanks for the lift and for all your help. I don't suppose you'll be able to come to the funeral, but we're going to live-stream it. I'll send you the link.'

$$\ast\ast\ast$$

'Mr Max Barker?'

Max blinked in the sunlight as he stared round at the two uniformed police officers that were standing at his front door.

'Yes,' he answered after a lengthy pause. 'What is it? Has somebody died?'

One of the officers held out a piece of paper towards him. 'This is a warrant to search this house and your taxi and any other vehicles that you own.'

'Why? What's this all about?' Max snatched the paper and stared down at it. Then he looked up again and noticed a police van parked a little way down the road. At a signal from the man who had handed him the warrant, more uniformed police seemed to pour out if it.

'If you wouldn't mind stepping to one side, sir, and let us get on with our job.'

'But, but … Look, what is this? What d'you think you're doing, getting me out of my bed when I've been up all night with airport runs? And what gives you the right to ransack my house?'

'The law, sir – and this warrant. And we need you to come with us and answer a few questions. So perhaps you could go in and get dressed? We've no objection to taking you in your pyjamas, but you may prefer to have something a bit more formal for talking to the chief inspector.'

'But why? You've no right! I haven't done anything! I'm completely innocent! You can't just go round arresting innocent people like this.'

'If you're innocent, you've got nothing to worry about, have you, sir? But DCI Latham wants to talk to you urgently, so if you wouldn't mind? PC O'Connor will accompany you while you get changed and then we'll take you back to the station for a little chat with her.'

$$* * *$$

'Tyson Green, I'm arresting you on suspicion of the murder of Rania Ansari. You do not have to say anything, but it may harm your defence if you do not mention when questioned something that you later rely on in court. Anything you do say may be given in evidence. Now get up out of that bed and get some clothes on.'

Tyson opened his eyes and stared up at the massive uniformed officer who was looming over his bed, staring down at him. He had been playing *Thoria* until the early hours and was not yet fully awake. He reached out his hand for his phone, but before he could grasp it the police officer's hand closed over his and took it from him.

'We'll be needing this.' Tyson watched as the man held out the phone to a brown-skinned officer who took it and enclosed it in a plastic evidence bag. 'And that laptop. Do you have any other devices? Computers? Tablets? Smartphones?'

'J-just an iPad.' Tyson continued to stare round in bewilderment. 'What's going on? Who are you? Why are you taking all my stuff?'

'I'm PC Thomas and this is PC Hanif. We need your devices so that we can find out what you've been up to online. Now where did you say that iPad was?'

'It's – hang on! Don't you need a warrant to do that?'

'Voila!' Tyson screwed up his eyes in an effort to focus on the piece of paper that suddenly appeared in front of him. 'This is a warrant authorising us to search these premises and to seize property to gather evidence in connection with our investigation,' the towering police officer told him. 'Your father is currently assisting our team downstairs. We just need to check over this room and then we'll be done. If you don't want to tell us where to find that iPad, it's up to you, but we may make a bit of mess looking for it.'

'It's in my bag – over there on the chair.'

'Thank you. That's much better. Bag it up, Hanif.'

PC Hanif opened the rucksack and peered inside. He soon found the iPad and sealed it into an evidence bag. 'I'll give your father receipts for all the items, and they'll be returned when we've finished with them.'

'But my phone!' Tyson threw off the duvet and swung his legs over the edge of the bed, pushing himself up into the sitting position. 'I've got to have my phone! You *can't* take it! I need it!' He made a lunge towards the desk where Hanif had put down the phone and laptop while he dealt with the iPad.

Thomas stepped in front of him, took hold of both his arms and expertly pulled them round to his back. 'Do you want me to put the handcuffs on you?' he breathed into Tyson's ear. 'Or are you going to come quietly? I'm sure your parents would prefer it if the neighbours don't get to see their son being marched out to the car with his hands cuffed. If you're sensible and co-operate, nobody need even know that this is an arrest. Do you understand?'

Tyson swallowed hard twice and then nodded. With enormous relief he felt the constable's grip on his wrists loosen.

'OK. Now get dressed and we'll get going. DCI Latham doesn't like to be kept waiting.'

$$***$$

'Mrs Casey, is Liam in?' Sandra Latham smiled amiably at Liam's mother as she opened the door to see who the early morning callers were. 'As I told you yesterday, we need to ask him a few more questions. And we also need to borrow any equipment that he has access to that can connect to the internet – computers, tablets, that sort of thing. PC Jones here will give you a receipt for anything that we take, and they'll be returned to you as soon as our IT experts have finished with them.'

Clarissa Casey looked momentarily as if she were about to argue, but thought better of it and made way for the two police officers to enter. Most likely she wanted to get Lee Jones's police uniform out of sight before the neighbours saw him and tongues started to wag.

'Come into the kitchen. We're just finishing breakfast. Liam's got school today. Couldn't this wait until later?'

'I'm afraid not. Three young women are dead, and we think that your Liam can give us the information that we need to prosecute the people responsible. Any delay could lead to more innocent victims being killed.'

On entering the kitchen, Sandra saw Paul Casey and his son sitting on stools on opposite sides of a peninsular breakfast bar. Liam, dressed in his school uniform, had an almost empty bowl of cereal in front of him, while his father was in the act of raising a cup of coffee to his lips. He put it back down on the table when he saw the visitors and treated them to a hostile stare.

'The inspector needs to speak to you again, Liam.' His mother told him.

'Have you brought my phone back?'

'No, I'm afraid not,' Sandra replied apologetically. She knew how important their smartphones were to teenagers. Liam would feel bereft until it was returned to him, but it might well contain the key to this strange conspiracy that had left three families scarred by grief. 'Our experts are still examining it. We can't return it until they've got all the data they need. And do you have a computer or a tablet at all? An iPad perhaps? Or a laptop for school?'

'He's got Paul's old desktop, that's all,' Clarissa answered for him. 'It's in his bedroom.'

'Could you show PC Jones the way? As I said, we'll need to take it away, but we'll return it as soon as we can.'

'What about his homework?' demanded Paul. 'He'll need it over the weekend, won't you Liam?'

'I'm sorry, Mr Casey, but I have to insist. There are computers in the library that he could use if he needs one.'

'What right have you coming in here taking our property?' Paul got down off his stool and came across to Sandra. He glared into her face from only a few inches away. 'Where's your warrant?'

'Here, sir.' Lee stepped forward and presented him with a piece of paper. 'This is a warrant to search these premises. Under Section 19 of the Police and Criminal Evidence Act, we have a right to seize property that is evidence in relation to an offence.'

'Don't worry,' Sandra added. 'Provided you all co-operate, we don't intend to search the whole house. We just need to have a look round Liam's room and to take away any devices that may contain information about his online activity over the past few months.'

'I wasn't going to hurt her!' Liam blurted out suddenly. All eyes turned on him as he pushed away his unfinished breakfast and held his head in his hands. 'I told you! It was just a game! Or that's what I thought it was. Did they really kill those other girls? Was it really Aragorn and Knight Crusader who did it?'

'You tell me,' Sandra answered. 'Did the game involve them leaving tokens at the scene to show they'd completed the quest? Were those tokens chess pieces?'

Tears began to fall from Liam's eyes as he slowly nodded. 'Yes,' he said in an almost inaudible whisper.

$$***$$

'Yes? Who is it?' The voice on the intercom outside the tall Victorian house in which Corey Macdonald occupied the second floor flat sounded a little surprised but neither hostile nor scared.

'DC Oliver Ransome. We spoke yesterday. Can you let us in?'

'OK. Just a minute.' There was a pause and then the sound of a buzzer. 'OK. Push the door now.'

Ollie pushed open the front door and entered the building, followed by Charlotte Simpson. They headed up the steep staircase, trying to tread softly so as not to attract the attention of the occupants of the other flats. Corey Macdonald was waiting for them on the second-floor landing.

'Will this take long?' he asked anxiously. 'I need to leave for school.'

'I'm sorry, Mr Macdonald, but I'm afraid you'd better ring them to say you won't be in today,' Charlotte told him. 'We need you to answer some more questions.'

'But I told DC Ransome yesterday, I don't know anything about those horrible murders. I just play computer games. I don't act them out in real life!'

'We'll talk about that later, back at the station. Let's all go inside and you can make that phone call while we have a quick look round.'

Charlotte stepped past him through the open door of the flat. The bewildered Macdonald followed her inside, still protesting.

'You've no right! I've done nothing. I'm completely innocent. What about the kids in my class?'

'The sooner you ring the school, the better chance they'll have of getting a supply teacher in for them,' Charlotte said implacably.

She looked round the room. 'We'll need to take that laptop. I'll bag it up and write out a receipt while you make that call.'

$$***$$

'Haven't you persecuted him enough?' growled Graham Daniels, as two uniformed officers headed up the stairs to Guy's attic room.

'He's told you everything he knows. He's got nothing to do with those attacks. Our lawyer will take your lot to the cleaners over this!'

'I'm sorry, sir,' PC Anwar apologised. 'DCI Latham has more questions for your son. Some new evidence has come to light.'

He stood barring the way while Sergeant Sara Farrow hurried on up the stairs. They heard the sound of voices above, then footsteps descending and soon Guy was on his way out in the company of the two officers.

'You don't have to go with them,' Graham called after his son. 'This is police harassment.'

'It's alright, Dad. I want to help get this cleared up.'

'Tell them you won't answer any questions without your solicitor. I'll ring them right now.'

'It's alright, Dad,' Guy repeated. 'I'm not under arrest. I'm just—'

'*Helping the police with their enquiries,*' his father cut in. 'That's what it always says on the news just before they announce that they're charging someone. Don't be so naïve. They're only saying that to put you off your guard. I'm getting on to George right away. He'll soon tell them what's what. And you're not to say a word until he gets there – d'you hear?'

'Yes, Dad.' Guy sounded submissive, but he did not meet his father's eye. Instead, he looked towards Sara who could have sworn he gave her a quick wink. He was beginning to enjoy his role in this operation.

✳✳✳

'It's all set up. The cameras in each interview room are linked to these monitors here, and everything's also being transmitted to

Oxford. This monitor shows the Oxford interview room, and this one is for you to communicate directly with DI Lepage down there. You need this headset so that you can talk to him without creating an echo. You control which interview you're listening in on here.'

Sandra surveyed the array of screens in front of her. Interview Room 1 was empty. It looked as if Tyson had not yet been processed following his arrival at the police station.

In Room 2 Liam was sitting between his mother and a man whom Sandra recognised as Arnold Beattie, a lawyer from a firm in West Derby. It looked as if Liam's parents had chosen to see that he had someone other than the duty solicitor to provide him with legal advice this time. They each had a cup of some brown coloured liquid in front of them – Sandra could not tell whether they had opted for tea or coffee – and there was a plate of biscuits in the centre of the table. A uniformed office stood in a corner of the room watching them discretely as they waited for the interview to start.

In Room 3 Max Barker and DC John Fisher faced each other across an identical table. Max had declined the offer of a solicitor, preferring to brazen things out with indignant protestations of innocence which, in his view, would be compromised if he were to admit his need of legal advice.

Finally, Interview Room 4 held a shocked-looking Corey Macdonald, shifting nervously in his seat and looking round at the uniformed officer standing next to the door. He too had been provided with refreshments, but his hand shook so much as he attempted to lift the cup to his lips that he gave up and set it back down on the table. He was waiting for the arrival of the duty solicitor.

Sandra picked up her phone. It was time for the final showdown to begin.

$$* * *$$

John Fisher in Interview Room 3 returned his phone to his pocket and fixed his eyes on the suspect. Although he was a police officer of more than thirty years standing, he had not been in CID for long and this was the first time that he was leading on an interview with a murder suspect. He was determined not to blow his chances of producing a breakthrough.

'Mr Barker, please could you recap exactly what you did when you arrived at Greenbank Student Village with Yasmeen Osmani?'

'I pulled up outside. She paid the fare, and got out. I offered to walk her to her room, seeing as it was dark, but she said no, she'd be OK on her own. I watched until she was inside the gate, just in case, and then I drove back into town.'

'Are you sure that you didn't follow her inside the student village?'

'Quite sure. I watched her go inside, then I drove back to Lime Street.'

'How do you explain the fact that our forensics team found the print of one of the shoes that you told us you were wearing that night in the mud at the edge of the lawn close to where Yasmeen's body was found?'

'Someone else must wear same kind of shoes as me.'

'In the same size?'

'Lots of people take size ten.'

'With the same pattern of wear on the bottom of them?'

'Why not?' Max shrugged nonchalantly. But John detected a slight quiver of nervousness in his voice.

'Our forensics team have taken samples of soil from the soles of your shoes. They're going to test them against the soil in the

Student Village. If they match it will prove that you went inside the grounds. Do you still say that you stayed outside?'

'Yes. I didn't go in and you can't prove I did.'

'We'll just have to wait and see, won't we?'

They eyed each other across the table. John, remembered Sandra's advice to him: "Silence is your friend in an interview. Most people are frightened of silence and won't be able to resist saying something to fill the gap." So, he resisted the temptation to argue or to repeat his accusation and sat in silence with his eyes firmly fixed on the taxi-driver's face.

Max dropped his gaze and began picking at a hangnail on his thumb, but he said nothing.

'Do you recognise this?' John deposited a plastic bag on the table and pushed it towards Max, who stared down at it for a few seconds before putting out a hand and smoothing down the plastic to see inside better.

He looked up at John, his confidence apparently restored. 'It's a castle from a chess set.'

'We found an identical castle in a chess set in your house.'

'That old thing?' Was it his imagination or was that a forced brightness in Max's voice, designed to convince him that the chess piece meant nothing to him? 'I'd forgotten I still had it. I haven't played with it for ages. Some of the pieces are missing.'

'Yes, I know – including one of the castles.'

'Really?'

'You'll be pleased to know that the team who searched your house found the pawn that you dropped down the back of the sofa and the bishop that rolled under the wardrobe in your bedroom. We didn't manage to find the pair to this, though.' John pointed down at the castle in the evidence bag.

'That's a pity. I used to enjoy a game of chess.'

Max seemed to have got his confidence back. John felt that he was playing with him. It was clever of him to have "lost" the other pieces from the chess set to disguise the missing rook.

'This chess piece was found on the ground next to Yasmeen Osmani's body. We believe that the killer left it there as a sign to his confederates that he was responsible for her death. You were with her only a few minutes before she was killed. You left a footprint only a few feet away from where she was found, and one of your chess pieces was lying next to the body. Why don't you save us all a lot of wasted time and admit that it was you who killed her?'

'Because it wasn't me. I told you! I watched her go inside the student village and then I drove back to Lime Street. I wanted to get back in time to meet the next London train.'

'And did you?'

'Nah! By the time I got there they'd all gone. But there was a Birmingham train came in and I picked up a lady from that. Took her to Allerton.'

'Can you give me the address?'

'It was … Canterbury Park. I don't remember the number.'

'Did she give you her name?'

'No, but she paid by card. I'll have the receipt.'

'Thanks. We're going to need that. Where will we find it?'

'On my phone. Everything's electronic these days – no paper bills.'

'OK. We'll check that out. Now, tell me about this game you've been playing – Thoria, is it called …?'

✳✳✳

'We've got some DNA results back from the lab,' Charlotte told Tyson. 'There are traces of your DNA on the hijab that Rania Ansari was wearing the day she died – the hijab with which she was strangled. How do you account for that?'

'No comment.'

'We have CCTV showing you leaving the Henry Cotton Building shortly after Rania left that evening, and a witness who remembers seeing you coming out of Fontenoy street into Dale Street between twenty minutes and half an hour later. It takes about two minutes to do that walk. What took you so long?'

'No comment.'

Charlotte decided to try a different approach. 'Your mum tells me you were a whizz at chess when you were at school. She showed me a trophy that you won. She's very proud of you. She says you're the first one in the family to go to university, and she's really looking forward to seeing you graduate.'

Tyson grunted and looked uncomfortable.

'She tried to get out the chess set you used to play with,' Charlotte went on, 'but she couldn't find it. Neither could our officers when they searched the house. Do you know where it is?'

'No.' Tyson mumbled.

'She did tell us that this knight looks just like the ones in that set.' Charlotte set down the white knight that Poppy had found next to Rania's body on the table in front of Tyson. 'Do you know where we found this?'

Tyson shrugged.

'Have a guess.'

'Dunno.'

'Are you sure?'

Silence.

'Then let me tell you.' Charlotte put the evidence bag back in her briefcase and looked intently towards Tyson. 'It was lying next to Rania Ansari's body when her friend found her the next morning.'

'So?'

'We think that her killer left it there to let the others in his little group know that he'd done it. Your gaming name is *Knight Crusader*, isn't it? It would be natural for you to choose to leave a knight as your calling card.'

'No comment.'

'Your friend Alfie was in the chess club at school too, wasn't he?'

Another shrug from Tyson.

'And now you're both beta-testers for Guy Daniels' computer games. What's Alfie's gaming name? Aragorn? Necromancer? Silver bullet?'

'Why don't you ask him?'

'We will – or rather the police in Oxford will. They're talking to him right now. And we've got all the other Beta-testers in interview rooms here: Corey, Max, Liam. Liam has been *very* helpful, but he claims you weren't supposed to actually kill your victims – just to get their hijabs off their heads. *Is* that what your little game was all about? Was that what you planned to do, but then Rania fought back? Did you get carried away and strangle her by mistake?'

'I told you – it wasn't me.'

$$* * *$$

'There was a chess set out on the table in your living room when we searched your flat, Mr Macdonald,' Oliver said, leaning across the table in Interview Room 4. 'What were you planning to do with that?'

'Play chess – what else?'

'Who with?'

'With whom,' Corey corrected him automatically. 'I teach Year 6. A few of the brightest kids could do with something beyond the curriculum to stretch them. I'm going to introduce them to chess.'

'I see.' Oliver allowed the words to hang there for a few moments before continuing. 'Were you aware that there have been three murders in the last three weeks in which a chess piece was left beside the victim's body?'

'I'd read about it, yes.'

'Would it interest you to learn that a fourth murder was only narrowly averted two days ago, and that the perpetrator was carrying a chess piece when he was caught?'

'If you've caught your killer, why have you arrested me?'

'Because it wasn't a simple case of serial killing, was it, Mr Macdonald? It was a conspiracy.'

'I'm sorry; I don't know what you mean.' Corey Macdonald looked round in bewilderment, first at Ransome and then at the solicitor sitting beside him, whom he appeared to find almost as intimidating as the police.

'I mean that you and the rest of your little group of gamers decided to play *Thoria* for real, with Muslim women in hijabs as the Sarcenians.'

'That's a load of ….' Corey turned very white and he put his hand to his mouth in horror.

'A load of what?' asked Oliver, pressing his advantage.

'Nonsense,' Corey whimpered. 'It has to be!' he added a little louder, as if trying to convince himself that what he was saying was true. 'They couldn't have … They can't have been serious! Are you telling me that they really did …?'

'Really did what, Mr Macdonald?'

Corey took a long draught of water from the plastic cup on the table in front of him. Oliver waited patiently, confident that his suspect was about to come clean. Gradually the colour returned to Corey's cheeks and his breathing slowed and became less erratic. He put down the cup and looked up at Oliver.

'Please believe me when I tell you that I thought it was all just talk. I never in a million years thought they meant it for real.'

'OK.' Oliver nodded encouragingly.

'It was *Roadkill* started it. He made it sound like a joke. He said he felt as if he was living in Thoria sometimes, the way there were so many immigrants around these days. And you could never tell which ones might be terrorists. He knew someone who was killed in the Manchester Arena bombing. He said it made him sick whenever he saw Muslims walking around as if they owned the place.'

'I see,' Oliver murmured encouragingly. 'And how did the others react – *Knight Crusader* and *Aragorn* and … what was the other one?'

'*Necromancer*. He never seemed very sure about it. I think he was probably as disgusted as I was at some of the things that *Roadkill* and *Knight Crusader* were saying about Muslims, but he didn't like to say so.'

'So, it was *Roadkill* and *Knight Crusader* who were making the running in this conspiracy?'

'I suppose so,' Corey agreed reluctantly. 'Except that I never thought of it as a conspiracy. I thought they were just, well, fantasising. We were all playing a fantasy game, after all. Anyway, I told them they could count me out of anything like that.'

'Like what?' Corey did not answer, so Oliver repeated, 'like what? I mean, if you thought it was all fantasy, why did you need to opt out?'

'I just didn't like the way they were talking – as if "Muslim" and "terrorist" were synonyms. And ….' There was a long pause. 'And I did just wonder if they might … well … do something on social media or something like that. Target women whose profile pictures had hijabs in them, for example. It never occurred to me that it could go beyond trolling or something like that.'

'And after you told them you weren't playing ball with their scheme?'

'They stopped including me in their messaging. You can check all that, if you like. You've got my phone. It's all there.'

'And when exactly was this? When did you stop being part of the group?'

'Weeks ago – before Easter. As I said, you can check on my phone.'

$$***$$

'Do you believe him?'

Everyone was taking a breather from the intensity of the interviews, and comparing notes in a joint case conference between the Liverpool and Oxford investigating teams. Andy was keen to know whether Corey could be treated as a reliable witness rather than a suspect.

'I think I do,' Oliver answered cautiously. 'I've seen the messages on Liam's phone, and *Silver Bullet* does drop out some time back in March.'

'And what about Liam?' Andy asked. 'Do we buy his story that he thought they were only supposed to use persuasion to get the women to take off their hijabs?'

'It doesn't seem very plausible after three murders,' Alice commented contemptuously. 'He *must* have known what was going on by then.'

'I'm not so sure,' Sandra disagreed. 'It's amazing how people manage to deceive themselves when they're under pressure from their peers. He's seen how Corey was excluded when he dared to question what they were doing, remember. And by the time the reports started coming out about the chess pieces, which was the first he could have been sure that the murders really were part of their game, he was already in it up to his neck.'

'But he *must* have known then,' Alice argued. 'It would have been far too much of a coincidence to have someone else going round killing Muslims and leaving chess pieces lying around.'

'O – ka-a-ay,' Sandra said slowly. 'What if he did realise by then what his friends were doing? That doesn't prove that he was planning to kill anyone himself. He could be telling the truth when he says that he was only going to pull off Nadia's hijab and take a photo of her with his chess piece to show to the others.'

'It's still pretty damning if he knew they were responsible for the killings and didn't tell anyone,' Andy observed.

'I agree.' Sandra tried to force out of her mind the memory that kept intruding on her consciousness, of her daughter, Philippa, being questioned by a store detective after stealing clothes that were not even in her size, egged on by so-called *friends* from her school. Liam was so young. And teenagers were so vulnerable to peer-pressure. What had really been going on in Liam's mind on Wednesday evening? Had he really not made the connection between the so-called *game* that he was playing with his friends and the deaths of three women not much older than himself? 'But it *is* a bit different knowing who committed a crime and doing nothing about getting them arrested and committing the crime yourself.'

'If he'd come to the police after Tyson Green killed Rania, it could've saved two lives.' Andy was not prepared to be so understanding

'What do you think, Bryony?' Sandra asked. 'You've been talking to him today. Is he lying when he says he didn't know the others were actually killing people?'

'That's certainly what he *wants* to believe, but I don't know. It hardly seems possible, does it? And was he so scared of the others that he went through with attacking his ex-girlfriend just because it was part of this weird game they were playing? I just don't get it at all – and neither does his mum! I can see it on her face. She just can't believe he could be so stupid as to go along with it all. She's scared – dead scared – that he's going to be going down for life.'

'OK. Let's leave Liam for the moment. I think I'd like to have a chat with him myself later.' Sandra turned her attention back to Andy's face on the screen in front of her. 'How did your interview with Alfie go? I was watching one of the other rooms, so I didn't see it.'

'Quite well, I think,' Andy answered cautiously. 'At first, he stuck to his story that he just went to the pub and stayed until closing time, but he got rattled when we showed him the CCTV footage that proved he went past the door and then came back a few minutes later. He claims he was going to a different place a bit further on and then he realised how late it was and turned back to make sure he didn't miss last orders. He's conferring with his solicitor now. I think it's possible she'll be advising him to turn Queen's Evidence.'

'You mean King's Evidence, sir!' the musical Welsh accent of DS Iestyn Williams cut across Andy's words. 'And I agree with you. Alfie's almost ready to throw in the towel and admit everything, and I think his lawyer will be telling him that's his best option.'

'Thank you, sergeant,' Andy said curtly. 'And thank you for the reminder that, with the coronation tomorrow and another bank holiday on Monday, we could really do with getting some results from these interviews today. Did he say anything about the other suspects? Did he admit that they were playing some sort of game together?'

'He confirmed that he and Tyson knew each other and that their gaming names are *Aragorn* and *Knight Crusader*. He claims not to know who the other beta-testers are in real life, but I got a feeling that he did recognise Liam's name when I put it to him that they'd been to the same school.'

'He got really rattled when we showed him some texts from his phone,' Alice put in. 'He and Tyson weren't just communicating through the game; they were using ordinary text messages and WhatsApp. Back in March Tyson asked Rania Ansari out, but she turned him down, and he moaned about it to his friend Alfie!'

'He asked her out, and she turned him down?' murmured Sandra. 'And last summer, Guy asked Mariam Ali out, and she turned *him* down. And—'

'And Nadia Karim was going out with Liam and then she dumped him!' Charlotte cut in excitedly. 'You've got it, Sand! They've all been rejected by Muslim girls and they don't like it.'

'Alfie and Zahra were both reading English,' Alice added. 'So they probably knew each other. I wonder if he asked her out and was rejected too. We could ask her friends.'

'There certainly does appear to be something of a pattern emerging,' Andy agreed. 'But I'm not sure that it helps us much. We're still relying too much on circumstantial evidence: missing pieces from chess sets, unaccounted-for periods of time, coded messages that defence lawyers would have no difficulty putting a perfectly innocent spin on.'

'There's the DNA on Rania's hijab,' Charlotte pointed out, 'and I've just heard that they've found a partial fingerprint on the chess piece that was lying next to her, which is a match to Tyson's forefinger. They're a bit more than just circumstantial.'

'And what about the footprint in the Student Village?' added Fisher. 'That's hard evidence, isn't it? And Max Barker doesn't have any explanation for it being there. He's still just insisting over and over again that he didn't follow Yasmeen inside the Student Village.'

'Mmm,' mused Sandra. 'But Max and Tyson are certainly looking like the hardest nuts to crack in all this. They've both imbibed the dogma that the safest thing to say when you're accused of a crime is nothing at all. I think we're more likely to get somewhere if we concentrate on Liam and Alfie – particularly Liam. He's got the most to gain from co-operating with us, because he hasn't actually killed anyone. The others are bound to know that they're facing a life sentence even if they plead guilty.'

'But there are life sentences and life sentences,' Andy pointed out. 'I'm hoping that Alfie's lawyer is impressing on him the need to convince the judge that he should be given a low tariff.' He looked at his watch. 'I think they've had long enough to discuss that. I'd like to get back in there and see if I can persuade him to talk.'

'Sounds good to me,' agreed Sandra. 'And I'm going to try my hand at cajoling Liam. Come with me Bryony; you seem to be building some sort of rapport. Charlotte and Ollie, go back to the student village and see if you can find anyone who was around the night Yasmeen was killed and saw Max following her in. Maybe someone looking out of their window? Or someone passing by outside who saw the empty car? And John! That was good work with Barker. Now can you check out his story about his next fare? See if the other drivers at the Lime Street taxi rank remember what time he got down there; and see if you can track down the lady he dropped off in Allerton. We may be able to prove that he couldn't have set off right away like he said he did.'

∗∗∗

'Our Liam wants to tell you everything – don't you, Liam? He's really sorry – aren't you, Liam? He just got caught up in something that he couldn't get out of! That's right isn't it, Liam?'

Mrs Casey gave Sandra no time to introduce herself or to announce that she was resuming the interview with her son. The moment the detectives entered the room, she leaped to her feet and began her impassioned plea on Liam's behalf. Sandra waved her back down into her chair and took a seat on the other side of the table. Bryony did the same.

'Sit down, Mrs Casey. All in good time.' She looked round at Liam and the lawyer. 'I'm going to re-start the interview now that we've all had a break. Is that OK with you all? Nobody needs a trip to the loo before we start? Right! Good. Now, Liam, let me just remind you that you are being interviewed under caution. Do you understand what that means?'

Liam nodded.

'And this interview is being recorded.' Sandra glanced up at the video camera on the wall. 'And the recording can be used in evidence. Do you understand what that means?'

Liam nodded again. Then, in response to a nudge from his mother, he mumbled, 'It means you might play it to the judge – in court.'

'Something like that.' Sandra nodded. 'Good. So, now, what was it you wanted to tell me?'

'I – I *do* know who the others are – you know, the other beta-testers, some of them anyway.'

'Go on. What are their names?'

'T-Tyson Green, Alfie Prescott, M-Max … I don't know what his last name is.'

'Why didn't you tell us this before?' Bryony asked. 'It would have saved us a lot of time.'

'I didn't want to get them into trouble. You don't grass on your mates, do you?'

'And they were your mates?' Sandra stepped in, speaking more gently than Bryony had. 'Did you only know them through playing computer games together, or had you met them in real life?'

'Tyson and Alfie were at my school. We were all in the chess club. Tyson was captain when we won a cup for the school.'

'They were two years older,' Mrs Casey interjected. 'They led our Liam astray. Getting him into all that online gaming stuff. It was interfering with his schoolwork – keeping him up all night playing on his phone.'

'Thank you, Mrs Casey, but Liam has to tell his own story.' Sandra smiled at the young man – just a boy really – with a look that conveyed the thought *Parents! They can be so-o-o embarrassing!* 'And what about Max? How did you get to know him?'

'I *don't* know him. It was Alfie got him into beta-testing. He drives a taxi. Alfie's at Oxford University. He's dead clever like that. He caught Max's cab at Lime Street when he came back after his first term and they got talking about computer games and Alfie told him Guy was looking for more beta-testers. I've never met Max. I don't even know what he looks like. All I know is his gaming name – *Roadkill*. I don't like it – it sounds sort of … creepy.'

'And the others? What are their gaming names?'

'Alfie's is *Aragorn* – out of The Lord of the Rings. That's what gave me the idea of *Necromancer*. Tyson said I ought to be Frodo or Pippin, because I was only small, like a hobbit. But I'm not that small, am I?'

Liam's voice rose in indignation as he recalled his friend's taunt. Sandra wondered if there had been a degree of bullying involved in his relationship with the older boys. That could explain his reluctance to *grass on them* as he put it, even when he began to suspect them of something as serious as murder.

'And the others?' she pressed him gently. 'Tyson? And wasn't there another one?'

'Tyson's name was *Knight Crusader*.'

'And there was one more, wasn't there?'

'There was a guy called *Silver Bullet*, but I don't know his real name. He never wanted to talk about anything outside the game.'

'So, he wouldn't have been involved in this little conspiracy that the rest of you hatched?' Bryony asked. 'The one where you each had to get a Muslim woman alone and pull off her hijab and strangle her with it?'

'It wasn't a conspiracy!' Liam's face turned very white and then blushed red. 'It was just a game! We were just pretending that they were Sarcenians – like in *Thoria* – and we had to get them to take off their hijabs to turn them into Thorians. I never knew they were really killing anyone. Are you sure about that? Couldn't it have been someone else? A coincidence?'

He looked from Sandra to Bryony and back again with pleading in his eyes, willing this nightmare to stop.

'Tell me about the chess pieces,' Sandra said quietly. 'You each had to leave a different one behind after you'd completed your challenge, is that right?'

'Yes. They said I had to be the bishop, because I'd been an altar boy when I was a kid. Tyson said he was *Knight Crusader* so he'd have to be the knight, and *Roadkill* wanted the castle. That left Alfie with the king or the queen. He didn't like the idea of being a queen, but Tyson said he ought to be pleased we were letting him be the most powerful piece on the board.'

'OK. Can we recap, to make sure I've got this straight?' Sandra leaned forward and started writing on a page of her notebook. 'The beta-testers are Tyson Green, Alfie Prescott, Max Barker, you, and one more that you don't know?'

Liam nodded.

'And their gaming names are Knight Crusader, Aragorn, Roadkill, Necromancer and Silver Bullet?'

Another nod.

'And you each had a chess piece assigned to you, and they were knight, queen, castle and bishop?' Sandra finished writing and turned the page round for Liam to read. 'Have I got all that right?'

$$***$$

'That was DCI Latham,' Mariam came back into the room and put down her phone on the table next to her plate. She looked round at the others. They were gathered in the newly-refurbished kitchen in the Knotty Ash house, eating their last meal together before Bernie and Peter left for Oxford. 'They're charging them all with murder. Well, except for Liam. He's been charged with attempted murder and stalking. They've let him go home, but they're keeping the others in custody.'

'Even Guy?' asked Peter. 'I thought he was helping them to get the evidence together to prosecute the others. Do they really think they'll convince a jury that he intended his game to incite them to kill in real life?'

'It was Guy she wanted to talk to me about,' Mariam told him. 'She wanted to check that I'd be willing to stand up in court and answer questions about that incident in the park last July. She thinks that will demonstrate that he was thinking of Muslims in hijabs when he wrote a game in which the villains were brown-skinned women being controlled remotely by voices in their helmets.'

'And are you?' Dominic asked at once. 'You said you didn't want him prosecuted for what he did to you.'

'I didn't think it mattered then. I still don't now. What if he was genuinely trying to help me? What if he was just misguided?'

'And what if he planned the whole thing?' demanded Lucy. 'Maybe he *is* the mastermind behind a campaign to kill Muslim women? He shouldn't be allowed to get away with it just because he's cleverer at covering his tracks than the others.'

'But isn't it better to forgive?' Mariam argued. 'Doesn't the Qur'an tell us that forgiving is better than paying someone back?'

'I think you can forgive at a personal level, but still help to bring him to justice,' Bernie suggested. 'To help stop it happening to anyone else.'

'That's right,' agreed Peter. 'If forgiving meant never reporting offences to the police or giving evidence in court, there would be nothing to stop criminals from just carrying on stealing and killing and maiming other people. And my whole career hunting them down, would have been a waste of time, because none of the robbers and rapists and murderers that I caught would ever have been prosecuted. It's not just between you and him – not in the law. In a criminal trial, it's the crown that prosecutes, not the victim, because the offence is against the whole of society, not just the victim.'

'And that's why it's the judge, not the victim, who decides what sentence a defendant gets if they're found guilty,' Bernie added.

'But Nicole was so certain that he didn't mean any harm,' Mariam argued.

'And he'll have his chance to convince the jury of that in court,' Bernie said firmly. 'But it seems to me that he needs to understand the effect that his game had on the others, even if he didn't mean it to.'

'And he *did* actually assault you,' Lucy added. 'He needs to realise that too.'

'Yes, I know.' Mariam paused and looked down at the food on her plate. 'Anyway, I told Sandra I'd do it, so that's that.'

CHECK MATE

14. POSTSCRIPT

Tahmina shook out her umbrella and propped it up by a radiator to dry. A chilly, cavernous church hall on a rainy November evening didn't seem like an auspicious venue for what might turn out to be a difficult meeting with only a handful of people present. But, Cheryl, the Restorative Justice co-ordinator, had insisted that it should take place on neutral territory, and this was what she had come up with.

'I suppose we sit here.' Mariam pointed at a circle of six plastic chairs.

'Looks like it,' Lucy agreed, sitting down and taking out her phone. 'We're a bit early. He's probably not here yet.'

'Here you are!' Cheryl's cheery voice echoed from the bare brick walls as she came in backwards, pushing the door open with her body, her hands occupied with carrying a tray of cardboard cups. 'Two teas with no sugar and one white coffee with one sugar. I hope I've got that right?'

'Perfect!' Tamina assured her, stepping forward to relieve her of the tray. 'Let's put this down on that table over there, or …. I know! Why don't you girls bring that low table over and put it in the middle of the circle, where we'll all be able to reach it.'

Soon the furniture was rearranged in accordance with Tahmina's instructions and they all sat down together, facing the remaining two chairs across the table. Cheryl's phone buzzed and she checked her messages.

'That's John – Guy's probation officer – they're in the foyer. I'll go and meet them.' She turned to look at Mariam. 'Are you ready? Or do you need a few minutes to prepare yourself?'

'I'm fine,' Mariam assured her. 'Go ahead and bring him in.'

They sat nervously waiting, sipping their drinks and watching the door through which Cheryl had departed.

'I suppose she'll be getting them drinks,' Lucy said, after a few minutes.

'Perhaps he's got cold feet,' Tahmina suggested. 'I couldn't blame him. It must be nerve-racking wondering what we're going to say to him.'

'I'm still not sure what I want to say to him,' said Mariam. 'I'm more interested in hearing what he's got to say. I want to know why he did it, and how he feels about those others latching on to his game and playing it out for real.'

'*I'd* like to be sure that he really didn't know what they were up to.' Lucy said, still unconvinced that the court had been right to acquit Guy of any involvement in the sequence of murders. 'And I wish we could talk to those others – the ones who actually did go on to kill. Did they really see their victims as nothing more than avatars in a computer game? I'm glad they got life sentences.'

'But I'm glad that that younger boy – Liam – wasn't sent to jail,' Tahmina added. 'He was so young and so obviously under pressure from the others to join in with something he didn't like at all.'

'I think Nadia was very brave the way she spoke up for him,' Mariam nodded. 'I was really proud of her.'

'Yes,' Lucy agreed. 'I think anyone who watched the trial ought to have been impressed by the contrast between the forgivingness and empathy on the side of the Muslim witnesses and the arrogance of the likes of Max Barker and Tyson Green.'

The door opened and a man came in. He stood holding it wide. They waited. At last, appearing very nervous, Guy Daniels stepped across the threshold. He paused momentarily before walking across the floor towards the circle of chairs, his feet making no sound in their grey canvas shoes. Cheryl scuttled after him, while John, the probation officer, followed at a more sedate pace.

'Sit down.' Cheryl pulled out a chair on the far side of the circle from Mariam. 'I'll put your drink down here. And the plate of biscuits. Help yourselves everyone!'

After the cardboard cups, Lucy was pleasantly surprised to see that the biscuits were not the standard institutional selection – plain digestive or rich tea with the occasional custard cream – but a rather upmarket choice of chocolate-coated biscuits together with some unusual-looking home-made cookies.

'The coconut cookies are gluten-free,' Cheryl explained, seeing her eyeing them suspiciously.

'You made them yourself?' asked Tahmina. 'You must give me the recipe. My sister has coeliac disease and I'm always on the lookout for new things to make for her.'

'I'll email it to you,' Cheryl promised. 'Now help yourselves – please!' She looked round hopefully at the little group sitting on their uncomfortable chairs, clutching their paper cups.

'What do we do next?' Lucy asked bluntly.

'Well, how about some introductions? I'm Cheryl Campbell. Please, call me Cheryl. I think I've spoken to most of you before. I'm going to be facilitating this session. I hope you've all read the list of ground rules that I sent you, but I'll just summarise quickly. The most important thing is that this meeting is confidential. Don't repeat anything that's said here to anyone outside. The others are really just basic respect: don't interrupt when someone else is speaking, be prepared to listen as well as speaking, don't put words into other people's mouths or try to speak for them, be honest. Are you all OK with those?'

There was a general nodding of heads in agreement.

'Good. Now let's go round the room and each of you tell the others who you are and why you're here. What do you each hope to get out of this session? John – would you like to kick off for us?'

'OK. I'm John Wilson. I'm Guy's probation officer and my job is to keep an eye on him and help keep him out of trouble. I'm here to support him in what's likely to be a difficult meeting for him.'

'Guy?' Cheryl looked towards the young man, who, at the sound of his name, jerked his head up from contemplating the grey and white vinyl tiles on the floor and looked about him with the terrified expression of a hunted deer. 'Thank you for agreeing to come. Would you like to tell the group what you're hoping to get out of this?'

'I – er – I – well … I just want them to know I'm not a racist, and I never wanted anyone to get hurt.'

'OK. That's great.' Cheryl turned to Lucy, who was next around the circle. 'And what about you? Could you tell Guy and John who you are and why you're here?'

'I'm Lucy Ali, Mariam's sister-in-law. I was with Mariam when he assaulted her. I'm here to support Mariam and I want to know why he did it. And I want to know why he wrote that stupid computer game portraying Muslims as monsters.'

Guy opened his mouth to protest, but John put out his hand and touched him on the arm, applying gentle pressure to warn him to remain silent. Guy closed his mouth and lowered his eyes.

'Thank you, Lucy. And Guy, you'll have a chance to answer that in a few minutes. But let's finish the introductions.'

She switched her gaze to Mariam, who looked across at Guy and said, 'I'm Mariam – but I think you all know that already. I'm not all that bothered about the incident in St John's Gardens. I just want to understand why two of my friends are dead now.'

'OK. Thank you. And lastly …?'

'I'm Tahmina Ali. I'm Mariam's mum. I'm here to support her and, like Lucy, I'd like to know why Guy made his alien invaders look like my daughter and her friends. Couldn't he see what effect it might have on people who played his game?'

'OK. Good. Guy? Do you want to respond to any of that?'

'Yeah.' There was a long pause. 'Yes, I do. I – I just want to say … I really, really never thought …. Thoria is just a game! I don't know why they started killing people for real. I never meant that to happen. And I'm really, really sorry about your friends!'

'But why did you make your Sarcenians look like Muslim women?' Lucy demanded. 'Why did you make those ridiculous brain-washing helmets look just like hijabs? Why do all the Sarcenians have brown skin when all the Thorians are blond white people?'

'I didn't!' Guy protested instinctively.

'Really?' Lucy's hackles were rising. 'That's certainly what they look like to me! And that's obviously what they looked like to your beta-testers. Why else would they pick on Muslim women when they decided to act out your game in real life?'

'Let's all calm down, please,' Cheryl intervened. 'Remember, we're here to listen to the other person's point of view. Guy, do you have anything else to add to what you just said?'

'Not really,' Guy mumbled. Then he looked up and caught Mariam's eye. 'At least, I suppose I sort of *was* thinking about hijabs when I thought of the helmets. I'd been reading about the way Muslim girls are conditioned to wear them and not allowed to decide things for themselves and forced into arranged marriages. And it made me think, it's as if those hijabs gave the men control over their brains.'

'And was that what you were thinking when you tried to snatch Mariam's off her head?' Lucy tried, only partially successfully, to speak calmly and not to raise her voice.

'Sort of, I suppose. But it was more, sort of, *symbolic*. Like, if you took off your hijab it was a sign that you were going to make your own decisions, not just do what other people told you. ... Like those girls protesting in Iran,' he added, as if hit by sudden inspiration. 'I'd been watching videos of them, and reading about their government putting them in jail and torturing them for daring to go out without them on.'

'But *nobody* was telling *me* to wear a hijab,' Mariam said simply. 'Look at my mum! She doesn't wear one. She never has.'

Guy stared at Tahmina as if seeing her for the first time.

'Would you like to know why I cover my head?' Mariam asked.

'Because of your religion?'

'No. And not because of my Pakistani heritage either. And definitely not because anyone told me to.'

'So, why then?'

'I'll show you.' Mariam took out the pin that secured her hijab and began to unwind the length of fabric from her head. Guy watched intently. Nobody spoke.

As the final layer dropped down around Mariam's shoulders, Guy gave an involuntary gasp and turned his face away to avoid staring at the bald and scarred patches on her scalp.

'What happened?' he croaked through suddenly dry lips.

Lucy was about to jump in with a reply, but Mariam was quicker. 'Someone threw acid over a group of us, a few years back. I was lucky; it only went on the back of my head. One of our friends got it full in her face. The lesions got infected and it turned to sepsis. She died.'

'I – I – I'm so, so sorry! I didn't know!'

'No, why would you?' Mariam's voice was gentle, but unyielding. 'But I *told* you I wasn't being forced to cover my head, and you didn't believe me. Why?'

Guy sat silently watching as she wound her hijab round her head again and pinned it in place.

'I don't know,' he mumbled at last. 'I suppose I thought … I thought you'd been brainwashed by ….' He glanced guiltily towards Tahmina. 'I thought your parents must have made you think you had to wear it because of your religion.'

'Chance'd be a fine thing!' Tahmina grinned. 'I know better than to try to force either of my kids to do anything!'

'Especially not marriage,' Lucy added. 'They've both married Christians, you know!'

Guy stared at her, lost for words.

'Lucy's married to my brother,' Mariam explained, sharing her mother's amusement at his confusion. 'And I married her second cousin.'

Guy stared round at the three women, finally fixing on Tahmina. 'And you don't mind?'

'Why would I? Lucy and Dom have been the best possible friends for Mariam and Ibrahim through some pretty difficult times. I couldn't wish for a better son- or daughter-in-law.'

'And you're –,' he turned to Lucy. 'You're not one of them – a Muslim, I mean?'

Lucy shook her head. She was grinning too by now.

'So, why do you wear that – that – you know!' He nodded towards the lime green hijab that covered her head. 'Did the acid go over you too?'

'No.' Smiling, Lucy took off her hijab and allowed her long blond curls to fall loose about her shoulders. 'I'm showing solidarity with all the women who get shouted at and spat on in the street because they choose to wear one. And I'm proving that I've got a right to wear whatever I choose to wear without being judged for it. And I wanted to know what it feels like to have people thinking you must be a terrorist just because you dress differently from them.'

Guy said nothing, so Lucy continued. 'The funny thing is, a lot of people react quite differently when they see me in my hijab from when they see Mariam. They often stare, but they don't usually edge away or choose to stand rather than sit next to me on the bus. Which makes me think it's brown-skinned people they really don't like.'

Under the steady gaze of Lucy's blue eyes, Guy felt compelled to respond. 'Maybe they feel like my nan. There weren't any brown-skinned people here when she was young. Now she's surrounded by them and she feels like a foreigner in her own country. It's not that she's a racist – she just doesn't feel safe with all these people jabbering away in languages she can't understand.'

'Well, tell her from me that they're much more likely to be swapping samosa recipes than plotting to plant bombs,' Tahmina said, continuing to smile warmly towards him. 'I'm sure that they are all just very ordinary boring people who don't want to intimidate anyone.'

'We're all just the same underneath,' Mariam added. 'Wearing different clothes and speaking a different language doesn't change that.'

'I bet when your nan was a girl, all the women round her used to cover their heads when they went out!' Lucy put in suddenly. 'And I bet a lot of them wore headscarves, just like this one. I've seen a photo from the fifties of the queen standing next to a horse wearing one.'

'I'm not saying she's right about it,' Guy protested. 'I'm just saying that's the way she feels. And it doesn't seem right to me that she's still living in the same house, in the same town, but now she can't talk to her neighbours and she feels like she's a prisoner in a foreign country.'

'Maybe she just needs someone to introduce her to her neighbours,' suggested Tahmina. 'They may be feeling just as shy as she is.'

'But they're not like you,' Guy argued, looking at Tahmina's navy-blue trouser suite and cream blouse. 'You've adjusted your lifestyle to fit in. No one would know you weren't born here!'

'I was,' Tahmina told him. 'I'm as British as you are. I'm as British as your nan!'

There was a long silence.

'O-ka-a-ay,' Cheryl said slowly. 'Let's have a breather, shall we? And perhaps you can all think about whether you've got what you were hoping for out of this meeting.'

She picked up the plate of biscuits and held it out to each of the others in turn.

'Would anyone like another drink?' There were shaking heads all round, so she continued. 'OK. I'll go round the room again and you can each tell me if you've got anything else you want to say or any more questions you want to ask. Shall we take you first this time, Guy? Is there anything you want to add?'

'No, not really. I just want them to know how sorry I am about what those idiots did. I and want them to believe that I never meant anything like that to happen. And I'm really sorry about what happened to Mariam. I don't know why anyone would want to do something like that to her.'

'Thank you, Guy.' Cheryl paused for a moment before shifting her gaze to the other side of the table. 'Tahmina?'

'I'd like to thank Guy for being so honest with us. And ...,' Tahmina looked towards Guy as she added, 'And I'd love to meet your nan and help her to get to know her neighbours – if she'd like me to.'

Guy looked back for a few seconds and then nodded briefly. 'Thanks,' he mumbled. 'I'll ask her, but ....'

'Mariam?' Cheryl broke the awkward silence that followed.

'I accept that Guy didn't mean his game to make people want to kill Muslims, but I don't understand how he could've not known that they'd think that the Sarcenians represented people like me. Like Lucy said, they look like Muslim women from South Asia and the Thorians look like white people.' Mariam looked towards Guy, who instantly dropped his gaze and appeared to be staring at her feet. 'How could you not have realised that your game would attract people with racist and Islamophobic views?'

'And that it would confirm them in those views,' added Lucy. 'Maybe you couldn't be expected to predict that your game would make anyone kill people, but how could you not realise that it might encourage them to think that Muslims are legitimate targets for their hate? And can't you see how dehumanising it is for Muslim women to have people seeing them in that way?'

'OK. That's enough,' Cheryl held up her hand. 'Let's give Guy a chance to respond, shall we? Guy?'

'I dunno,' Guy mumbled, appearing to address a dark stain on one of the white floor tiles. Then, after a long pause, he raised his head and looked towards Mariam. 'Please believe me! I can see now how it looks, but I never thought of that; really I didn't! It was just a game – a fantasy game in a fantasy world. And it wasn't about killing people at all – not even in the game! That was what made it different – more subtle – than other games. You didn't win by killing the Sarcenians; it was all about recuing them from their controlling overlords and turning them into Thorians.'

'But Mariam and Tahmina and their friends *have* turned themselves into Thorians,' Lucy broke in. 'They've done what you want them to do. They speak English; they wear western clothes; Tahmina's a nurse and Mariam will soon be a doctor – treating white British people in the National Health Service. But that doesn't stop people putting dog excrement through their letter box or spray-painting their front door with obscenities or shouting abuse in the street. You write a game in which the good guys are all white-skinned and blue-eyed, and the evil invaders are brown-skinned people wearing stereotypical Muslim head coverings, and you expect us to believe that it never occurred to you that the people who play it won't think that it's really about sending the dirty Pakis home? Do you think we're–'

'That's enough, Lucy,' Cheryl cut in. 'Let's just cool it, shall we? Remember what we said at the beginning – we all show respect to each other, and we *listen* to what the other person has to say. Now Guy, do you want to say anything about what Lucy just said?'

'I – I just want them to believe that I didn't mean it like that. When you're writing a computer game you have to make the two sides look different, so people can tell them apart. I suppose maybe I was thinking about this idea I had that Muslim women were being forced to wear hijabs when I designed the brain washing helmets, but I wasn't consciously trying to make the Sarcenians look like Muslims – not really.'

'Why?' asked Tahmina, the moment he stopped speaking. 'Why do the two sides have to look different? Why couldn't you write a game where you can't tell whether someone is a goodie or a baddie?'

'Like in real life,' Lucy added.

'So, part of the game would be working out who you needed to be scared of and who you could trust,' Mariam suggested. 'And then trying to change the dangerous ones without letting them hurt you.'

Guy frowned in concentration. 'Ye-e-es,' he said at last. 'That might work ….'

THANK YOU

Thank you for taking the time to read *Lethal Quests* If you enjoyed it, please consider telling your friends or posting a short review. Word of mouth is an author's best friend and much appreciated. Thank you,

Judy

ACKNOWLEDGEMENTS

I would like to thank many Facebook friends, especially those from the *Pesky Methodist* group, for their support and encouragement and for suggesting ideas for my books. In particular, Heather Rotherham, Jill Hudson, Bronwyn Coveney, Jo Opsimath, Lucy Brown-Beard, Carol Rowe, Deborah Adeniji, Jenny Spouge, John Fenn, Ann Smith, Edwin Hird, Liz Parkinson and Katy Brookes-Duncan all provided me with useful comments on my proposed titles and cover designs, which enabled me to come up with significant improvements in both.

Quotations from the Qur'an are from the translation by M.A.S. Abdel Haleem, Oxford World Classics, 2004.

Every effort has been made to trace copyright holders of any quotations from writing other than my own. The publishers will be glad to rectify in future editions any errors or omissions brought to their attention.

DISCLAIMER

This book is a work of fiction. Any references to real people, events, establishments, organisations or locales are intended only to provide a sense of authenticity and are used fictitiously. All the characters and events are entirely invented by the author. Any resemblances to persons living or dead are purely coincidental.

Many of the locations and institutions that feature in this book are real. Their inhabitants and employees, however, are purely fictional. In particular:

- The Stanley Mosque and Islamic Centre is a figment of my imagination, as are its imams and other members;

- Mount Street Chambers and the barristers and clerks who work there are purely fictional;

- None of the police officers depicted here are based on real members of Merseyside Police or any other police service;

- No students or staff from any of the universities featured in this book are based on real people from those or any other educational establishment.

MORE BOOKS FROM JUDY FORD

This is the fifteenth **Bernie Fazakerley Mystery**. The others are:

1. Two Little Dickie Birds: a murder mystery for DI Peter Johns and his Sergeant, Paul Godwin.

2. **Murder of a Martian**: Peter and Jonah solve a double murder and Peter meets Martin Riess for the first time.

3. **Grave Offence**: Peter investigates an assault and a suspicious death, while Jonah is in rehab in the spinal injuries centre.

4. **Awayday**: a traditional detective story set among the dons of Lichfield College.

5. **Death on the Algarve:** a mystery for Bernie and her friends to tackle while on holiday in Portugal.

6. **Mystery over the Mersey**: a murder mystery set in Liverpool.

7. **Sorrowful Mystery**: Jonah investigates a child abduction and Peter embarks on a new journey of faith.

8. **In my Liverpool Home**: Bernie and her friends return to Liverpool to investigate a suspicious death in Aunty Dot's Care Home.

9. **Organ Failure**: a body is discovered under the organ in St Cyprian's Church and Jonah is called in to investigate.

10. **Rainbow Warrior**: One of their friends is injured in a hit-and-run incident and Jonah is convinced that this is attempted murder.

11. **Admission of Innocence**: Father Damien calls Peter and Jonah out of retirement to solve a murder case and prevent a miscarriage of justice.

12. **Lethal Mix**: Three of Lucy's student friends are injured in an anti-Muslim hate crime in Liverpool. Jonah, Peter and

Bernie assist Merseyside Police to bring their attacker to justice.

13. **A Secret Gardener?** Bernie's friend Martin discovers a body in the Fellows' Garden of his Oxford College.

14. **Crowd of Witnesses**: Jonah decides to write his memoirs, beginning with a murder investigation from 1982.

Bernie, Lucy and their friends also appear in seven other novels:

- **Changing Scenes of Life**: Jonah Porter's life story, told through the medium of his favourite hymns.

- **Despise not your Mother**: the story of Bernie's quest to learn about her first husband's past.

- **Weed Killers**, **Lost in Lockdown**, and **Victim Statements** form a trilogy of novels about the aftermath of the murders of two young men.

- **Just Another Knife Crime** and **Just Another Suicide** are the first two in a series of books starring a younger generation of police officers from Thames Valley.

And there's a book of short stories, in which Peter Johns narrates his side of the story:

- **My Life of Crime**: the collected memoirs of DI Peter Johns. This includes some episodes that appear in other books, but told from a new perspective, as well as some completely new stories.

You can find all these on Judy Ford's **Amazon Author page** and on her **website**.

Visit the Bernie Fazakerley Publications **Facebook page**.

GLOSSARY OF ARABIC WORDS AND PHRASES

As-Salaamu-Alaykum – Peace be upon you, a traditional Arabic greeting, to which the response is **wa-alaykumu-salaam** meaning "and upon you be peace".

Allahu Akbar – God is the greatest.

Alayhi al-Salaam – Peace be upon him. This phrase, or its abbreviation "a.s.", is often used by Muslims after the names of prophets as a sign of respect. The English abbreviation, pbuh, is also sometimes used.

Bismillah ar-Rahman ar-Rahim – In the name of God, the lord of mercy, the giver of mercy. A phrase used to inaugurate many tasks, especially prayer. It appears at the start of all but one of the chapters of the Qur'an.

Dua – supplication to God.

Hadith – a record of the acts and sayings of the prophet Muhammad. The literal meaning is "news?" or "story". The hadiths are used within the Muslim community as a source of guidance and provide the basis for much Islamic law.

Halal – lawful, permitted. This word is frequently used in the context of permissible food and drink.

Haram – forbidden, in contrast with *halal* (permitted).

Hijab – barrier or partition. In Islam, it is used to describe the principle of modesty. Hence, it has come to be used for the head covering worn by many Muslim women.

Hidayah – God-given guidance.

Insha'Allah – God willing

Jummah – Literally "congregation", *Jummah* is also used to denote Friday, the day of congregation.

Khutbah – sermon.

Maghrib – The *salah al-maghrib* is the sunset prayer, one of five daily prayers that are obligatory for practising Muslims.

Mahr – the marriage gift given by a man to his wife as part of the marriage contract.

Nikah – Marriage, literally "conjoining" or "uniting"

Salla Allahu alayhi wa sallam – Peace and blessings of Allah be upon him. Muslims often say this phrase (often abbreviated "saw" or "pbuh") after saying the name of a prophet of Islam.

Salah al-Jummah – Friday prayers, said by Muslims in congregation (the literal meaning of *Jummah*) in a mosque or other gathering place.

Shahada – the solemn declaration of faith in God. Converts to Islam make this declaration in front of witnesses in order to be received into the faith.

Subhana Rabbiyal Adhim – Glory be to my Lord, the exalted.

Subhanahu Wa Ta'ala – Glory to Him, the Exalted. This phrase is often used when speaking of God (Allah). It may be abbreviated as "Allah (SWT)".

Sunnah – "tradition" or "way". This word is used to describe the words and actions of the prophet Mohammed, which forms a model for the behaviour of his followers.

Taqwa – the state of being fully conscious of God. Sometimes rendered in English as "God-fearing" or 'righteousness".

Umma – the worldwide community of Muslims (literally "nation")

Wa-Alaykumu-Salaam – and upon you be peace, the traditional response to the greeting **As-Salaamu-Alaykum**

Wudu – ritual washing performed by Muslims before prayer

Yawm al-Jummah – Friday (literally "day of congregation")

Zakah – Charity. The obligation to give alms is one of the five pillars of Islam (the foundation of Muslim life).

FAZAKERLEY FAMILY TREE

ABOUT THE AUTHOR

Like her main character, Bernie Fazakerley, Judy Ford is an Oxford graduate and a mathematician. Unlike Bernie, Judy grew up in a middle-class family in the South London stockbroker belt. After moving to the North West and working in Liverpool, Judy fell in love with the Scouse people and created Bernie to reflect their unique qualities. She has worked in academia and in the NHS.

As a Methodist Local Preacher, Judy often tells her congregation, "I see my role as asking the questions and leaving you to think out your own answers." She carries this philosophy forward into her writing and she hopes that readers will find themselves challenged to think as well as being entertained.

Printed in Great Britain
by Amazon